DON DIABLO

G·K
Hall
&Co.

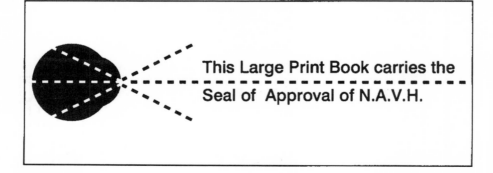

This Large Print Book carries the
Seal of Approval of N.A.V.H.

DON DIABLO

A Western Story

MAX BRAND™

G.K. Hall & Co. • Waterville, Maine

Published in 2002 by arrangement with Golden West Literary Agency.

G.K. Hall Large Print Western Series.

The text of this Large Print edition is unabridged.
Other aspects of the book may vary from the original edition.

Set in 16 pt. Plantin by Al Chase.

Printed in the United States on permanent paper.

Library of Congress Cataloging-in-Publication Data

Brand, Max, 1892–1944.
   Don Diablo: a western story / Max Brand.
     p. cm.
   ISBN 0-7838-8948-8 (lg. print : hc : alk. paper)
   1. Outlaws — Fiction. 2. Large type books. I. Title.
PS3511.A87 D66 2002
823'.912—dc21   2001039243

Western
Brand, Max, 1892-1944.
Don Diablo [large print] : a
western story

Table of Contents

Editor's Note

Throughout his writing career Frederick Faust featured series characters in his contributions to Street & Smith's *Western Story Magazine*. Among these creations are Bull Hunter, Ronicky Doone, James Geraldi, Chip, Speedy, and Reata. Faust's output for 1932 consisted of fourteen serials and twenty-three short novels, all of which appeared in *Western Story Magazine*. In the April 9, 1932 issue of *Western Story Magazine* in a short novel entitled "Mountain Raiders" Faust introduced readers to Jim Tyler, an outlaw hero who would also appear in two more stories — "Rawhide Bound" in the *Western Story Magazine* issue dated 4/23/32 and "Greaser Trail" in the 5/21/32 issue, for which Faust's original title, "The Trail of Death," has now been restored. All three stories appeared under Faust's Peter Henry Morland byline. In this compilation all three Jim Tyler stories appear together for the first time in book form.

Mountain Raiders

I

"The Enigma"

Turning his head from his Mexican visitor, Tobias Reed looked through the window of his office across the sun shimmer of the roofs of Santa Anna toward the mountains. They were as nakedly beautiful as ever they had been, and the clear browns and blues and mauves held out to him as definite a suggestion of the wealth he knew to be in them as ever they had done in the past. His straining eyes, even at this distance, could see the glint of the sun along huge strata that were worth the plumbing for hidden treasures of silver.

Already he had done much. The United Mine Companies of Santa Anna had opened half a dozen shafts, here and there among the ridges, and every one of them, with a single exception, had been working in bonanza for some time. But there were other difficulties to be dealt with in old Mexico besides the mere finding of the precious metals. The young Mexican, who now sat in the office with Reed, symbolized to the geologist all of those extra difficulties.

Handsome, smooth-spoken, gentle of manner, with a large and trusting eye, nevertheless, Ramón Díaz was to Tobias Reed an enigma, a representative of a strange country and a strange people that he, Reed, never could understand. For that matter, Tobias Reed knew little except his subject and certain types of men and women to be found in New England. The great Southwest was to him a book almost as closely sealed as old Mexico itself.

His eyes dropped from the glories of the mountains, with half their beauty lost to him now. Falling back across the glimmering roofs of the town, his glance rested on a tall man seated in the cool of an arcade across the way.

Sometimes, when we are most troubled inwardly, we give all the more particular attention to exterior objects. And now the mind of Tobias Reed rested suddenly, with keen force, upon that man across the street. He was not Mexican; certainly he was not New England; he was, in fact, typical of the Southwest.

Once, through a strong glass, the geologist had studied the ways of a great-winged buzzard, circling high above a valley. Now he felt a similarity between that bird and this man across the street; that is to say, there was the same sense of perfect impassivity, combined with an occasional quick turn of the head and keen darting of the eye that assured a watcher that every sense was constantly on the alert and in both the man and the bird there was great size without great weight. Desert sun had starved them both of all superfluous flesh, and there remained only the skeleton and the powerful, tireless, elastic muscles.

There was, too, about the man as about the bird, a sense of cruel power. His face was very lean, almost as a matter of course. The nose was arched. One felt that this was a predatory being. His very repose, united with that nervous intensity at all times, made Tobias Reed think a little of a cat watching beside a rat hole.

What was the rat hole in this case? For what was that lean, long fellow waiting? Well, he was only one more mystery to be added to the long list of unexplained marvels that Tobias Reed had been adding up in his memory ever since he had crossed the Mississippi River into the land of little rain. But there was something both stimulating and clean about that fellow, dangerous though he might be, and in the case of that Mexican who sat with Tobias Reed. . . .

He turned his head, at this moment, back toward his visitor. "Beg pardon," said Tobias Reed. "I had to take a minute off to think things over."

"Why, of course," said Ramón Díaz. "One must think, and I have another half hour before . . . I must go."

The pause before the last three words, the little, polite gesture that accompanied them, the graceful and deprecatory bending of the head to one side — to Tobias Reed these were all perfectly and entirely Mexican. Half an hour to make up his mind upon such a question as this?

"Look here, Díaz," he said, "if I go to the rest of the chief holders of stock and tell 'em I've raised the cost of production, there'll be a howl that'll split the sky."

Díaz half closed his eyes and leaned back his head, the better to show the expression of intense sympathy and pain that filled him when he thought of the predicament of the other.

"Ah, my friend," he said, "if only I could help you. But, you see, I know that there is nothing for me to gain. I receive messages and I pass them on to you. That is all. I am simply a transmitter."

He waved his graceful hands, and again a sudden deep, dark wave of doubt and suspicion flooded the mind of Tobias Reed. He was a practical man. People, even in Mexico, were not likely to be so disinterested as this handsome young man appeared to be. If there were one lie, there might be nothing but lies behind the rest.

Reed shook his head. He heard the voice of the visitor going on smoothly. "Ten thousand dollars a month for protection is a very great deal of money to pay, of course. A very great deal. And to ask you to pay twenty thousand seems to me . . . why, a dreadful thing. But there it is. That terrible El Tigre, he is growing stronger and stronger day by day. He gathers to himself every discontented soul. He stands off there in the midst of the mountains, and he points to the riches that you clever American miners are tearing out of the hard, flinty ribs of our Mexico, day by day. He incites his men to madness, telling them that all of his wealth ought to remain south of the Río Grande . . . that it is theirs, in fact. As El Tigre, that diabolical man, gathers strength, it is necessary for Beltran Vizcaya to gather strength, also. He wants to guard those mines well and thoroughly, and so far, at least, you admit that he has done it well, *señor?*"

"He's done it well enough. We haven't lost an ounce, so far as I know, since we began to pay protection."

Ramón Díaz settled back in his chair and waved his hands, as though to emphasize the importance of that point. "Pardon me," he said, and glanced at his watch. Then he sat upon the edge of his chair, as one anxious to conclude an interview all of whose points had been thoroughly talked over.

Still the Yankee mind of Tobias Reed retained doubts. "Do you mean to say," he asked, "that El Tigre's getting so strong that Vizcaya has to double his own force to keep those robbing, murdering demons away from the mines?"

"That is it, and that is why Vizcaya now asks for double the amount of money, for protection. I, personally, am very sorry for you, *Señor* Reed. But, on the other hand, one thinks of the tons and tons of silver that, every month, you and your friends take out of the rocks. Vizcaya asks for not more than one dollar in ten, after all, and that is not such a very high percentage, no?" He raised his thin eyebrows as he spoke. It was only now and then that the English of Díaz failed of perfection.

"Ten percent!" cried Reed. He was a little

11

man. There was nothing long about him, except his neck. Now he added a little height by jerking up and down in his chair and whacking his fist on his desk for emphasis.

"Ten percent?" he echoed again. "Do you think that it costs us nothing to take that silver out of the ground? Do you think that those *peones* are laboring every day for nothing, and that the rail line costs nothing, or the smelting? Do you think that we have no stockholders back in the States who will inquire into this business of protection and call it dirty graft?"

Díaz shrugged his shoulders and rose from his chair, slowly.

"I am very sorry for you, *señor,*" he said again in his gentle voice, although perhaps his eyes were a shade less caressing now. "But, as I said before, I am only conveying a message to you. Your answer is nothing to me, except that I should be sorry to see the mines ruined by a raid from that demon of an El Tigre. The scoundrel has ruined more than one rich mine owner." He turned toward the door.

"Wait one minute," said Reed, slipping far down in his chair with a groan. "Twenty thousand dollars a month . . . nearly a thousand dollars a day," he muttered. Leaning his head on his hand, his blank, desperate eyes looked vaguely across the street. There he saw that same thin, long fellow sitting in unchanged posture. Again he was reminded of a bird, not the foul buzzard, but the great sailing hawk that slides through the air with an oiled and effortless ease. Ah, to have such a fellow as that to stand between him — at a good, stiff, honest salary — and the machinations of the famous El Tigre, that ever-hungered bandit.

As Reed watched, a figure slipped through the shadowy doorway behind the Southwesterner, moving with a stealthy, cat-like air. A double-barreled shotgun was in his hands. In a stinging instant, the truth rushed upon Tobias Reed. Murder! That was what it meant. He would have shouted, but his throat refused to respond. He only gasped and made a soft, whistling noise.

At that instant, as the shotgun was carefully being raised, Reed was able to observe that the quiet but apparently alert air of the American stranger was by no means an illusion of his mind, for the tall man suddenly wheeled out of his chair and flung himself at the stalker. There was a roar from both barrels of the gun, but the American did not fall. It was the Mexican who dropped. People rushed out of the doorway and surrounded them, but Reed was able to make out through the confusion how the American was picking up the fallen figure by the coat collar and how the Mexican hung limply down, like a wet rag, his head falling loosely over to one side.

Suddenly Reed rose to his feet. His voice was high. He cried to Díaz: "Tell Vizcaya that he's another robber as bad as El Tigre. I won't pay him a penny. From this minute, not even what he was getting before. From this time on, I'll have men I know about me."

13

II

"The New Employee"

Díaz shook hands with a sadly affectionate air in which there was a suggestion of despair. "You are excited, *Señor* Reed. And it is no wonder. I hope that everything may be well. Indeed, I hope so very greatly." Then he left, only pausing at the door as if to add another word, but apparently changing his mind about it.

Tobias Reed was left sadly shaken. He could see, in his mind's eye, the sneaking, cat-like approach of ragged, savage figures through the mountain gloom toward the mines. He could see the final rush, the stabbing of the guards; he could hear the screams.

He pressed a button. A bell rang. A youngster entered and stood in the doorway, shifting from one foot to the other in his straw sandals.

"There was a fight across the street," explained Reed, in such Spanish as he could muster. "You go find out what happened, and tell the tall American that I would like to see him here . . . something that may be to his own interest. Hurry!"

The boy was gone in an instant. Very suddenly, hardly five minutes later, he was back

14

again in the same doorway, his eyes abnormally large and bright. "He is coming, *señor!* He is coming! The very man who killed José Leone. The very man . . . he comes. You hear his steps?"

The boy disappeared. In the doorway stood the same tall, spare, wide-shouldered form that the miner had seen across the street. Seen at close hand, he did not seem quite so big. There was a dusty quiet about him. Reed could find in his mind no other word for it.

He went forward and extended his hand. "My name's Tobias Reed," he said.

"Everybody down here knows who you are, Mister Reed," said the other. "I'm Jim Tyler." He added: "And nobody down here knows anything about me." He did not smile when he said this. He did not leave it to be inferred that there was a great deal that people might learn about him, one of these days.

"Sit down," Reed said.

"Thanks."

His visitor took a chair in a corner and sat with his wide-brimmed sombrero on his knees. Reed noticed with pleasure that the man was neatly dressed. He was apparently a cowpuncher. Reed did not follow his example and sit down. He felt, somehow, if he seated himself, he would sink altogether out of the ken of this grave-eyed young man.

"I was sitting at that desk, watching, when the man sneaked out behind you," he said. "I thought that I'd let you know, in case you should

15

need an eyewitness during the investigation."

"Thanks," said Jim Tyler. "But there won't be any investigation."

"What?"

"No, there'll be no investigation."

"But I thought that you killed the man!"

"No. I was a half inch too far to the side, and that's a pity, because he certainly needs killing, that José Leone. There won't be any investigation. He's been needing a killing for a long time."

"Ah-ha," murmured Reed, and because he did not understand, he blinked his eyes rapidly and nodded in agreement. "Might I ask why he wanted to kill you, Mister Tyler?" he continued.

"Me? Oh, just a little wrangle about a horse."

"Ah-ha, a horse, eh? They're very keen about their horses, I know."

"Little horse deal back north of the Río Grande," Tyler said. "That was all."

"And he followed you all this way south?"

"No, he was here all the time." Tyler stopped speaking, as though the matter was completely clear. Seeing the baffled look of his companion, he added calmly: "It was another fellow up there. Friend of this one. He stole a couple of my horses one day. That was all."

"Ah-ha," Reed murmured again. "But I should think that you would be the one with a grievance, then, and not the horse thief and this Leone? I don't understand at all."

For one instant a look half of weariness and

16

half of grimness came into the eyes of Tyler. At last he shrugged his wide shoulders and said: "You see, I followed the horse thief and got back the horses all right." He paused. He seemed to be wondering whether the remainder of the yarn was worth the telling, but finally he concluded, cheerfully: "The thief got a slug through the right thigh, and afterward he had to have that leg cut off at the hip. It cripples him a good deal, I guess, having only one leg. Instead of stealing horses and rustling cows, he's got to sit on a leather pad and learn how to make shoes, or something like that."

Here he made a definite end of the story by taking out a sack of tobacco and a package of wheat-straw papers. He offered these materials to the miner, who refused with thanks. Then Reed watched the lean, hard fingers maneuver deftly and with lightning speed, as he made the cigarette and lighted it — all in two or three seconds. There was Jim Tyler breathing out a great lungful of smoke and fixing his alert but unexcited eyes upon Reed.

The latter hardly knew what to say. If the matter of José Leone was such a mere ripple on the surface of his life, what would it take to stir this young man?

Reed said: "I sent for you partly to tell you that I was a witness and that I'd be glad to help if I could . . . if I were needed."

"Thanks again," said Tyler. "Other people saw it, though. And nobody would ask twice

17

about Leone. It's only a pity that I pulled the shot so far to the right. He needs killing, is all." And he waited again.

"Mister Tyler," said the geologist, "while I sat here and looked at you, I was in the middle of a lot of trouble, and I wondered if you would be the sort of a man who could help me out of it. Later, when I saw the way that you handled that murdering hound that sneaked up behind you, I began to feel pretty sure that you were the man. Do you mind telling me what your business is?"

"Punching cows," the other responded promptly.

"Is that all you do?" asked the miner.

Jim Tyler grew at trifle thoughtful. Then he answered: "Why, no, now that I think of it. I've done other things. I was a lumberjack in Canada for a while and did a little trapping in British Columbia. I've washed gold in the Klondike, and I tried to raise blood horses for the polo players. I've done a little farming, teaming, and mining. Matter of fact, I've done a good many things, but all I understand is cows, really."

He was perfectly grave. There was no affectation, none of the professional yearning to create surprise and to astonish the audience that is often a fault in the Southwesterner. He was merely stating facts with a perfect frankness.

"You know one other thing pretty well," said Reed slowly.

"What's that?"

"How to get yourself out of a chair and into a

fight in quick order . . . how to get out a gun so fast that the other man doesn't know where you found it. I saw that with my own eyes, a few minutes ago."

"That's not a help to me. That's a trouble to me," said Tyler. "People that can't pull a gun or shoot straight never get into bad trouble."

"Don't they?"

"No."

"I can't pull a gun, and I couldn't hit the side of a mountain if I did make a fast draw. But I'm in trouble."

"I'm sorry to hear that."

"Would you be sorry enough to take wages and help me out?"

"I've got two or three hundred dollars left," answered Tyler. "I'm not taking a job for a while."

Reed sighed. He felt that there was very little use in trying to persuade this man. But he went on: "I mean big pay."

"How big?" asked Tyler.

"You can be tempted, can you?"

"Yes, and I love to fall," Tyler said with continued gravity. "What's the trouble?"

"Protection," Reed answered.

Tyler waited.

"I mean," said Reed, "there's a bandit out there in the mountains called El Tigre."

"I've heard of him."

"And he's trying to get at my mines. And I've got to pay a fellow called Vizcaya to keep him away."

"Vizcaya can't keep El Tigre away," the other said calmly.

"Can't he?"

"No, he can't."

"You know 'em both?"

"Yes."

"Well, he can keep El Tigre away!" exclaimed Reed, smiting his hands together. "El Tigre raided us twice. We lost a fortune both times. But since Vizcaya came on the job, El Tigre has been kept away. We haven't lost a penny. But we've had to pay ten thousand a month protection. And now they've tried to raise the rate to twenty thousand."

"That's a lot of money for El Tigre," Tyler said.

"For Vizcaya," Reed corrected. "You've got the names mixed."

"No, I haven't."

"I tell you," Reed went on nervously angry, but trying to be patient, "that I'm paying Vizcaya ten thousand a month to give me protection against El Tigre."

"I tell you," said the other, "that Vizcaya never got that money."

"What?"

"El Tigre got it," said Tyler.

"How do you know that?"

"By knowing the pair of 'em."

"You know 'em both?"

"Yes."

Reed slumped heavily down into a chair. "It beats me," he said.

"El Tigre has beaten a lot of people," said Tyler.

"Then the whole thing. . . ."

"Oh, just the old game. They're good at it, south of the Río Grande. A frame-up. That's all."

"Curse these Mexicans!" shouted Reed, suddenly exploding.

"Don't curse 'em," Tyler answered. "Some of the finest gentlemen . . . and ladies . . . that I've ever known have been Mexican."

"Have they?"

"Yes."

The little man cried out in despair, or close to it. "Tyler," he said, "I've sent word to 'em that I won't pay the twenty thousand and, what's more, that I won't pay the ten thousand any longer, either."

"Then you'll be raided," said Tyler.

Reed groaned. "What's a man to do?" he said. "I thought, when I spotted you, that perhaps I'd found the man who might help me."

"Well, I might try my hand."

"Would you? Guard the mines?"

"Yes. I'd need some time to pick up men to help me."

"You have till tonight. You can write your own ticket."

"Thanks," said Tyler. "We'll talk finances after we see how well I can handle the job, and how hard it may turn out to be."

"You mean," said the geologist, "that you're

not going to ask for definite wages?"

"No," replied Tyler. "I don't need wages, just now. I told you I had a couple of hundred in my pocket. But if this is a good job, we'll fix the rate of pay later on. These fellows I get . . . how high can I go in paying them?"

"Anything you say . . . in reason."

"Is five dollars a day reason?"

"Of course, it is. Cheap, to me, unless you hire a whole army."

"About a dozen or twenty men ought to be enough."

"Can you find that many trustworthy Americans in this place?" asked the miner.

"Trustworthy Americans?" Tyler echoed, showing his first real surprise. "Trustworthy gunmen are what I'm going to look for. I don't care what their nationality is. But there are plenty of Americans around here, too, of one sort or another." He stood up. "Is that all, Mister Reed?"

"Wait a minute. I've got to give you authorization and some cash."

"All right, I'll wait for that." He went to the window and stood there, holding his hat behind the small of his back.

Reed sat at his desk, scribbling furiously a note to the general manager at the mines, ordering complete confidence to be placed in James Tyler. Then he paused, and cold sweat started out on his face. How could he tell that this man was worthy of confidence and was not another robber, in fact? He looked up at the outline of the broad shoulders against the window. He looked down at the lean, brown hands that held the hat. Then he went on writing, with more haste than before.

III

"Into the Mountains"

Tyler jogged his mustang down the street, turned out of the town, and headed it straight for the mountains. The level became a foothill slope, the slope became a steep grade, and the grade led him to a gap among the heights. Here was the long, winding, interior valley at one end of which the mines were located. But he was not headed toward the mines. Instead, he scanned those vast heights and depths in search, as it were, of elusive game.

He saw a shepherd sitting on a rock, not far off, with a few goats pastured here and there. Tyler rode up to him and waved his hand. The shepherd stood up and waved in answer. He was a big man with a gloomy, black brow and rather ruddy cheeks.

"Friend," Tyler called, "I am looking for El Tigre! Tell me where to find him."

The shepherd stared. "El Tigre?" he said. "El Tigre is not one of my goats. How could I tell where to find him?"

"It's not your business," agreed Tyler, "but then, as you sit here, day after day, keeping watch, you are not staying for nothing. There is some reason. And what is the reason? El Tigre, of course. He posts you here. He pays you, so you can tell me where he's to be found."

Under those shadowy brows, the eyes narrowed. "You say that I work for him?"

"I tell you the truth."

"That I watch here for him, day after day?"

"Of course."

"You are a fool!" the shepherd said hotly.

"Say that again," Tyler stated, and a gun was in his hand.

The shepherd had made a similar movement, but the gun he was drawing was not half out of his clothes before he saw that he was hopelessly beaten. His scowl grew blacker than before.

"What makes you think that I have anything to do with El Tigre?" he asked. "What makes you think that I watch here for him every day?"

"Because," said the other, "the grass is eaten down very close, all about here, and you could get better grazing by going half a mile. Also, there are twenty cigarette stubs all about, some of them nearly lost in the dust. You haven't smoked that many in part of a single day. What I see are the remainders of hundreds . . . the rest have disappeared. More than that, shepherds can't afford to buy revolvers with silver and gold chasing on the handles."

The calmness with which he spoke this, as well as the words themselves, seemed to make a great impression on the shepherd. He said: "You want to find El Tigre. Why?"

"To talk to him."

25

"Only that, eh?"

"If I came to fight him," Tyler said, "would I come alone?"

"True," said the other. "You are a friend, then?"

"No, I am neither . . . just now. Simply a *gringo* who wants to speak with him."

"Come," the big man stated suddenly. "We have wasted enough time." He whistled. Up from a copse of brush suddenly jumped a fine-limbed mountain horse that came trotting like a dog toward its master. The shepherd stepped, or rather jumped, into the saddle, and rode off with his legs dangling, for he used no stirrups, only the hull of a saddle. As he rode, he kept his face turned toward Tyler.

"You have eyes, *señor*," he said, "and also you have a hand!" There was admiration as well as anger in him.

"Thank you," Tyler responded.

"And now," said the shepherd, "you may be taking me into worse trouble than I ever had before in my life."

"Why?"

"I am taking you to El Tigre, and, if he's angry because of that, he will have me skinned alive."

"I've heard that he really has done that, *amigo*," said Tyler.

The other shuddered. "There was a man, once, who tried to leave the band. I saw what happened to him . . . I and a great many others. Yes, the skin was taken off him little by little. It was wonderful how much blood he had in him, for he did not die until just before the end. *Hai*, the yelling. It was so thin and high, it was like a needle through the brain, stabbing and stabbing." He smiled and shook his head, adding: "All is in the hands of fate, *señor*."

"Listen to me," Tyler began.

"I listen," said the shepherd, "to any man who is so quick to make his gun do his bidding."

"Very good," Tyler continued. "What I want to say is if you have trouble with El Tigre, I'll be your friend."

"You?"

"Yes."

"You are kind."

"I mean what I say."

"Perhaps you do, but what good will your kind heart do me? What can you do against El Tigre, if he decides to leap on us both?"

"He won't decide to do that," said the American.

"Do you know him?"

"I know him very well."

"And he knows you?"

"He knows me very well, too. We are old acquaintances."

"Not friends, eh?"

"No, not friends."

"It is all very strange. You are riding toward his camp . . . and you are riding alone . . . and you are not his friend," said the shepherd. He broke off with a whistle, his only means of expressing his immense amazement.

"You see, *amigo*," Tyler said, "sometimes the only way in this world is to dig under the ground to stop the forest fire. It may be living in the roots of the trees."

"That I don't understand," said the shepherd.

"You may, though, later on."

They were cutting gradually up a long, rough slope, and now two men suddenly appeared above the heads of some ragged rocks. Their rifles covered the two who were advancing.

"I came for El Tigre," Tyler announced.

They stared at the shepherd. The latter made them a covert sign, and with sudden grins the outposts nodded and then fell in behind the two riders. All four now crossed a rocky crest, and Tyler saw beneath him a little wooded hollow from the center of which was rising a very thin column of smoke. He could guess that the great El Tigre was not far from that fire.

IV

"The Mountain Lair"

It was a low growth of trees through which they rode down, hardly more than high brush. Finally they came out into a clearing or, rather, a natural opening, with several shelters constructed around it and what was apparently a community fireplace in the middle. From this arose a steady fume of smoke, so thin that it would hardly rise to visibility above the heads of the surrounding summits, for it was fed with the driest of dry wood. Here at the fire were two women cooking, squatting beside a number of blackened pots, and off to the side several more were scrubbing out corn to make the tortilla meal without which a true Mexican can hardly live.

There was only one man in sight, and he was a grim figure in a black hat and a black coat, smoking a pipe. He made no motion when the stranger appeared with three companions.

"There is El Tigre," the shepherd said to the man he had guided. "But you know him, of course."

"Of course," said the other. With a wave of his hand to his escort, he rode straight toward the seated man.

He had seen from the corner of his eye that, as he left them, the three prepared their weapons. In case a signal were given, his life would be short, indeed. Nevertheless, he kept his head high as he rode on toward the man on the rock.

The latter, as he came nearer, took the pipe from his mouth and, as he lifted his head to stare at the horseman, the wind curled back the brim of his hat and showed a small, square face with extremely large eyes, round and bright, and a short but bristling mustache. In fact, there was an actual resemblance between his face and a cat's.

"Hello, *amigo*," the rider said, without dismounting.

"*Señor* Tyler," said the other, and stood up, smiling. It was a mechanical smile, and the wrinkles that appeared in his cheeks were as though carved there.

"I'm glad that you remember me," Tyler said, and slid from his horse.

"I never forget brave men," said the other. "You cost me a good many thousand dollars. Nevertheless, I am glad to see you again. You are not as big as I thought you were."

"I'm dried up by living too much in the sun," Tyler suggested.

The other shook his head. "No," he answered. "But men who are capable of action always look larger than life when they're busily employed. You were very busy, that other time when I saw you, my friend."

"It was a question of jump fast or die before I jumped," explained Tyler.

"You made a good deal of money out of it, I suppose?" El Tigre asked.

"I never take blood money, if that's what you mean."

"Ah, no?" El Tigre commented, lifting his brows.

"Never!"

"What brought you there that night, then, if I may ask?" As he spoke, he held up his pipe like a Chinaman, between upturned thumb and fore-finger, and then puffed at it slowly, seeming to find the fragrance of the tobacco so delicious that he never could have enough of it. All the while his round, over-bright eyes were fixed upon the face of the visitor.

"The reason that I came there that night was not a very good one," Tyler began. "When I saw the boy on that horse, I decided that the horse was too good for the rider. So I followed him."

"Eh?" queried the crafty El Tigre sharply.

"I thought," said the other, "that a horse like that was more than the boy was apt to keep, considering the country that he was riding through. I was sorry for the boy, and I followed along for that reason."

"Come, come, *señor*," said the bandit. "One does not throw one's life away for a cause like that. You were hired to protect that boy, or else he was your kin. You never would have done otherwise, what you did at the inn."

31

Tyler looked for a moment at the small, cat-like face of the other. Then he answered, very slowly: "I told you that I saw a young fool of a boy on a fine horse, and that I was afraid he would not keep the horse very long in that part of the world without protection."

"Ah, yes," murmured the Mexican. "I was not giving you the lie, *Señor* Tyler. I was merely hoping that you would be more frank with an old acquaintance."

"I intend to be as open as day."

"That is always the best way, I think. But will you tell me where you were hidden that night? How did you rise out of the floor?"

"I didn't rise out of the floor. I was simply sitting there among you at the time."

"*Señor* Tyler," El Tigre stated, "I looked each one of my men in the face as they came in."

"But I didn't come in, at first."

"No?"

"No."

"At what time later? When could you have come in?"

"One of the lamps went out, you remember?"

"Yes, I remember that. The thing began to sputter, and a draft caught it and knocked out the flame."

"Then a man came in with another lamp when you shouted, because there was nothing to see by except the flare of the fire."

"I remember that," El Tigre recalled. "It was one of the men of the inn. I remember his servant . . . I remember the way he came in, sheltering the flame of the new lamp."

"Exactly, sheltering it so that a shadow fell completely across his face like a mask."

"Ha?" El Tigre said.

"That was I. I brought the lamp in, when you shouted," said the American. "It was an old smoky one, with an untrimmed wick. You cursed me for bringing such a lamp, and I faded into the back of the room."

"That could not be all," the bandit insisted.

"It was. You were busy talking, just then, about what should be done with the boy. You remember that he lay tied in front of the fire?"

"Yes. I remember that."

"And so," Tyler explained, "as you grew more and more interested, I simply slipped into a chair at the back of the room. Nobody marked me. I was one of them. By degrees I worked forward from chair to chair. Most of the men were wearing their hats, you remember?"

"I remember!" exclaimed the bandit.

"So I picked up one of the sombreros that had been laid aside. It fitted me well enough that I pulled down the brim so that it flopped in front of my eyes. I might as well have been fitted out with a mask of black velvet, it hid my face so well, unless someone chose to look close and hard at me. And no one chose to do that. I had shed the apron at the first moment. I was there dressed like the rest of you. As for the servant, when I went to the back of the room and opened the door and slammed it again, it appears that I had run out of the place in fear of your curses."

El Tigre sat down again. He rested his elbow on his knee. His eyes half closed and, except for the pipe stem, that he kept fuming under his nose, he looked more like a cat than ever, a cat warming itself at a good fire.

"Now I understand," he said. "Yes, I understand now. For a man without fear, such a thing was possible, of course."

"It wasn't a matter of the absence of fear . . . it was the question of too great a curiosity, *Señor* Tigre. I had to find out what happened to the boy, or what was about to happen to him. I thought, when I went into the room, that he'd been put out of the way already."

"Murdered?"

"Yes."

"And then?"

"I wanted to find out who had turned the trick."

"And kill him for it, eh?" the Mexican asked gently.

"Exactly that," said the American, and looked calmly into the round, bright, cat-like eyes of the other.

El Tigre smiled and looked down. He inhaled a long breath of the smoke and let it fume gradually out at mouth and lips. "Very good!" he said. "Very good, indeed!" Then, gradually, he lifted his gaze once more to the face of Tyler. "How many men did you shoot that night, after you knocked the chimney off the lamp and left the room dark. Do you know?"

"Several. I don't know how many."

"Five," El Tigre announced, after making a pause. "You shot five men." Then he added: "They were all shot in the legs. Why was that, *Señor* Tyler? At that range, even by the crazy, jumping light of the fire, you could have worked with a better marksmanship than that."

"I wanted to make the confusion worse, that was all," Tyler confessed. "If I dropped a man with a bullet through the body, he was dead, and that was all there was to it. But one man with a bullet through a leg will wriggle about more than a snake with its head off and upset the aim of a lot of other people. That was what happened. The whole room was in confusion. I was able to get to the water bucket and throw the water on the fire. Then there was complete darkness, and the rest was easy."

"Easy?" exclaimed the other. "I don't see that it was easy at all! Lights were brought in on the run a few seconds later. The window was still locked on the inside. You could not have got out through the door without being seen. How did you make yourself and the boy disappear?"

"You forget the big fireplace, with the pile of wood that was drying at one side of it, inside the chimney hood. I had simply dragged the boy back there with me. We almost suffocated, but we did not have to stay there long. When you got the lights and saw that the boy and myself had

35

both disappeared, those of you who could run hurried out to find the trail. The servants of the inn at once carried out the wounded. In two minutes that room was empty. Then the boy and I stepped out from our covert. Of course, I had cut the ropes that tied him while we waited, and given him a gun so that he could help to fight his way out, in case we were smoked from cover."

"But I remember, when the lights came on, the fireplace was boiling full of white smoke and steam!" exclaimed the bandit.

"Mostly steam, I think," Tyler insisted, "and a man can breathe steam and keep on living, for a few minutes. It wasn't comfortable, but we just managed to last it out. Then we walked out."

"Where?"

"I opened the door of the room, and we went down the hall."

"Ha! You have no weak nerves, *señor!*"

"It was a matter of necessity. We found one servant in the hallway, but he seemed to think that we were part of the men of El Tigre. He paid no attention to us, but hurried on to clean up the bloodstains before they soaked into the floor. We turned out the side door. Your people had looked to make sure that the horses were all in place at the hitching rack in front of the inn. Then you rushed back to the stable. Well, *señor,* we simply helped ourselves from the line of horses. He took his own Thoroughbred. And I felt it would be better to borrow yours, because we might need to ride fast before the morning came."

"So, so, so," El Tigre murmured, and a strange smile came in his eyes, but not at all in his face.

"That is the whole truth about the matter," said Tyler.

"And the money we had taken from him, did you get that, also?"

"Yes. Just before I started shooting, I scooped it up from the table where it had been placed to be divided as soon as the boy was disposed of."

"It is all perfectly clear," El Tigre remarked, "but there remains a greater mystery, which I think that you cannot clear up so well."

"What is that?"

"The mystery of how you dare to come to me again, *señor?*"

V

"A Challenge"

"That is easily explained, too," Tyler said. He sat down beside the Mexican and dropped his hands into the pockets of his coat, took them out again with the materials to make a cigarette, and manufactured one with lightning speed. Soon he was smoking, taking it in with great breaths.

"I listen," said the other.

"You'll hear, too," Tyler said. "The fact is, *Señor* Tigre, that I've taken over the protection of the American mines. You've heard already that the protection of that so-called Vizcaya is not wanted?"

El Tigre stroked his mustache with a delicate forefinger. He smiled, as though the hair had tickled the tip of his finger.

"Good," he said.

"I'm glad that you think so," said the other. "I was afraid that you might not like it."

"You have taken over the mines, and, therefore, you come to tell me that it is foolish for me to try to make any more money from them, the way that I have done in the past. Is that so?"

"That is so."

"Heaven be praised," El Tigre said, "that I

38

have met a man who has no fear, even if he should happen to be a fool."

"Am I a fool, Tigre?"

"Do you think that you can frighten me off?"

"You're getting only ten thousand a month. At least half of that you have to split here and there . . . to keep the *rurales* from interfering and to buy off this man and that. Out of your five thousand a month, you have to pay your men. That doesn't leave you very much for yourself."

"My men are cheaply kept," El Tigre assured.

"The glory of working for you is the biggest part of their pay, of course," said the American, in his grave manner.

"Exactly," the Mexican replied. "I find that I make a reasonable amount of money each month. Besides, now that they have given up paying for protection, I shall loot the mines and take off several months' pay at one stroke. After that, they'll be glad to begin payments once more, at double the old rate."

"You see, Tigre," the American said, "that you may be arguing falsely about all this. Suppose, for instance. . . ." He paused.

"Yes, yes. Suppose?"

"Suppose, when you come to rob the mines, you are only able to gather not silver, but little chunks of lead, fired straight at the heart or at the head?"

"Suppose, suppose," El Tigre said. And then he laughed with a soft purring sound in his voice. "Why should I suppose such things, when I know that they cannot be true? I shall raid the mines when I please, *amigo*. They are mine, to take when I will, and what I will!"

"*Señor* Tigre, you are rash," said the other.

"You are rash to say so," answered the Mexican.

"I say it again. You are rash."

"I don't think so. You are the rash one, *Señor* Tyler. Brave and frank in coming to tell me about the past, but wild and foolish to tell me about the future, when you see that there are three of my men over there, two with rifles and one with a revolver. Which of them, which of those heaven-born idiots, dared to guide you up to this place?"

"The shepherd," Tyler answered, "but he only did it after I put a gun under his nose, and because he was sure that he would be walking me into a trap."

"Perhaps he is not a fool, then, *señor*," suggested the other. "Perhaps you are the fool, my friend?"

"Gently, gently, Tigre. I am not a fool until I am proved a fool."

"I lift my finger, and you are a dead man, *señor*, protector of the mines!"

"Lift your finger, and you are dead first, Tigre," said his companion.

"Ah?"

"Don't move that hand of yours, *amigo*," said the American. "We sit here and talk patiently and calmly, one with another, like old friends. You observe that my right hand is free and at ease, and only a thousandth part of a second from the trigger of a revolver, Tigre. Do not move, unless you wish to forget that, or unless you wish to have a little duel of speed with me. I know that your way with a gun is excellent, but I prefer my own. Give me the draw from a spring holster under the coat, to the draw from a holster at the hip. You are old-fashioned in that one thing, El Tigre. In all others, you are my admiration."

The lips of the Mexican parted, his white teeth shone. But there was neither pleasure nor mirth in his smile. "You begin to interest me, *Señor* Tyler," he said. "You begin to interest me more than anything under the blue of that sky." He raised his hand and pointed, but the hand moved very slowly, indeed.

"Thank you," Tyler answered. "I am glad of that. The good Providence that takes care of us, Tigre, has given me very little . . . no talents, no cleverness of wits, no brains to make money, no skill to lead or impress other men, but in exchange for all that I lack it has given to me one small thing."

"What is that?"

"The ability to take a little revolver quickly from beneath my coat and the talent to shoot the bullets in it rapidly and straight at a mark. I hope that today you will not be the mark."

"And if you were able to draw your gun before I drew mine . . . which I doubt," El Tigre taunted, "you would immediately be riddled

41

with bullets from those rifles."

"Perhaps. I never expected a long life. But I'm not sure that they would hit me. There is such a thing as buck fever. And when they saw you fall dead, I would be something more than a deer in their eyes. I would run at the side of that mustang over the brow of the hill. If they shot well, they might send some lead into the poor horse, but I would bet on my chances of getting into the rough rocks. From that point . . . well, it is hard to catch a man in this country, Tigre, as you well know."

"Your spirit is high," El Tigre said. He looked at Tyler, and in the eyes of the American he saw a faint gleam of yellowish fire. He had seen that light before, in his days, and always just before a man took his life in his hands. A faint chill entered the spinal marrow of the bandit. "You talk well," he said. "But still I don't make you out."

"There are several causes that brought me here today. One of them was to make sure that you are really at work here, that another man has not borrowed your name and reputation for a time. Then, again, I have been able to see the faces of four of your people. Ah, there are three more running out from that hut. That makes seven. I have a good memory for faces. Not for print, but for faces, Tigre. You yourself may disappear. You may give up this camp, also, but you cannot make seven other faces disappear. Sooner or later I should find one of them, and they would bring me to the trail of the master quickly enough."

"You talk well," El Tigre repeated, but a glare was coming in his own eyes.

"I now know that you are here, in person. I know that I can recognize seven of your people and, in addition, I offer you a suggestion."

"And that is?"

"To give up the mines."

"Ah?" The Mexican sneered, but the sneer was faint.

"You see," Tyler went on, arguing softly, "I know that you are intelligent enough to change your mind. You do not jump over cliffs, and neither do you rush against a thick wall. Now, while you are here pretending that there was a Vizcaya giving the mine protection, stealing a few sheep and goats to feed your men, and getting your money paid in hand every month, the game was worthwhile. But, with me against you, is it worthwhile? I've pointed out that your profits can never have been very great. Now, if you attempt the mines, you find me in them, and my fighting men. Men ready to die, men ready to shoot straight. Is the game worthwhile? I ask you as a practical man. You may attack us once or twice, but if you do, sooner or later, I find your place in the hills and raid it in my turn. And many men shall die. Is it worthwhile, Tigre?"

"As a matter of business, perhaps not," said the other. "But then, *señor*, you forget another thing."

"What is that?" said the American.

"My honor!" El Tigre stated.

43

VI

"The Innkeeper"

"Your honor? Your honor?" murmured Tyler.
Then he added: "You mean your business reputation, eh? That's worth a great deal to you, naturally."

"Yes, naturally," answered the robber. He
shrugged his narrow shoulders, and there was
again that faint flicker of amusement in his
round, bright, inhuman eyes.

"Well," Tyler said, "I can understand that,
too. If you pull out of this game about the mines,
no matter how little you make on it and no
matter how many teeth you break, you'll lose
hundreds of thousands of dollars' worth of reputation."

"Besides," El Tigre answered, "since we're
being so perfectly frank, there's the little matter
between you and me."

"Of course, you want to even things up?"

"Of course," said the bandit.

Tyler stood up. "I've put the cards on the
table, Tigre."

"I thank you for it."

"For instance, I might have come the first time
with a dozen rifles."

44

"That's true, but you would never have come over the rim of the hill, if you'd brought so many. You are leaving, *Señor* Tyler?"

"I am going back to organize the defense of the mines. Yes. Good bye, *Señor* Tigre."

"Good bye," said the Mexican. "I wish you every possible good luck and fortune, until we meet again."

"Shall I ask you to walk up to the ridge of the hill with me?" Tyler asked. "Or will you let me ride away from here?"

El Tigre smiled, looking more like a cat than ever. "I'll walk with you to the top of the hill. I have no desire to kill you now, Tyler. It would be too casual, too out of hand. I want you to wait for a time and taste things in progress."

"Good old fellow," said the American.

He walked uphill among the rocks, with the black cloak and the wide black hat at his shoulder. When they reached the crest, he turned, and held out his hand. El Tigre took it without the slightest hesitation and gave it a warm pressure.

"What a brave man you are, *Señor* Tyler," said the Mexican.

"You are the king of the robbers of the whole world, Tigre," said the American. "What a pleasure to have seen you so close, face to face." He mounted. He took off his hat and bowed to the cat face of the bandit, then he reined his horse sidewise down the slope, still keeping his face turned toward El Tigre, still bowing with hat in

45

hand, like a courtier, until the horse was safely behind an outthrust of big rocks.

From that point, Tyler rode like a snipe down the wind, dodging his horse from one covert of rocks to another, until he made sure that there was no pursuit, no attempt at picking him off with a long-range shot. When he was sure of this, he drew the goat-footed mustang back to an easy jog, and so turned down the valley, through the gap, and back to the town of Santa Anna.

As he went along, he began to sing. It was not very much of a musical feat, that singing. It was, in fact, rather more of a nasal whine, but it pleased the ear of Jim Tyler so much, that he sang louder and louder, his head upon one side, his eyes half closed. So, singing of "Sweet Adeline," for whom he pined, he came back into Santa Anna.

He was content. The world had for him the flavor of wine. He was delighted with the whole face of existence, because he knew that there lay before him enough adventure to fill even his strong and empty hands.

He went to a *fonda* at the edge of the town. It was not very big, and it was not very clean, on the outside, but in the damp coolness of the interior all was as neat as a pin and the floor continually whitened with scrubbing. There in the *fonda* he sat at a little table on which he rested both of his elbows and talked to the proprietor as the latter brought him a glass of beer.

"Antonio," he said, "do you know me?"

The proprietor colored a little. "I have never seen you before, *señor*," he said, "but I am glad that you know my name."

"You name is over your door," Tyler said. "Can you guess at mine?"

"*Señor,*" said the other, "may I call you The Wolf?"

"It's a name that's been given to me," admitted Tyler. "I'm not proud of it, but, at least, it makes me known to you. By what token, Antonio?"

"I have heard many people speak of you, *señor*, of your face and the strength of your shoulders, the lightness and length of your body. I have heard a great deal about you for many years, *señor*."

"But never a word of kindness?"

"Oh, yes, I am sure."

"Never a word of kindness, Antonio, I know that. Be honest."

"In fact, *señor*, men are not often kind when they speak in fear."

"In fear?"

"The whole world fears the. . . ." He paused, the dreadful name sticking behind his teeth.

"What man did you last hear speak of me, Antonio?"

"Ah, *señor*, I would make no trouble. Not I. Not for worlds would I be the cause that blood should be. . . ."

"Antonio, will you try to believe me? These people who don't like me, at least they have given me the name of being an honest man? Is that true?"

"Your honor is a perfect thing, *señor,* of course. Everyone knows that."

"Now, then, Antonio, I want to speak to you something that you must believe."

"I shall believe every word, and gladly, *señor.*"

"Very well, then. There are in town, here in Santa Anna, certain good men and strong men, a little wild in their ways, now and then, most of them given to drinking hard liquor, fond of whisky or tequila or such stuff. They are generally fast, rough riders, and high-handed in their manners."

"No doubt, *señor,*" said the proprietor of the inn. "I suppose that there are such men to be found in every town in this part of the world."

"But a few more in Santa Anna," suggested Tyler. "A few more here, I dare say, and you've heard a certain number of them curse the name of The Wolf, swearing that they would cut his throat, have you not?"

"I have heard many men curse you, *señor.* I am sorry for it, but I have heard them, it is true."

"Why should you be sorry, Antonio?" Tyler asked. "If men aren't my friends, it pleases me that they're my hearty enemies. It gives life spice, and I wouldn't have it otherwise. Not I."

"*Señor,*" said Antonio, "I believe what you say."

"Now, then, listen to me carefully," said Tyler.

48

"With all my heart, *señor*."

"Of the men you have heard curse me, there are some who stood out above the rest, are there not?"

"Certainly, *señor*."

"Brave men, good riders, quick with their guns, ready to fight anything from a panther to a man."

"Such men there are among them, of course."

"Then, Antonio, I want you to make a list of their names . . . not for my eyes, mind you, but for your own. And I want you to pick out a dozen or twenty from among them all. Not sneaking cutthroats, but brave, upstanding men. The more they hate me, the better. I have a good use for them. When you can get in touch with them, send them straight to the office of that American down the street, that *Señor* Reed."

The innkeeper was dazed. However, shaking his head as though to clear away the mists of confusion, he said that he would do all he was bidden. Then his hand was presently closing over ten dollars, and he was watching the American step from the cool, thick gloom of the *fonda* into the brilliant shock of the sunshine in the street.

Antonio lifted the coin; it glinted brightly like mellow sunshine under his eyes. "What work of Satan goes forward now?" he murmured. "But then, what other sort of work can one expect from The Wolf?"

VII

"The Rat Retires"

Tyler went down to the office of Tobias Reed with his mustang stepping at his heels. Still, as he went, he was singing softly, "Sweet Adeline." His eyes were misted by the high notes, as he stepped into the sanctum of Reed.

The little man jumped up from his desk and came hurrying forward. "What have you done now, Tyler?" he asked. "A long time has passed. I suppose that you've been finding men?"

"I've set somebody else at finding the men for me," Tyler replied. "In the meantime, I've been up to the hills, and I've chatted with El Tigre, seen some of his men, and made sure that this fellow Vizcaya is, as I thought he would prove to be, merely a sham behind which El Tigre works more safely. Vizcaya is not protecting you . . . he's simply helping El Tigre to extort more money. If you were able to look into the thing, you'd find out that the men who are supposed to be hired by Vizcaya are really the men of El Tigre. And one of these days you'll find it out to your cost."

"The scoundrel!" Reed hissed. "I'll have him jailed."

"I don't think," said Tyler, "that the jail in Santa Anna would hold him very long."

"Heaven deliver us," Reed muttered. "Now I begin to think of it, I remember that the man who's been coming to me in the name of Vizcaya is the man who runs the jail here. He's one of the politicians and officials."

"Beware of 'em in Mexico," Tyler said. "Beware of 'em in our own country, too, for that matter, I suppose."

"There, there!" Reed shouted, pointing suddenly. "There he rides down the street at this moment!"

Jim Tyler looked, and through the window he saw the gallant form of *Señor* Ramón Díaz mounted on a prancing, fine-limbed charger, while at his side rode a dark-skinned little beauty of a Mexican girl, looking rather grave as she stared up from enormous black eyes toward her escort.

"That's Ramón Díaz," Reed explained. "D'you think that he looks like a rascal?"

"I never could tell a rascal from an honest man, by the face," Tyler confessed. "That is, not a rascal worth his salt. But this Díaz is almost too handsome to be true. Who's the sad beauty with him, now?"

The couple had passed out of view by this time.

"That's the daughter of rich old Gonzales, Anita Gonzales. Her father is the wise one who bought land for a hundred miles along the course of the railroad before it was built. He bought it for nothing, and after the railroad went through, well, it was worth something. Change an acre price from ten cents to five dollars and it's not much on a small scale, but it's worthwhile when there's half a million acres on the book."

"A wise man," Tyler nodded, grinning. "And she's something to Díaz? Fiancée?"

"I don't think so. The way I have the story," said the other, "she's engaged to the dearest friend of Díaz, and that friend is the young revolutionary, Pedro Salvatore."

"I've heard of him."

"Yes, everybody's heard of him. He's about the only one of the lot who's fighting for the good of Mexico, rather than the good of his own pocketbook."

"He's real, is he?"

"Real as steel, I understand. I saw him once before he joined the revolutionists. He had a fine look about him, he stood straight, and he had a good pair of eyes. He looked like a man to me."

"You find 'em that way in Mexico," agreed Tyler, "and, when you find 'em, they're the best in the world, almost."

A boy slipped into the room, to announce that Mr. Ramón Díaz was about to enter.

"I'll go out," Tyler said.

"Stay where you are," Reed said, scowling. "You might be interested in seeing this fellow closer at hand. Maybe you can make more sense out of him than I can."

"I can make out this much," Tyler said at once, "if he claims to be representing any Beltran Vizcaya, he's a liar, the king of liars."

The door opened again, and Díaz came into the room. He started a little at the sight of Tyler.

"Friend of mine from the north," said the miner abruptly, by way of introduction. "Tyler, this is Ramón Díaz."

The two shook hands. The big, magnificently black eyes of Díaz went softly, swiftly over the form of the tall American.

"I came for a little quiet and private chat, Mister Reed," Díaz stated. "I'll wait until another time, when you're not engaged?"

"Sit down and tell me what's on your mind. Tyler, here, is such a friend of mine that he might as well know anything that you've got to say."

"Ah, but this is about Vizcaya." He said it softly. He raised one forefinger as he spoke, to instill caution to approaching such a dangerous topic.

The miner, however, merely scowled back at the Mexican youth. "What about Vizcaya?" he asked. "Did you send him word that I wouldn't have his protection any more at any price?"

"I've sent the word," said Díaz. "Vizcaya flew into a terrible passion, to begin with. He swore that he'd have the blood of any man who suspected him of being a mere extortionist. Mexican honor has tender points, Mister Reed, and

I'm afraid that you touched Beltran Vizcaya rather deeply."

"Did I?" Reed said with an ominous terseness.

"I'm afraid that you did," continued the Mexican suavely. "However, I managed to soothe him. I knew, when you flew into a little temper, that you might regret it later on. I was sorry about it, and thought that I'd better simply leave you to cool off, Mister Reed. In the meantime, I talked seriously with Vizcaya. As you know, he's a man of common sense and practical mind. Finally I was able to point out to him that if he were willing to take a somewhat larger chance, he might be able to hold off the danger of El Tigre with the men he already has, somewhat increased. To be frank, he didn't like the danger involved. But at length he was persuaded that the thing could be done for only half of the advance that he had originally thought would be necessary." Díaz laughed a little in the most genuine and open manner. "You see," he continued, "that I am something of a diplomat in your behalf, Mister Reed."

"Thanks," Reed said very shortly.

"And so, sir, Vizcaya is now ready to guarantee protection to the mines for fifteen thousand a month. That's the lowest figure I could reduce him to."

Reed turned and looked at Tyler. The tall American was smiling in a way that did not illumine his eyes.

"How much of that money does Vizcaya get

for his bluff?" asked Tyler.

"What?" Díaz asked.

"How much, Díaz?"

"I don't understand this," Díaz said with dignity and bewilderment at once. "Is your friend authorized to talk for you, Mister Reed?"

"Seems so," Reed said bluntly.

Díaz drew in a breath, and at the same time he drew his gloves slowly through the tight grip of his left hand. It was plain that he was very much displeased.

"I understand you to ask," he said to Tyler, "how much *Señor* Vizcaya gets for his . . . bluff? Did you use that word in regard to an honorable gentleman?"

"Honorable. Stuff and nonsense," Tyler stated calmly. "What does Vizcaya get? Two or three hundred dollars out of the whole thing, or would it be as much as five hundred? He's a cheap worker, I understand."

Díaz stared. He made no answer.

"Go on and speak up, Díaz," urged Tyler.

"You speak in a manner as one who wishes to insult," the Mexican said at last.

"I'm glad that you have such a fast brain, Díaz," Tyler answered. "Go-between rats like you are pretty slow at understanding insults, though, as far as my experience goes."

"Saints!" groaned the Mexican. He drew himself up on tiptoe; his right hand doubled into a tight fist.

"Don't bluff when you're playing a real game

with real money on the table," Tyler said. "I've been up in the hills, and I've seen your cat-faced friend, El Tigre."

It was a home shot that seemed to strike the young Mexican to the very heart. He turned a pale, sallow, greenish color, and his chest that had been distended with anger suddenly collapsed.

"El Tigre!" he gasped.

"Yeah, that explodes some of your pride, eh?" Tyler asked. "You brazen little four-flusher, get out of this office, and stay out. If there were a decent law in the land, we'd have you in stripes for this job of yours . . . extortion, Díaz. It's by far the dirtiest game of all."

Díaz, it appeared, was a man of some courage. He had taken the shock of the first revelation badly, but now he rallied under the repeated insults. He ground his teeth and stamped on the floor. "Perhaps," he said, "you are one of the hired brigands of El Tigre, but that will not permit you to enter Santa Anna and insult. By heaven, you'll find out that there is a law in the land and. . . ."

The door of the office flew open with a crash. In the opening stood a huge man with a peeled red face that looked raw, except where the pigment had collected in great blotches of freckles. The dust of recent riding lay thickly upon his shoulders. His sweat had blackened his flannel shirt, and in places the salt of that sweat had dried in layers whiter than the alkali dust. He wore upon either thigh a big gun. An ammunition belt sagged at an angle over his hips. In every respect he looked like a man capable of desperate action. And now his loud voice roared out.

"What fool says that The Wolf is in town?"

He might himself have worn, it seemed, even a worse name than this. As he glanced around, his eyes fell on Tyler.

Díaz, in the meantime, was muttering: "The Wolf? That fiend? Who speaks of him?"

"By the eternal, high-jumping thunder," roared the big man in the doorway. "It's The Wolf himself! Tyler, confound you, I dunno whether to curse you or to shake hands with you!"

"Either way goes for me," Tyler said, slowly rising from his chair.

"It's so dog-gone far south," said the other, "that I'm gonna forget the way that you trimmed me in the old days, Jim. I gotta admit that I'm glad to see you, and there's my hand on it, if you want it. Or if you don't, I'll make it a fist."

Tyler readily stepped forward and grasped the burly hand of the other. He smiled with genuine pleasure as he looked into that red face and the red-stained eyes of the intruder. "I'm glad to see you, Bull," he said. He glanced aside, at the others. "This is Tommy Jones, sometimes called Bull Jones. Mister Díaz . . . Mister Reed."

The big man waved his hand and said —
"Howdy." — to the others. That was all. Then

he turned toward Díaz.

The latter was moving softly through the doorway into the hall.

"What's the matter with friend pussyfoot?" asked Jones.

"He smells trouble," Tyler said, "and he's going home to his own safe rat hole."

VIII

"The Gunmen"

Jones, more often called Bull, was not alone, and behind him came in no less than six other men. They were of varying sorts. Three were Americans. There was a one-eyed Portuguese with a tattoo mark covering half of one cheek. There was a sleek, lean Malay, and there was a shining black Negro, who addressed Tyler as "master," and seemed to mean what he said.

All of these men looked on Tyler with a burning interest.

It seemed to Reed that they were as keen as chickens that see a grain of wheat and are eager to pick it up.

Tyler made them a speech in the presence of Reed, a speech that the little man was never to forget to his death day.

Tyler, alias The Wolf, said: "All you fellows are old acquaintances of mine. I remember you, Mickey, in the shaft of the mine, when you lighted the fuse and ran for it."

"I didn't get far," Mickey said. "You planted me with a chunk of lead. The whole gang got out, and I was the last. I dunno how I managed to crawl. I dunno why you let me crawl, seeing that I'd tried to trap the lot of you."

"You were dead game, Mickey," Tyler said, "and the way you ambled along on one leg and two hands, I thought that such a fellow needed to have a fair chance at living his life. So I didn't tap you on the head as I went by. But all of you fellows I've known, here and there, under difficult circumstances, more or less."

"More, not less," Bull Jones said. "Always more, brother Tyler. There ain't doubt about that. Why, boys, I spent a half hour trying to bash his head in with a crowbar in an old quarry, and he didn't have nothing but his empty hands, and the walls was a lot too steep for him to climb out. How we got down in there was a different kind of a yarn, Jimmy, eh?"

"Quite different," Tyler agreed.

"And every time that I swung that crowbar, he managed to dodge sideways or under the swing of it, and get clean away."

"No, you clipped me over the head with it once," Tyler corrected.

"Yeah, that's right, I nicked him alongside of the head with it once, and he dropped, and the blood came spurting out, and I thought that I'd brained him. But when I gave the bar another heave to make sure by smashing the skull of his to bits, damn my hide, if he didn't come to life enough to roll out of my way and, a second later, there he was again, playing tag with me. Finally I swung too wide, and he got in at me before I could recover, and then it was a different story.

I ain't a baby, but then I ain't a wildcat, either. And I was considerable bruised and clawed before you finished with me, Tyler."

"That's all in the past," Tyler said, "and. . . ."

"It's in the past," said the other, "but I'm gonna have a couple of acres of your scalp for it, just the same."

"Good! Every one of you that wants a fair and square showdown with me, can have it any time," said Tyler. "I'm at his service, and I mean what I say."

There was a general rumbling murmur of content at this, but Reed could not help noticing that none of the men immediately demanded satisfaction.

Then Tyler went on: "You can have all the chances at me that you want, but, in the meantime, I take it that most of you boys are out of luck, or you wouldn't be down here in Santa Anna."

"Take me," Bull Jones said. "I wouldn't be in any trouble at all, except that I missed the head of a sheriff I was shooting at and only blowed off his ear. So he took after me, and the trail was pretty warm, till I got over the river."

"I was selling mighty good dollar bills for forty cents apiece," the Negro put in. "And damn my bad luck, Master Tyler, the bulls got hold of some of them bills and put a magnifyin' glass onto 'em, and what they saw was a picture that was just as pretty as what the government mint prints, but not quite the same. And they got riled

61

up, they did. I tell you what, boss, it don't matter about the state police, but the federal agents, they ain't particular where they step, so long as they can catch you by the hair of the head."

"I've noticed that myself a lot of times," Tyler said. "The federal agents are always nuisances. They never seem to get discouraged. A sheriff can be a pest, but a marshal, he's a regular nerve disease. He never gets out of your system."

There was another general muttering of assent at this. Several others started to speak at once, but Tobias Reed began to realize that every one of these precious fellows was a breaker of the law who had fled south of the Río Grande until the storm had blown over.

Tyler continued: "I take it that none of you fellows would be above turning an honest penny?"

"Depends on how honest it is," Bull Jones said.

"Yeah, that's the idea," said a man named Bud Wynne, who had a grin that stretched, almost literally, from ear to ear. "It's gotta be sort of honest."

"This is dead honest," Tyler assured them. "How would you fellows like to step on the side of the law and be private police for a little while?"

"Working with you, Jim?" asked the Portuguese.

"With me, friend," Tyler affirmed.

"I wouldn't even mind being a policeman," said the Portuguese, "if you'll show me on the job how you handle your Colt."

"I'll show you all how I handle it, I hope, before the job's ended," Tyler said. "The idea is this. My friend here, Mister Tobias Reed, is the president of a company of Americans who have some silver mines in the mountains yonder. And there's that fellow, El Tigre, who thinks that he wants a part of the profits. That's all right, too, but he doesn't go about it the way that an honest thug should. He doesn't simply raid the mines, but he works a gag . . . that is to say, he hires a second-rate thug to pretend to protect the mines from him, El Tigre, and the thug collects several thousand dollars a month for the protection. Now, boys, what I want to do is to get fifteen or twenty of you together, all of the same pure quill, and give Mister Reed protection . . . and while we're protecting the mines, we'll try our hands at running down El Tigre, if we can manage it. Does that sound to you?"

"What's in it?" asked one of the men.

"Five dollars a day."

A general groan was the response.

"What do you make out of it?" asked Bull Jones.

"Not a penny, I think," Tyler said, "except that El Tigre is another old acquaintance of mine, and we'll never rest easy, either of us, until he or I is dead. Is that clear?"

"That's clear," Wynne said. "Five bucks a day will do for me, if that's the lay-out. I always liked to be in on a grudge fight."

The others agreed with one voice.

"I expected more of you than that," Tyler said. "Antonio ought to be able to put his hand on more than this little group of hand-painted beauties."

"Tod Murphy ain't anywhere far," said one.

"Spill Lessing is around, somewhere," said another.

"And Ernesto Baccigalupi."

Half a dozen other names rattled off the tongues of the men.

"That's all straight, then," Tyler said. "You fellows rustle around town, and see who you can get. I don't want a man that's not a proved man. Every one of you is perfect. I know that because I've tested you all myself, one time or another, and a warm time I've had of it with you all. I've had to have seven spare lives to live through the hands of the seven of you. I want another seven or a dozen of the same, if you can find that many around this tough little town. Meet me at Antonio's, at the *fonda,* in about an hour. Every man with his horse, his rifle, and his revolvers. I'll buy the ammunition before I leave the town."

"What bonus to the gent that plasters El Tigre and breaks up the game that way?" asked Bull Jones.

"Five thousand bucks, and my friendship to the end of time."

"I'll chuck the money for the sake of the second part of that reward," Jones stated. "I come here thinking that I wanted to cut your throat, Tyler. But I've changed my mind. It's the kind of a leather throat that looks like it would turn any razor edge."

He laughed as he spoke, and yet there was a great deal of meaning in what he said. The rest joined in his mirth, with approving nods, and the whole group now herded out of the office and into the street, which presently was ringing with their voices.

Tyler, standing close to the window, laughed as he listened to them, his head bowed a little toward the floor, a singular smile on his lips.

"What do you think, Tyler?" Reed asked anxiously.

"I don't know. What do you think?"

"That I never saw such a precious collection of rascals in all my born days."

"Nor I," Tyler agreed. "When I'm with 'em, we're the flower of the penitentiary world, as you might say."

"Have you ever served time, Tyler?" Reed asked.

"Never, and I never shall."

"Ah, but, man, man, how can you tell, living the wild life that you do?"

"I can tell easily enough," said the other, with a shrug of those wide, lean-muscled shoulders of his. "I can tell, because I always keep one last bullet inside the revolver. That's labeled for papa, to be used at home." He chuckled as he said this, then, raising his head, he went on: "You've seen my men, Reed, and you may not like their looks exactly, but every one of 'em is a killer . . . every one of 'em is a man I know. You trust me, and I'll trust them . . . and among the lot of us, I'm going to make those mountains entirely too hot for El Tigre!"

IX

"At the Mines"

Ned Cardigan was thirty-two years old, good Welsh fighting stock, although an American by birth, training, and education, and now holding down his first big job as manager and chief engineer of the United Mines.

This evening, he walked up and down in front of the shacks at the end of the valley in which the mines stood, very ill at ease. His assistant Sam Gloster walked with him. It was a gloomy time of day; in fact, one could hardly say whether it was day or night, for it was the moment between the two. The sun was down. The last color was gone from the sky. The mountains were turned almost entirely from brown to black. Yet there was still sufficient sunshine in the upper air to make the big moon, now nearing the three-quarters, hardly brighter than a patch of cloud in the middle of the day.

Before the two, as they strode up and down, turning with a military precision at the end of their beat, lay the broader and more open part of the valley; behind them was the ragged ravine in which the five mines were situated. They could still see, even by this light, the skeleton supports of the trolleys that swung down from the higher mines along the ravine walls to carry the ore cars and their precious loads down to the easier level. And behind them, sometimes distantly, and sometimes near at hand, the voices of the laborers. The Mexican *peones* were redeeming the work of the day with songs, practical jests that brought wolfish howls of merriment, and setting up, in short, a little babble of sound in the ravine. But all of those sounds were dwarfed and muffled and uncertain, compared with the immensity of the mountains around the place, and the spread of the starry sky. Something else made the mirth seem, to the manager and his assistant, worse than a mockery.

Cardigan, as he strode up and down, repeatedly rattled a paper that he held in his hand. It read:

Dear Cardigan:

I have reason to think that Vizcaya is simply an extortionist. Today, through Ramón Díaz, he asked for double the protection money. Twenty thousand dollars a month! I lost my temper and refused. Later, he sent around Díaz to offer lower terms . . . fifteen thousand. Perhaps he could be haggled down to twelve. But that doesn't matter. I think it's all extortion. I have found a fellow unlike anybody I've ever met in my life, and it's his idea that El Tigre is simply using Vizcaya as a cat's-paw.

The scoundrels have bled us long enough. The man who opened my eyes to the matter is the strange fellow of whom I speak above. His name is James Tyler. It appears that he's known south of the Río Grande as The Wolf. I have turned the protection of the mines over to him, and he'll be on hand this evening to take charge of the defense. Trust him in everything.

He makes little demand for money, but wants to have an absolute authority. I have written out a little paper that he carries with him, investing him with the authority that he requires, but I'm sending you this notice so that you will assist him in every way possible. He says that he'll make the mountains too hot to hold El Tigre, and I cannot help believing in him, for he seems to be the sort of man who will do what he says!

Take care of yourself. I wish that I could be out there, because I imagine that the next few days will be dangerous. As soon as I've attended to the last shipping matters and brought in the new consignments, I am coming straight out, and I dare say that I'll arrive before the actual fighting begins, if any really takes place.

Yours faithfully,
Tobias Reed
president

The last word of all gave the letter a redoubled

69

meaning. Usually the letters from Reed were simply signed with his initials. This writing of the name in full, and the word "president," scribbled in his own hand under the signature, seemed to show that Reed wanted the letter to receive special and official attention. Ordinarily he gave his underlings very much of a free hand, but now it appeared that he wished to assert himself.

"What do you think of it?" Cardigan asked finally.

"I think," Sam Gloster replied, "that it's a lot of rot, Ned. I think that Reed's out of his depth. I've thought so for a long time, but this is the proof to me." Cardigan groaned. "It's this way, Ned," Gloster continued. "Reed has spent his entire life among law-abiding people. He can't make head or tail out of wild country like this. It baffles him. He was probably a fool to start paying such a high rate for protection at the first scare. If there was fighting to do, that was the time to do it. Now he's delayed too long. The grafters are going to make sure of their profits. Ten thousand dollars a month! Why, it's a huge fortune to 'em! And that demon of an El Tigre, can you imagine him giving up a juicy chance like this without a hard fight, now that he knows how much meat there is in the game? But suddenly Reed has met some schemer, some interloper, and let himself be persuaded to right-about-face. It's time, Cardigan, that the stockholders knew how badly things are apt to go with a scary old chap like Reed at the head of things."

Again Cardigan groaned. "I've thought of all these things," he said. "Did you notice the nickname of this fellow whom Reed has picked up to be our chief guard and caretaker?"

"The Wolf," answered Gloster. "A fine nickname for a trustworthy man to have."

"What to do?" Cardigan pondered aloud. "I've made a few moves already."

"The laborers you armed, eh?"

"Yes, there are some of them who have a knack with guns. I found them out. About a dozen, altogether, seemed to me to be men who might stand up in an emergency. We have treated them pretty well, and paid them more than the average. And now it seems to me they'll be willing to pay us back with some real action."

"It's a good idea," Gloster agreed. "But the worst of it is that, for all we know, this fellow they call The Wolf may be hand in glove with El Tigre. It may all be a plan between the pair of 'em. Have you asked any of the men if they ever heard of The Wolf?"

"No, I haven't."

"There's José, the watchman. Let's ask him."

They approached the darkening form that stood near the entrance of the First Luck, as this mine was called, for here Reed had struck his first good ore.

"José, did you ever hear of a fellow nicknamed The Wolf?" said the manager. They could see the start of the watchman.

Then he answered: "*Hai!* And who has not?"

"I haven't, for one," Gloster shot back. "Who is he?"

"The Wolf," said the watchman, speaking slowly, "is a man or a demon who lives on fighting the way that we live on bread and meat and *pulque*. That is what he is."

"What's he done, José?"

"Killed men," said the other.

"Wanted by the law?"

"No. I don't think so. Not usually. If he's wanted by Mexican law, he's north in the States. If he's wanted by that law, he's south of the Río Grande."

Cardigan turned away with his companion.

"There you have it," Gloster stated.

"Yes," answered Cardigan. "Here comes a troop of riders now . . . the precious Tyler, alias The Wolf, I suppose."

It was a group of six riders, who loomed through the twilight. Some came on at a brisk trot, and some were cantering. The iron-shod hoofs now and then struck sparks out of the valley rocks.

"Halloo!" Cardigan called.

"Stop here!" answered a voice in decisive tones.

The troop halted. One man advanced.

"Hello!" he called out.

"Hello!" Cardigan called back.

"Who are you?"

"Cardigan. Are you The Wolf?"

"My name is Jim Tyler." He came closer, dismounted. They heard the rustling of cigarette papers; he was making his smoke in the thickening dusk as swiftly as though in the daylight.

"This is Gloster, my assistant," Cardigan said.

"Glad to know you, gentlemen," said Tyler. "Reed told me about you."

"Is this the crowd that you've brought to look after the mines?" asked Cardigan.

"This is part of 'em. I hope for more, later on."

"Six men to . . . to hold this valley against El Tigre and his wildcats?" Cardigan exclaimed.

"We may manage to hold it," said the other.

"Look at the width of the valley here," Cardigan said. "Do you mean to say that six men can outpost this place and keep those clever ruffians from slipping through?"

"One can't tell," Tyler replied. "I hope so." He lighted a match. They saw by the flare of it the lean, grim face of the man, and instinctively they glanced at one another. All their fears, they felt, were confirmed.

"I'll tell you what," Cardigan began, "I have a dozen men together, under arms, the pick of the laborers in the mines. They can all handle guns, and I've given out rifles to them. They'll be a reinforcement for your end. You can tell me what you want me to do with 'em."

"Get their rifles first, and then disband 'em, and tell 'em to turn in and sleep. Tell them that there won't be any trouble tonight," Tyler responded.

"Can you read El Tigre's mind? Don't you think that he may make his jump this very night to teach us our lesson?" asked Gloster.

"Of course, he'll make his jump tonight," Tyler replied. "The first jump, at least. And that's why we don't want to have his hired spies mixed up with our fighting men."

"Tyler," Cardigan said, "I'm afraid that I don't follow your line of reasoning."

"You don't have to follow it," Tyler answered dryly. "Just do as you're told. I'm not in a humor for arguing."

X

"The Attack"

Gloster broke into the dull silence that followed this last abrupt reply from Tyler: "Cardigan, you see how it is. Reed takes the responsibility off your shoulders and puts it entirely on Tyler here. There's nothing that you can do. If Tyler wants to throw away any help that we could give him, that's his business. Your hands are tied."

"That's correct," broke in Jim Tyler. "Get your men together and take the rifles away from 'em. Your mine laborers are half of 'em spies who'd join El Tigre in a minute. That's all I have to say." He turned and rode away.

José, the watchman, said quietly: "Yes, *señor*. That is The Wolf."

"I wish Satan had him now," Cardigan hissed through his teeth. "The infernal, impudent puppy! Look at the width of this valley, Gloster. Why, El Tigre's men can rush through this gap like waves from the sea."

"What are you going to do?" his assistant asked.

"I'm going to get my own rifle and stay here at the mouth of the shaft of the First Luck. We'll beat them off from this place, if possible . . .

they'll probably gut the rest of the mines, and in the morning they may get this one, too. But if you'll stand by me, Gloster, we'll take the chance."

"I'll stand by you," Gloster asserted. "I'll go up the valley to the bunkhouses and get the guns away from your armed gang. Then I'll come back here."

"Hurry, Gloster! You never can tell how soon the bandits will rush us. Before long, I imagine. If I were El Tigre, I'd begin this very minute, between dusk and moonshine."

In fact, as Gloster hurried away up the slope, the shoulders of the mountains were splotched with silver, and the little rivulets of water that ran down the slopes appeared with a twisting gleam as the last light of day disappeared. There was just enough light, as it appeared to Cardigan, to insure the walking of ghosts. Tragedy, he felt, was literally in the air. As he sat there, before the mouth of the First Luck, he ground his teeth and groaned in despair to think of the undoing of all his work; he knew what a savage mob could do in the way of sabotage. There was a plentiful supply of explosives, and the shaft of each mine could be smashed in with a few well-placed charges of dynamite.

In the meantime, the brutal Jim Tyler had strung his handful of men across the valley. Either these fellows were great heroes, or else the whole affair was a mere sham, and they were working hand in glove with the men of El Tigre.

76

But suppose that they attempted to make good their position?

He could see them, dimly, posted behind rocks here and there, resting at ease under the brightening moon, some of them working at their weapons as though to make sure that they were in proper condition. In fact, they had the air of efficient workers who knew their business, but it was perfectly clear to the mind of Cardigan that such a scattering could never hold back the rush of determined men in far greater numbers.

The men of El Tigre were sure to be determined enough. They always exhibited, rumor said, a sort of fanatical contempt for life when they were working under the eye of their leader. Besides, the roughness of the ground would enable them to approach with comparative safety. In his mind's eye, Cardigan saw an approaching line of fire that would seep in around the islands of defense, surround them, and wash over them one by one.

He began to grip the handles of his revolver and wish that Sam Gloster would hurry back, bringing the rifles. Revolvers seemed singularly blind and weak weapons, when the distances were so great. Then, down in the valley, he heard the snort of a horse, astonishingly close at hand. He stared and suddenly he made out a throng of riders — two score, three score! How could they have come so quickly up the valley? It was as though they had risen up out of the ground.

The heart of Cardigan beat violently. Here

was the thing that he had been visualizing, but all of his mental pictures had been far wrong. There was a ghostly calmness about this approach. The men dismounted. It was all very orderly. It was like the work of regular troops. Half a dozen horses were left in the charge of one keeper. A dozen of those keepers were stretched across the valley, a dozen groups of horses. He had under-estimated the force of the attack by one half, at least. The men were going forward on foot; the ground was alive with them for a moment, then they were blotted out. So it seemed, but after a moment, straining his eyes, he could make out man after man, but only in glimpses, as the followers of El Tigre moved forward, each taking advantage of what cover lay before him.

Then the rifles began. It was a mere scattering of shots from the defenders. Were they shooting to kill, or were they merely putting up a sham, firing high over the heads of the advancing fighters? It seemed to Cardigan, as he froze his grip on the butt of his Colt revolver, that there was a hollow popping sound to those explosions, as though the rifles were loaded merely with blank cartridges. Up the valley another sound came to his ears, the confused clamor of the voices of the *peones,* yelling with fear.

A nearer sound split the air as a bolt of lightning cracks the sky across from side to side. It was the death shriek of one of El Tigre's men. Up he bounded like a jumping jack, his arms flung above his head. It seemed to Cardigan that he could see the man go dead at the height of his spring, falling limply back among the rocks.

A deep, hoarse shout of anger came from the attackers. They had not fired a shot, up to this moment, but now there was a sudden and continued fusillade. Wasp-like noises darted about the head of Cardigan and set him ducking. He fell upon the ground and lay flat on his stomach, thrusting the revolver straight out ahead of him toward the mêlée. He was sure that he was helpless. He wanted to run. But the old fighting strain in his blood kept him there, an icy statue of a man.

They were coming on more rapidly now. He could see the rascals dodging from rock to rock. They fired every moment. And the defenders replied steadily. From each of their posts it seemed the twinkling of a firefly that sparkled dimly through the ghostly moonshine. Well, they were fighting, indeed! There was no treason here. As for Tyler, the man was a daredevil, indeed, to venture into such a deathtrap, so unprovided with the necessary means of resistance. He would die. They would all die.

Up the slope toward his own position, Cardigan could see three — no, there were four or five men coming. He shut his eyes, then opened them. He snarled like an angry dog. For the first time in his life, he fired at a human target. A brief howl answered him. By heaven, they were in revolver range, and the affair would be over quickly now. He had five bullets left. He would save them for close range, he said to himself.

Just then thunder rolled lower down in the valley. No, it was the rushing of hoofs, armed hoofs that made a clangor against the rock floor of the ravine. He glanced in the direction of the sound and saw a round dozen of horsemen sweeping down the slope straight at the horses of the enemy.

Ah, that was Tyler. That was his scheme, then. Cardigan began to laugh — short, deep sounds coming from the hollow of his throat. How beautiful it was to trap the trappers.

That whole body of horses was swept away in an instant. What resistance could men make when their hands were already full? Off to the side the herd of horses rushed. From the ravine before the mines, with howls and yells of rage and excitement, the whole body of the attackers whirled back, running hard to save their mounts. It was their natural instinct. For how can a Mexican live contented when he knows that he is reduced to locomotion on foot alone?

As they ran, those evil rascals, Tyler's men pursued them, charging after the fugitives on horseback. There was no attempt at resistance. It was a rout. The riders charged across the ravine, and the hunted Mexicans took like goats to the sides. They threw away their rifles, their revolvers, even their heavy hunting knives were left behind, as they scrambled with foot and hand to climb to safety.

And so it was all over. Like magic the thing had an ending, and Cardigan, standing up, looked with dazed eyes and a dizzy brain at the moonlit valley and listened to the sickening groans of the wounded. Better that these groans should come from the bandits than from honest men, but it was horrible in any case.

He stepped forward. Behind a rock, a figure stirred on the ground; a shuddering voice said: "Water, *señor*, in the kind name of the saints."

That was his own victim. He pulled the canteen from his side, knelt, and pressed it to the lips of the man. The latter drank, the lank black hair falling back from a brutal face.

"Ah, *señor*, I give you thanks," said the Mexican on the ground, and extended his hand.

Cardigan grasped it, for he felt that he had to do with a dying man, when suddenly he was jerked closer and a knife flashed in the moonlight. He had only the canteen for a weapon; the weight of that he dashed into the face of the traitor as the knife grazed his side. The other fell back, twisting, cursing, blinded by the blow, and Cardigan stepped away as one steps when he has come too close to a coiled rattlesnake.

XI

"After Victory"

They brought in the dead and wounded. Among the victors, there were five wounded, but none seriously. Of the men of El Tigre, there were seven dead, and just over twenty wounded; so much more costly it is to run away than to stand and fight.

The mine laborers came down, chattering and laughing and yelling to one another, wild with excitement and relief. They carried in the dead and assisted the wounded to shelter. The dead were laid out in an empty powder shack; a whole bunkhouse was turned over to the wounded, and nurses were appointed to attend them. The company doctor had enough work to keep him busy until morning. Then the captured weapons were brought in, and five dozen horses were herded into the livestock corrals of the mining company. It was a cheap victory, no doubt. From one viewpoint, it could hardly have been cheaper. The only great expense had been in the thinking of Tyler. After all, he deserved his title of The Wolf.

How neatly the man had worked up the scheme and fitted the parts of it together. All had come out exactly as planned. El Tigre's very beard was singed, his reputation was smashed, for the time being, and his crowd scattered. They would not be likely to reassemble again in a hurry, not in those mountains, at least.

Cardigan went looking for the victor, and found him in the long bunkhouse, where the wounded were lying, attended by the doctor and nursed by some of the *peones* of the mines. At the farther end of the room, in a dimness through which the lamplight hardly penetrated, Cardigan saw him, on his knees beside one of his victims — a youth of eighteen or twenty, tall, with a handsome face and a noble brow. His dark eyes looked straight up toward the ceiling.

"As for my name," he was saying, "it does not matter. I shall soon be dead. No man will know."

"You'll not die, boy," Tyler said.

"No?" The boy laughed a little, softly. Then he said: "If they put bandages on the bullet hole, I'll tear them off again. I won't live in the *calabozo*. No one shall ever have a chance to know what I have done."

"You're not going to live in the jail," Tyler said. "As soon as you can ride a horse, you're going your own way. You understand?"

"Free?" asked the boy.

"Yes."

"*Señor,*" said the sick boy, "you laugh at me. I know what comes to the men of El Tigre. I know that they die, every man. It is not even a trial, but a shooting squad, as soon as justice lays its hands on them."

"Enough men have died. There are seven dead," Tyler explained. "Four or five more of these poor rascals are going to die, too, from their wounds. But the rest go free, as soon as they can walk. I know what justice would do to 'em, and I'm going to keep justice away from 'em."

"Saints in heaven," said the boy. "You are The Wolf. You don't mean what you say."

"I give you my word, and my word is sacred."

"Shall I believe you?"

"Believe me."

"Then, the saints be kind to you. *Señor* Tyler, I am Hernando. . . ."

"Hush," Tyler said. "Are you sure that your father would like to have you speak the other name?"

"Do you know me, then?" asked young Hernando.

"I know brave men when I see them fight," Tyler assured the boy, "and I saw you fighting. You were the only one who did not run. As for the rest, I could guess what sent you into the mountains, Hernando."

"What, *señor*?"

"Your father is a stern man, is he not? And you, also, are proud."

"*Señor* Tyler, you know everything. I swore that I would never go back until. . . ."

"Then you can take back that swearing, Hernando. Go home."

"I had rather die, first."

"Perhaps you're right. In that case, I'll go home with you, or ahead of you, and prepare the way. Do you agree? Now be still. Everything is to be well. Trust me. When you are able to, tell these other poor fellows that not one of 'em is to be jailed. The dead will be dead, that's all. The living ought to have a new chance. I give you my honor that they shall have it. Good night, Hernando. Sleep well. I'm going to take care of you."

The quivering lips of Hernando could not answer. Tyler stood up in haste and turned away, to encounter Cardigan. His brow darkened a little, but, before Cardigan could speak, he said: "I am sorry that I was rude to you, Mister Cardigan. There was no time to make explanations. If I had told you my plans, everything might have been lost. My whole gamble was that El Tigre would try to rush the mines tonight, and that his outposts would think that the first group of men I brought into the ravine was all that I had on hand. Bud Wynne and his men, up there in the draw, were my aces up the sleeve, and I didn't dare to tell even you about it. There was one of the Mexicans in hearing distance all the while I was speaking to you."

"It's true," Cardigan said. "I have played the sulky fool, and for that I apologize. As for the spies and the traitors in the mines, I'm going to spot them and weed them out. The scoundrels."

"Don't do it, man. Let them be," Tyler urged. "They were willing to be traitors when they thought that El Tigre would get the upper hand. Either they had to work with him or be in danger of having their throats cut some night. But now he's an exploded bubble, at least for the moment. It will take him two or three years of lonely work on a smaller scale to reëstablish himself, the cat-faced ruffian. In the meantime, if you will let your people know that you understand all the time that they were communicating with El Tigre, that you simply laughed at him, and that you forgive them like bad children, they'll worship you . . . they'll look up to you as a father. Believe me, I know what I'm saying."

"I'll do as you suggest," answered Cardigan. "I'll do everything exactly as you suggest. If Reed knows what he's about, he'll give you a position here simply to handle the Mexican labor, Tyler. You can read the minds of these fellows."

"I'm ten years too old to start in on new work," Tyler answered. "And I'm ten years too young to settle down. I have to see a little more of life first, Cardigan."

"A little more of life," Cardigan murmured, and his eyes opened wide. For he knew that if he himself lived ten generations of active existence, he would never begin to learn what his companion already knew about the world. He left Tyler with that, and, although he was busy in one part of the ravine or another from that moment until dawn, he found no trace of The Wolf again.

Later on in the morning, he simply learned

that Tyler and eight picked men had taken a pair of fresh horses apiece and disappeared in the mountains. They were going hunting, they had said in parting, and Cardigan realized with a shiver of the nerves that their game walked on only two feet.

All of that day they were gone. In the evening they came back, exhausted, but with an air of contentment. They had found two of the temporary headquarters of El Tigre. They had not located that dangerous man in person, but they had scattered the few armed adherents of the chief that remained on guard. They had dismissed the women at the camps, warning them of the rout of the El Tigre forces. Incidentally, they had looted both camps.

It was not an inconsiderable booty that they had accumulated. There were jewels, a good deal of hard cash, and something worth having in the way of super-decorated saddles and some horses better than the ordinary.

That was the end of what people in Santa Anna, to this day, call the war of El Tigre. The bandit himself was still at large, but his wings were clipped, and his prestige almost ruined. As men pointed out, this had been accomplished in forty-eight sleepless hours by The Wolf.

XII

"The Traitor Again"

Tyler, returning to the mines at the end of that second day, ate heartily, smoked two cigarettes, rolled himself in blankets, and slept the round of the clock. Then he went off with his favorite mustang and rode to the verge of the pines, scattered along the sides of the mountains. There he selected a place of mottled sun and shadow, raked together a great quantity of pine needles, and lay down on them, spread-eagled.

He spent all the rest of that day in this fashion, sometimes half awake, sometimes deeply sleeping, sometimes rousing and sitting up anxiously to look all around him. Just as a wild animal will rest for a long time after a difficult season of labor, so this man rested while good health brought suppleness to his mind and his muscles. Times of strain put on us ten premature years of age suddenly, and those years had been put upon Jim Tyler, but now he deliberately threw aside the burden and came down in the evening, perfectly refreshed, to the mining camp.

He and his men ate with the others, then Tyler called them out to a campfire, and they sat around it while he declared his mind. He thought that each wounded man should receive two shares of the reward, whatever that reward might be. And Bud Wynne, who had acted as second in command, should get three shares. That would make twenty-five shares, altogether.

For division, they could offer the loot taken from the camp headquarters of El Tigre, which ought to amount, thought Tyler, to fifteen or twenty thousand dollars, unless he was very wrong about the value of certain, big, uncut emeralds that he had found. In addition, they had five or six dozen horses, most of them mustangs, but all of them of the finest quality. Those horses ought to sell for a good round sum, say, four or five thousand dollars. The company, too, was sure to pay a substantial bonus for work so well done and so quickly. Therefore, every one of the men under him could count, probably, on making something like fifteen hundred dollars, or even more, as the result of a single day of real labor. On the morrow, he would lead them back, with their horse herd, to the town of Santa Anna. When he had finished, he was roundly cheered.

"They ought to give you something pretty fat, Jim, for the work you've done on this job. Ten thousand wouldn't be too much," Bud Wynne suggested.

"Or twenty!" called another.

"Or thirty, considerin' they were paying ten thousand every month for protection!"

He raised his hand and hushed them. "Boys,"

he said, "I'll tell you something. I've made money in a lot of ways that the law doesn't like. But I never make money out of blood. It's just a little funny twist of the brain in me. But it's there."

"You mean," Wynne demanded, "that you'll not take a penny for the whole job?"

"Not a red cent," Tyler stated.

They gasped in surprise. There would have been further comment, except that at this moment Cardigan and Gloster came down to the fire, and between them walked a girl with a dark and lovely face. Even the firelit glimpses of it were enough to get that circle of ruffians to their feet.

Cardigan introduced her. "My friends, this is the *Señorita* Anita Gonzales, of Santa Anna," he said. "She has ridden out from the town by herself and she's come on the strangest errand that I've ever heard of. I don't know that it's legal, but I dare say that the legality of it will not bother you when you hear what she has to say."

They formed instantly into a semicircle, facing her, and she stepped up on a rock that raised her a foot or more above the level of the ground. She was so small that she seemed to need this extra height to hold their attention. So they stared at her, some looking through the actual flare of the fire, others at the sides of the semicircle having a better view.

"It is true that I am Anita Gonzales. It is also true that I am in terrible trouble," she said. "The law cannot help me. Nothing but courage and great hearts like yours can help me. And this is why. It is known to everyone in Santa Anna that I have been betrothed to Pedro Salvatore for more than a year. It is also known that our marriage was postponed because he disapproved of the ways of the government, and became the leader of a small body of other discontented men, revolutionaries.

"For a long time I had received scarcely a word from *Señor* Salvatore except messages that were brought to me, from time to time, by a dear friend of his, who remained true to him through everything. This friend finally arranged for Pedro to come to see me. This very day he came, in full sunlight, to the meeting place. But he had hardly arrived when we found that we were not alone. Men sprang up among the rocks. He was helpless in their hands, and they carried him off to the prison in the town."

She made her first pause. No one stirred. The dry wood of the fire crackled; there was a hissing where some resin flared suddenly in a point of yellow flame.

Then she went on: "The sentence was passed as soon as he was captured. He is to be shot at sunrise, as a traitor to Mexico. And that is why I have come to you. This is a terrible danger to me. There was another terrible danger, not long ago, that hung over all the district of Santa Anna . . . that was El Tigre. But you are the men who have removed that danger. You were not afraid

91

to face his men, his cruelty, and his cunning. And so I have come to you like a beggar to ask what you will do for Pedro Salvatore, and likewise for me.

"What can I offer you? The family of Salvatore is poor. My own father will not give money for what he considers a bad cause. I have no friends able to reward you with gold. There is nothing left to give except myself. And that I shall give. I shall marry the man who saves Pedro Salvatore . . . and gladly. I am not very wise, not very clever. But I have a faithful heart that will never forget to be grateful. Trust me, I shall never regret. I shall carry my head high. If I am very foolish, tell me so. I know that the prison is a terrible place. Water still runs in the old moat around it, and the walls are high. It is very well guarded. In the patio there are always armed men inside the building. It is true that the governor of the prison is a very dear friend of Pedro Salvatore. He is Ramón Díaz . . . and because of his friendship for us, because he brought Pedro Salvatore to see me, now Díaz himself is under arrest. His lieutenant governs the prison. The kind saints alone know what danger lies before Díaz. Perhaps I should come here asking for his sake, also. But there is only one great grief and one great fear before me. Tell me if I have come uselessly to you?"

They watched her with bright, excited eyes, but nearly every head was shaken. They remembered the tall, heavy walls of the old fortress castle, now made into the prison of Santa Anna. They remembered the heavy guard of picked men. They remembered, perhaps more than all else, the record of the prison of Santa Anna. Its prisoners never escaped. So they looked not at one another, but at the beauty of the girl and at the flare of the fire.

"No one of us can possibly turn a trick of this sort," said one of the men. "I'd like to try it with anybody who'll help me. I'm crossing to the *señorita*'s side of the fire. Anybody else with me?"

It was James Tyler who now walked gravely around the side of the fire and, coming to the girl, was followed by four others. The names of two of them counted, Mickey Foster and Bud Wynne. The others, as will appear later on, were not really important. But here were five men standing before Anita Gonzales. They were not the five who would have been chosen from that crowd either for strength or beauty of body, but the iron was in them, the iron that lies in the heart of a brave man and that may be tempered by action into steel of any sort, supple, keen, never blunted by long use.

As they gathered, Jim Tyler turned about and said: "I knew you'd be with us, Bud. And you, Mickey, you Irish loafer. Still I'm surprised that half of the lot of them didn't come across, or even more than half. But I know the prison. I know the look of the walls. Besides, there's something about a prison that takes the heart out of people like us, merely to think about it. Boys, shall we pull aside where we can talk a little?"

"I'm going to get the horses ready, and the guns, and such stuff," Wynne said. "I'll have them waiting for you in a little while. You talk things over with *Señorita* Gonzales, Jim. Whatever you decide on will be the best, I know. I'll follow on wherever you lead."

As he walked away through the firelit darkness, tall Jim Tyler had brought the remaining three volunteers, together with the girl, to a little distance from the campfire. Now they stood in the chilly moonlight of the mountain valley, remote, as it seemed, from all the world of men. But it was of men that they were thinking, their cruelty and strength, the men against whom they would soon have to pit their own strength.

Anita Gonzales had lost the boldness that brought her from the town to the camp. When Tyler said to her — "You've told us everything that you know?" — she was only able to nod.

"That's all right, then," he replied. "Just try to answer what I ask you."

"*Señor,*" she said, "is it you who are The Wolf?"

"That's him, lady," Wynne answered. "You can say the name twice over, and you've only got half the truth about him, at that." And Wynne grinned widely from ear to ear, as Tyler went on: "About Ramón Díaz . . . ?"

"Ah, poor man!" the sad, musical voice of the girl said.

"About that same poor man, that Ramón Díaz," said Tyler. "Tell me, *señorita,* if you are

94

sure that he's a friend?"

"Alas, *señor*," she said, "is he not lying in chains, now, in the prison? Is it not most likely that he will be led out in front of the same firing squad that takes the life of Pedro Salvatore?"

"I know this much about Díaz," he said. "I know that he was the agent for Vizcaya, whoever that may be. . . ."

"I know him, also," said the girl. "It was he who was protecting the mines, *señor*. You surely have heard about that."

"I've heard how he protected 'em," he responded. "But I know that Díaz was his agent, and that Vizcaya worked with El Tigre . . . and I'd put my bet that Díaz was working hand in glove with the pair of 'em."

"Impossible!" cried the girl.

"Let me know this much, was there any reason that could have made anybody want to betray Pedro Salvatore? Any money reason?"

"There was the reward on his head. Ten thousand *pesos*. And my father, who disliked the match for me, offered as much as. . . ."

"No matter what your father would offer," Tyler said, "ten thousand *pesos* is enough to buy Díaz, body and soul. Trust him for that. Díaz was bought . . . Díaz sold Salvatore for the blood money . . . and Díaz is going to die. There's a tickle in the fingers of my right hand that tells me he's about to die."

"*¡Señor!*" cried the girl. "Ramón Díaz was the greatest friend. . . ."

95

"Hush," Tyler warned. "There's nothing else that you can tell us, except that you've lived in Santa Anna longer than any of the rest of us. So perhaps you can tell us about the plan of the building inside."

"Almost every stone I know," she said. "In the old days, when Díaz was first appointed to be head of it, Pedro and I used to inspect it with him. It is this way." She dropped to her knees and began to draw the plan upon the ground. Tyler leaned over her to watch the lines.

XIII

"The Ancient Prison"

Not more than a quarter of a mile from the prison of Santa Anna, beyond the outer verge of the town, there was a low-standing thicket of brush, and half concealed in this brush sat five men, staring toward the forbidding walls of the fortress. Up they went, breaking into the moonlit sky like a vast tower, for the prison had in the old days been built as a fortified residence and, therefore, it had been built on a hill, whose top was leveled for the structure. The five who watched the place smoked cigarettes and said nothing, until Tyler spoke: "Boys, the whole thing ties together in a knot in some way. I don't know why, but it does."

One of the men answered: "I reckon that there's five loose strings to that knot, and, when they're pulled taut, they'll be around our five necks, and no mistake."

"Maybe," Tyler muttered.

"What makes you think that everything pulls together in one knot, and what's in the knot?" asked Wynne.

"In the knot," Tyler said, "is El Tigre, first of all. He's the poison. He's the one that'll make the untying the hardest. There's no doubt about that."

"He's been licked, and all of his men with him," Wynne said.

"You don't lick a man when you lick the army that he's a part of," Tyler insisted. "El Tigre had his men together, and then they ran out on him. No doubt about that. They were tricked into running by that charge you made on their horses, Bud. But El Tigre alone might be more dangerous, by a whole lot, than the rest of the gang. I'd rather handle a mob than one real fighting man."

"Go on," Mickey Foster urged. "El Tigre, you say, is in the knot. Who else?"

"Vizcaya, the sneak and four-flusher, who pretended to be protecting the mines. He's certainly somewhere in it."

"Vizcaya, then. Who else?"

"Ramón Díaz, the governor of the prison, who's said to be under arrest now. That's utter nonsense."

"The girl ought to know," said one of the two nameless men in that group.

"The girl knows what she hears, and that's all," Tyler said. "Díaz, I'll lay my bet, framed the whole thing so that he would come under suspicion. The suspicion will be cleared up right away, as soon as poor Salvatore has been murdered by the direct orders of the lieutenant governor. Then, you'll see, Díaz will come out with a flourish, go and mourn at Salvatore's tomb, and try to marry this girl. Because she and Salvatore are in the knot, too."

"Hold on, Tyler," put in Wynne. "You're a bright fellow. But you can't read minds that well."

"I saw Díaz look her in the face the other day," Tyler replied. "That's how I know. You can't fool me, when I see a man look at a woman that he wants. That's the knot . . . El Tigre, Vizcaya, Díaz, the girl, and Pedro Salvatore, lying in there ready to die. That's the knot, but I don't know, yet, just how it's put together."

"When will you find out?"

"When we start in trying to untie the knot."

"And how are you going to do that?"

"By getting into that prison."

"Listen to me, partner," said one of the two nameless men, "have you got any secret that'll make the walls fall down, so's the five of us can get in?"

"I've got no secret that will do that," Tyler admitted, "but I'll tell you something."

"What's that?"

"Five of us are not going to try."

"No?"

"No, only three are going to try."

"What becomes of the other two?"

"The other two," Tyler said gently, "go where snakes and four-flushers always go when the pinch comes and the work gets hot. They go to the rear. They don't go forward." There was a dead pause, and after this Tyler added: "Bud and Mickey, you'll go ahead with me, I think. And we'll go alone. The other two don't count. I doubted 'em from the start. In a showdown you'll always find some sneaks who try to work in with the real stuff." He stood up as he spoke, and he received no answer.

Mickey and Wynne rose with him. Neither of the other two men raised his voice to dissent from the judgment of the leader. Tyler continued: "We've got the finest pair of hands in the world with us tonight, Mickey. Bud Wynne knows the mind of a lock better than anybody else. He knows 'em better than the locksmiths that make the damned things. And Bud is going to open a few doors for us. You've got your things along with you, Bud?"

"I've got what I usually use," Wynne said.

"You don't need a suitcase to carry the stuff, I see," Tyler commented, chuckling. "There's nothing that makes me so sick as one of those second-story boys who has to carry along fifteen pounds dead weight in the latest kind of steel gadgets. Bud, you're made after my own heart. Shall we start?"

"I'm ready to start," Mickey stated, clearing his throat nervously. "But I'd certainly like to know what's the plan of the campaign."

"Why, it's like all good campaigns," said the leader. "We make up our minds as we go along. That's all."

"I mean," Mickey said, "you know what the inside of the place is like . . . that is, if you can remember what the girl drew in the dirt, but where . . . ?"

100

"Every line is drawn in my mind," Tyler said. "I know every twist and winding."

"Sure?"

"Yes, sure."

"But do tell me whereabouts is the cell they've got this Salvatore in?"

"No idea in the world."

"You mean that after we get inside that place we'll have to open the door of every cell to find out?"

"No, we'll have to ask our way."

"What?"

"You know, Mickey," said the leader, "that everything looks impossible until you try it. Take the good luck that we have to start with . . . a bright, moonlit night, without a cloud in the sky."

"So's they can see us off the walls nearly a mile away, eh?"

"Look at the other side of it, Mickey. It's a bright moon shining, so that we can find our way into the place. Our way over the wall, for instance."

"Over the wall?" Mickey exclaimed.

"That's why I brought along these ropes. We may need 'em."

"Well," Wynne said, breaking in, "I'll be damned."

"Not a bit of it, Bud. You'll be saved. And so'll Salvatore, if we all pull together."

"I'm not quitting, but I'm not thinking, either," Mickey Foster said. "You can go ahead

101

and do our thinking for us. But don't even tell us what the thoughts are. What I've heard of 'em gives me chills and fever. Just blat out with what you want us to do, and we'll try to do it."

"That sounds to me, too," Wynne agreed. "If you can beat El Tigre, maybe you can beat the prison, too, but you'll be the first man in the world who's ever tried to."

"Of course," answered Tyler. "You know how it is with most jail breaks. The boys try to figure things out too far ahead. While they're still figuring, before they get a chance to act, somebody finds out about it, and the plot goes hang. It's like planning out your lie ahead of time. Never works that way. The only sort of a lie that ever turns the trick is one that you make up as you go along. That's the kind that has the bloom on it, like a peach. You know what I mean. Just fallen from the tree."

There was a groan from Mickey Foster.

"You're The Wolf, all right," he said. "When Satan gets you, Jim Tyler, he is going to get off his throne and give you right of way. Otherwise, you'll make the infernal regions too hot for him."

"Do we start?" Wynne asked through his teeth.

"We start," answered the leader. "So long, you other fellows. You may not like this part of the job, but perhaps you'll stand by here with the horses?"

"I'm through with the whole thing," one said.

"Maybe I'm yaller about walking up the side of a wall. I ain't no fly," said the other, "but if you boys tackle the job, I'll stay here with the horses to try to pick up the fragments of you whenever you fall off."

"Good man," Tyler stated. "Stick to that, and everything will come off just as easily as bark off a slippery elm."

He waved his hand. The three of them stepped forward through the moonlight, leaving the shelter of the brush. With the very first step from their refuge, it seemed as though the great walls of the place leaped closer to them and that eyes were fixed upon them from the parapets.

"They can see us, now," Mickey said.

"They could, if they looked very hard, but they've had a century or so to blind 'em," said Tyler. "At least, we've got to count on their eyes being closed."

"A century of what to close their eyes?" Wynne asked.

"A century of success," Tyler said. "They've always succeeded in keeping their prisoners all of that time. And that'll make every guard on the wall look on his walk as an excursion, not as a job."

They stopped talking. The walls grew and grew. They saw, from the higher inner part of the old building, the gleam of a few lights, and then, as they came closer under the walls, these disappeared, shut out by the rising parapets. Presently, working in between two walls, they saw before them the steep slope of the masonry, going upward, and below, just ahead, the flat sheen of the water of the old moat, fully twenty-five feet across. First they stared upward at the great walls. Then all three looked down at the water again.

"What'll you do now?" Wynne asked in a whisper.

"This," the leader said, and began immediately to strip off all of this clothes.

XIV

"The Moat"

Behind the steep bank of the nearest mound, shut off from observation by their very nearness to the wall, they stripped off boots and socks. Trousers alone remained on them, and their shirts. They tore the sleeves out of these or rolled them up to gain greater freedom.

It was Tyler who finished first and, sitting there, he actually made a cigarette and began to smoke it. The two watched him in amazement. "They won't be able to smell the smoke that far up in the sky," Tyler commented. "Don't worry, boys."

"Why should we worry?" Wynne asked. "We're standing with the noose around our necks already, so why should we care about a little smoke?"

Tyler actually chuckled, and he looked with a sort of affection upon the other two. He knew that he might search the world over without being able to find another pair who would follow into an adventure as mad as this one. Therefore, he gloried in their courage. They were his kind. The sun-burned brand of the Southwest was imprinted upon them. They were typical of their

105

section and of their race.

Suddenly Wynne said: "Look here, I want to put my hand on your wrist."

"That's all right," Tyler said. "Here's my hand." He held it out, and Wynne with a dexterous touch found the pulse. Then, almost savagely, he flung the arm away from him.

"Pulse as steady as though he was just sitting down to dinner after a good day's work," Wynne said to Mickey. "Tyler, I think that you'd rather be right here than any place else. You like it. Answer up bright and quick, now . . . you like it?"

"It's all right," Tyler responded. "You know, boys, you've got to have some salt and pepper on your meat."

"I knew almost the words that he'd say," muttered Wynne. "You teach me to like it, will you, brother?"

"You'll like it before we're done," the leader assured him. "Are you fellows ready?"

"We're ready."

"Stay here," Tyler stated. "Count a hundred and then go down to the edge of the moat. I'll have swum across it, by that time, and made a line fast on the other side. You can pull yourself along by that line. It'll take less time than swimming, with less noise, too."

"Can you swim, yourself, without making a noise?" asked Wynne.

"I was with the Indians for a while in Canada," Tyler explained. "They showed me how." He disappeared quickly between the mounds.

"He ain't human," Wynne said finally.

"He ain't human. He's an Indian," Foster commented. "I got a mind to give up the job right here and now."

"So have I. But I won't. And you won't, either."

"I wish I had the nerve to," Foster said. "But if I did, and got out of the place alive, I'd wanna kill myself. And if he died inside because of it, I'd kill myself anyway."

"That's it," Wynne said. "He gets us going, and he gets us coming, because he's a hundred percent man. Our time's up. I hope there ain't any slime on that water."

"I hope that there ain't no frogs in it," muttered Foster.

Between the two mounds, which were the remains, perhaps, of an outwork built there in the earlier days, they slipped quickly down to the edge of the water and saw clearly, in the moonlight, the rope lying on the bank. Lost in the black shadow close to the wall, they could barely make out the form of their companion who had already crossed.

Wynne tested the rope, found that it was tied fast on the other side, and stepped into the water. Then, leaning over, he thrust himself forward, pulling hand over hand. In a moment he was on the other side.

"Slime," he gasped to his companion.

"Yeah. A lot of blasted slime," Tyler said.

"But that's all right."

Foster followed quickly, gasping as he joined them. "Frogs, damn 'em! Listen to 'em croaking for me."

"That's good luck," answered Tyler. "Here we are, boys. Look at the easy job we've got. This old wall was built with such a slant to it that you could almost walk up without using your hands, and the whole surface is weathered and pitted. They never finished off these stones. Look at the handholds and the footholds. Why, it's a joke any ten-year-old would laugh at."

His whisper had hardly ended, before he began to climb, not rapidly, but with a cat-like assurance and ease that made his companions stare. He was well above them, before either of them started to follow. His body seemed to arch out against the moonlit sky overhead so that he looked, in fact, like a creature that walked on all fours, with some mysterious power of adhesion to that sheer surface.

Wynne muttered: "Well, I guess we're both goners . . . but I can't stay back when The Wolf's up there ahead of us. So here goes."

Up the wall he began to climb. It was by no means the easy task that the leader had made out in the beginning. To be sure, there were plenty of little indentations, but most of them were shallow and weathered smooth at the edges. Had it not been for the great slant of the wall, they would have fallen a dozen times. As it was, near the top, Foster lost his foothold and swung by the hands, back and forth like a pendulum, with a low and terrible undulation over the abyss beneath.

Yet, all three came to the top of the wall, and the two in the rear found that their master was already crouched on the outside of a crenellation of the old battlements. There was a deep ledge here, and he greeted his followers with a warning gesture that made them flatten themselves on that high and dangerous shelf. They understood the need for extreme caution, a moment later, when footfalls approached them. Above the battlements they saw the gleam of a shouldered rifle. It passed, and suddenly Tyler came to life.

He rose as a shadow rises, and in absolute silence he slipped through the embrasure and followed the guard. There was the sound of a heavy blow. That was all. There was no scuffle, no clang of a gun falling upon the stones.

Yet, when the two followed, they found their leader leaning over a prostate body, holding the muzzle of a revolver to the head of the man. The Mexican had sense enough not to cry out or was it the hand of Tyler at his throat? However, he was merely whispering oaths and brief prayers to the saints to have mercy on his soul.

Wynne and Foster heard Tyler say: "You're going to live. You're not going to be harmed. You understand?"

"The saints be thanked," said the guard. "Ask me questions, then, and you'll find that I can talk faster than water babbles down hill."

"Good," Tyler said. "First, how long is it before your relief?"

"Twenty minutes. I looked at my watch just now and made sure. It's the end of the watch that is the longest."

"Sit up here against the parapet. A man talks more easily, sitting up. So?"

The sentinel sat down as Tyler had indicated.

Then his questions followed rapidly. "How many men in this prison? How many guards?"

"Fifteen, *señor*."

"That's enough of 'em. How many prisoners?"

"Just over twenty, *señor*."

The fellow could hardly speak, his nerves were so shattered by the dripping apparition of this panther-like man who had leaped on him from behind and struck him down.

"Steady, brother," Tyler calmed the man. "There's no harm coming to you. Be quiet. How do you get from this place into the prison?"

"Down the steps, yonder, that slant across the inside of the wall, and so to the patio."

"Is there no other way? No door that opens from the wall?"

"There were three or four of them. They've all been walled up."

"Rotten luck," Tyler muttered.

Wynne and Foster glanced over the wall. They could see in the patio four figures seated around a small fire, for the night had turned cold. The firelight flickered up the stairs that went steeply down the inside of the wall. To walk down that stairway seemed like venturing straight into the mouth of a lion.

"Once in the patio, you find the door to the prison where?"

"Just opposite the outer gate."

"Will the door be open now?"

"No. It is never unlocked, except by order."

Tyler swore softly through his teeth. "I knew that we'd need you, Wynne. Who are those men in the patio?"

"*Señor* Vizcaya and three guards."

"Ah, Vizcaya. Does he have anything to do with the prison?"

"He was a great friend of the governor. The governor is now under arrest."

"Locked up?"

"Only confined to his room."

"I thought so. Now, there is a prisoner here called Pedro Salvatore."

"Ah, my soul," the guard whispered. "It told me that you came for him. For no other man within the walls could you have come."

"Where is Salvatore jailed?"

"One story below ground."

"Worse and worse. How do we find the cell?"

"Inside the entrance door, there is another door to the right, against the wall of the hallway."

"Locked?"

"No. You pass through it and go down three windings. Then you come to another door set into the wall, with an iron plate in the center of it, and air holes drilled through the plate."

"I understand. A dungeon cell, eh?"

"Yes, *señor*."

Tyler turned to his friends suddenly. "Partners," he said, "I thought we had one chance in ten. I see that we have only one chance in a thousand. Now's the time for both of you to turn back, if you want to."

XV

"Watch Your Step"

Neither of his followers stirred nor spoke a word, and there was moonshine enough for the up-turned eyes of Tyler to see the expression on their faces. He looked back at the guard, therefore, saying: "Now, then, once down there, and at the door of the cell of Salvatore, what is the very best way of getting out of the prison?"

"That is simple, *señor*. A man goes down to the bottom level, and from that place he finds at the end of the corridor a straight way that leads to steps. At the end of the steps there is a door that cannot be opened from the outside. On the inside there is always an armed man, but what is one armed man to three such as you are?"

When he had finished speaking, Tyler said calmly: "I'm going to tie and gag you, friend. You'll have air to breathe in plenty, and the cords won't stop the flow of the blood. Be easy and trust me." He was at work as he spoke, and in a moment the man lay trussed and helpless, his wild, big eyes staring up at them, the muscles of his throat working desperately as he strove to thrust out the gag with his tongue.

Tyler looked almost tenderly down on him.

Then he said: "We have sixteen or seventeen minutes left, boys. We have to use 'em. Down those stairs we go. Mind you, when men are close to a fire, the firelight is stronger than moonlight. Also, people see only what they expect to see, and nobody expects to see men sneaking down the inside stairs of this fortress. Stand up straight, and walk down calmly and steadily. Your bare feet will make no noise, and those fellows down there are so busy talking that, if they look up and see you coming down, they'll think nothing about it. If you skulk, they'll be ready with guns instantly, and then we're dead men, or worse than dead . . . we're captives. Come along, follow me. We might just as well start at once."

He stood up, and, stepping down the wall to the head of the stairway, he began to descend with a slow and easy movement. The others followed. Wet, dripping, cold in that chilly night air, their hearts were small enough in their bodies, but Tyler's confident manner drew them after him. Besides, they were now so far committed that to retreat was almost as difficult as to go forward under his guidance.

They were halfway down the steps, when one of the men at the fire in the courtyard looked directly up at them. His glance froze the blood of the two at the rear, but their feet went automatically in pursuit of the leader, who continued quietly to descend.

So he who had looked up bent his head again.

114

Was he whispering to his companions the strange sight that he had seen upon the stairs? No, for perhaps the shadow that fell within the wall had obscured everything of the three except the dimmest of outlines.

At any rate, their feet were presently treading on the cold stone of the court, and straight ahead, before the others, walked Tyler, with his head high and his stride steady. Within ten paces of the group of four about the fire they passed, and not one head was raised and turned to examine them in passing. So much will boldness do for bold men.

Now they were under the shadow of the inner arcade, where the steep shadow of the moon covered them as with a velvet curtain. They stood before the great door, and, at a gesture from Tyler, Wynne began to examine the lock. He did not need to drop to his knees, it was so high. Bending over, he held his ear close to the lock, while he probed at it with what seemed an insignificant splinter of steel. It was not for long, not half a minute did the scraping continue, before there was a slight rolling sound, and the door swung slowly, heavily out toward them.

They slipped in like three ghosts, closing the door behind them and drawing back the spring lock. It was shut. They were inside the power of the law now, inside the very circle of its arms. For the instant, not one of them was braver than the other. Tyler was as weak as the others.

A door clanked with a strong, metallic sound,

high above them. Voices were heard, here and there. A single light, suspended from the ceiling, showed them the big hallway that they had entered and the little round-topped door at the right through which they must pass, according to the instructions they had received from the guard. What if he had lied to them?

Danger was present about them, audibly, something like the hum of a dynamo at work. A faint, stale odor of cookery lay in the air like hoar frost, chilling the soul.

Tyler stepped to the round-topped door at the right. As had been predicted, it was unlocked and, opening it, he led the way down the stairs. They wound, circling slowly, at a sharp angle. They made two turns.

Then a voice stopped them, and clearly upon the ear of Tyler came the voice of Ramón Díaz, saying: "Salvatore, you are playing the fool."

"I play my own part, not yours," answered a man who spoke quietly, although there was despair in his muffled tone.

"If I say the word, you are free," Díaz said. "There is a side passage from the prison. I unlock your chains. I take you down the corridor. You walk out under the moat and onto the firm ground of freedom beyond. Do you hear?"

"I hear."

"All that you need to do . . . you understand?"

"All that I need to do," said Salvatore, in answer, "is to write what you want me to write. A letter to Anita, saying that my affair with her, all my pledges, were jokes and jests, and that I am through with the silly idea. I write that letter . . . you allow me to escape. You are there at her right hand, as the man suspected and arrested because of your devotion to me. She, with a broken heart, looks around her and sees no fit man except you. Oh, I understand, Ramón. To think of how I have trusted you and loved you."

"There is a time for emotion," said another voice that was familiar to Tyler's ear, "and there is a time to be practical. We are speaking to you of your life, Salvatore."

"And those who speak to me are traitors," Salvatore said sternly, "and murderers. I know your face, *Señor* Tigre. My blood curdles to see you with Díaz. Scoundrel that I know you to be now, Ramón, why have you taken this man for a confederate?"

"You sentimental fool," Díaz responded. "I didn't think that you'd know El Tigre, or I wouldn't have brought him. However, now that you know him, you may as well know that we've worked together for years. You've always wondered at the money that I've been able to spend, Pedro. Here's the answer. Think of it in the cold of the morning, when they strip you to your shirt and stand you against the patio wall to face the firing squad. You dog, I've always hated you, if you want to know the truth. I'm almost glad that you've refused to make the bargain with me. What difference does it make? You die in the prison. I escape death but, so far as anyone knows, only by the skin of my teeth, because I'm known to be your friend . . . you, the fine gentleman, the patriot, the noble soul. You die, and some of your nobility sticks to my fingers, so to speak. Will she be able to resist me and my broken heart? We shall have one thing to unite us, always . . . the thought of you, Salvatore. Ha!" His laughter was one short, diabolical sound. Then he said: "Close the door, Tigre. It has a spring lock. Close the door, and be done with him. I'll succeed as well with his death as if he should live and write a lying letter to the girl. Close the door, and let him die in the morning, as the law dictates."

"Díaz," the voice of El Tigre said, "I admire you. You have the good sense to use the law."

There was the metallic sound of a lock clicking shut in heavy steel.

The voice of El Tigre continued, while the footfalls began, moving away from the trio who listened, spellbound. "If I knew of some such thing as the law to put on the trail of that *gringo,* Ramón . . . ah, if I only knew that."

"I hate him, also," Díaz said. "And the two of us, when we work together, when have we failed? Trust me and the future, *Señor* Tigre!"

"Good," said El Tigre. "I was willing. . . ." His voice died out suddenly, as though something had hushed that precious pair, although, no doubt, it was simply that they had turned a sudden corner.

Now Jim Tyler went swiftly down the steps in

his bare feet until he came, exactly as the guard had promised, to a door set into the wall, a door in the center of which was a steel plate pierced with breathing holes.

"You, Wynne," said the leader.

This time Bud Wynne was on his knees, instantly, before the door, working with the small probe at the lock.

"Who is there?" said the voice of Salvatore loudly.

"Friends," Tyler answered, putting his lips close to the air holes in the steel plate. "In the name of all the saints, be quiet."

"Friends?" Salvatore echoed in a voice of wonder. "Sent by whom?"

Gringos," Tyler said, "sent by Anita Gonzales. Be still, or I'll. . . ."

Wynne looked up with the faintest of stifled groans.

"Can't you handle it?" Tyler muttered, sweat glistening on his face. "Have we come this far for nothing?"

"I can't handle it," said Wynne, "unless. . . ." He began his probing again, apparently caught up by a new idea. As he worked, he canted his head to one side, like a musician listening to distant and beautiful music that must be heard, lest an immortal idea should perish from the ken of man.

It was at this moment that a dull voice echoed up the stairway, saying in Mexican: "Why should we leave food for a man who'll be dead

119

before it's digested?"

"That's what I should say," a second voice answered, "but, after all, there's the job to be done and good pay for a lazy life that. . . ."

What he was to say was blotted out, for at the moment two men clambered into view up the circular stairs. At the same moment, the door of the cell clicked and sprang open, as though thrust out by a spring. Tyler saw the captive, saw the light glisten on his chains inside, and in that very moment Wynne smashed the butt of his revolver against the head of the Mexican who turned the corner of the stairs.

Foster leaped like a cat at the second, missed, and the fellow ran, screaming with terror.

XVI

"The Rescue"

It was the end of hope. Wildly and far as a bugle call might pierce, that sound of shrieking ran through the old corridors and chambers of the prison. Wynne and Foster sprang down the steps; they looked back and saw that their leader, who had brought them through so many perils, was no longer with them.

Foster groaned. "He's trying to bring the greaser away, even now," he said. Out of the greatness of his heart, he turned and leaped back to the door of the open cell. "Tyler, in every name under the sky, come away as fast as you can run. The whole place will be up in another minute."

"All in good time," Tyler answered. "The game is up, and now let the dogs yell a while." There was not fear, but an actual exultation in his voice.

"Man, man, you think it's a game! If you won't come, if you're going to burden yourself with a man in chains, I'm off!" And Mickey Foster fled for his life. But Tyler did not stir.

There were chains on the wrists and chains on the legs of the prisoner. With only an uncertain gait could he run out of the cell. But he was not allowed to proceed before Tyler caught him by both shoulders and held him hard. In that instant he looked deeper, perhaps, than ever a man had looked before into another soul, and what he saw in the open brow and the clear, steady eyes brought the flash of a smile to his face. "You're worth it, and thanks for that," he said.

Worth what? Worth the danger, the death, no doubt, that lay at the end of this adventure for both of them. Having said it, however, the face of Jim Tyler became as joyous as that of a child on a Christmas morning. He linked his strong right hand under the pit of the other's arm, and so he helped him down the steps, Salvatore holding up the leg chains as he ran or stumbled forward. They reached the lowest level, two windings of the stairway down from the cell door. By now it seemed that the whole prison was alive. Doors were slamming above, and to either side, like great beats on the head of a hollow drum. Voices shouted, and they heard the explosion of guns, although from what quarter they could not tell. Still they rushed forward. Several times the man in chains would have fallen, but the iron grip of his rescuer upheld him.

They entered a long corridor. At the end of it, they saw the dull blink of moonlight, and well did Jim Tyler know, then, that he was nearing the promised exit from the prison. The might of a giant came into his hand, upholding, buoying his fettered companion. "There, there is your freedom!" he gasped, his lungs burning with the effort that he was making.

The way was clear before them. Then a door opened suddenly in the side of the corridor, and two men stepped out before them, rifles in hand.

"There! There!" screamed the voice of Ramón Díaz, who stood first of the pair. "Shoot! It's Salvatore, the traitor!" His rifle was rising as he spoke.

Into the free hand, the left hand of Tyler, flicked a gun, speaking from his hip, and Díaz fell dead, driven backward by the impact. His companion was carried downward by the fall. Over them ran the fugitives, reached steps, stumbled across a limp, still bleeding form that lay upon them — mute testimony that the guard had tried to do his duty but Wynne had downed him — and so through a doorway into the open light of the moon.

Tyler made one step back and slammed the door shut. Screamings and knockings came against it the next moment, in token that the companion of Díaz had regained his feet. That tumult which they had heard within the prison was more distant now that they were in the outer air.

They ran straight forward, Tyler guiding the way toward the thicket in which the horses were held, and hoping they were still there in readiness. No, even that would be too late, for now that ancient drawbridge that arched the moat dropped with a sound like thunder, close at hand, and riders sprang out into the night.

Other horses came looming, straight ahead. Then the eager voice of Bud Wynne was calling: "Here, here, into the saddle, and away! Away!"

The strength of a giant came into the arms and back of Tyler. He picked up his companion and literally flung him into the saddle. His own mustang was close at hand. In an instant the wind of a racing gallop was tearing at his face.

In the office of Mr. Tobias Reed there was, in the top right-hand drawer of his desk, a certain box in which were his choicest Havanas. This drawer he had now opened and offered to his caller.

Jim Tyler shook his head and proceeded, with the old deft touch, to make a cigarette of his own tobacco, powdered fine from long travel in a coat pocket.

"About that other thing, I won't argue, man," said Reed. "I've offered you twenty thousand. If that ain't enough . . . well . . . we'll raise it. But I know that the raising won't do any good. What you say about blood money, however, there's another thing. I been hearing some odd things about you, Tyler. Things about the jail break the other night, and in here, in the next room, there's a person that wants to speak to you, pretty badly."

He stepped to the door. When it was opened,

Anita Gonzales, looking smaller and more lovely than ever, but with all color gone from her face, stood staring at the tall young American.

"*Señorita* Gonzales," Tyler said, "I suppose I know what you've come to say to me. And that's all right, too. But maybe my friend, Mister Reed, will be able to tell you that I don't like blood money in any form. Here's a letter to you from a mutual friend of ours. Look at it, and I'll be back right away."

He stepped from the room, and the pale girl, opening the letter, read it, cried out, and suddenly thrust it into the hands of the little Yankee geologist.

"Look!" she cried. "That is the man!"

Reed saw on the paper:

You know that I am safe, my darling. And he who has saved me will take from me nothing but my love, and yours.

Pedro

"I don't understand," Reed said. "I only. . . ."

"Ah, but I do, I do," Anita said, running to the window. "Look! There is the explanation! His heart is too great for us common people to understand."

And Reed, hurrying to the window, saw a mustang loping down the street, and in the saddle, disappearing around the corner, the form of a tall rider, light in the saddle, but with broad shoulders.

Rawhide Bound

I

"New Trouble"

When Jim Tyler came over the hills and down into the valley of the creek, he thought that he was proceeding toward a single mine, but, since it was sunset and, therefore, the end of the day's work, he heard the dull boom of several shots going off up and down the ravine. Thereby he learned that there were several shafts being developed.

This observation did not please him, for he was not a man to desire unknown society. Even the invitation of Tom Geary, who was under obligation to him and whom he believed to be a white man, he had hesitated before accepting.

Now he stood in his stirrups and raised his hand to peer up and down the creek. There was something about his lean face and his keen eyes that would have made the most casual observer think of a hawk peering into the dusk for game. There was also an intimation that the hawk might be aware that hunters and guns were abroad.

At last the sense of dusk falling made him shrug his wide shoulders and ride on. When he got down into the bottom of the ravine, he encountered a man driving a pair of burros up through the gloom toward the head of the valley.

"Hello, partner," Tyler said.

"Hello," grunted the man on foot.

"You know where Tom Geary located his claim?" Tyler asked.

"I know he had a sight more luck than was coming to him, is all I know," said the other, and he drove the burros on with curses.

Tyler waited a moment until he made sure that the man intended to make no further answer. Then a little, dull humming sound came into his throat. He brought his mustang to life with a stinging stroke of the spurs and jumped it ahead into the trail that lay before him.

"Mind what you're doin'!" shouted the driver of the burros, and he jerked a double-barreled shotgun out of the long holster strapped to one side of the rear burro. But to his bewilderment, the end of the long gun was suddenly grasped and jerked to the side. A smaller weapon, held close to his head, gleamed in the fading light.

"By the jumping thunder," Tyler said, "I've a mind to let you have it between the eyes, you skunk. I'm going to teach you some manners."

The driver of the burros tugged once at the shotgun, found that it was held by an iron grasp, and then stood still and folded his arms. "What you got on your mind, brother?" he asked calmly.

Tyler suddenly laughed. "You're an old-timer," he said. "I thought you were just one out of a new batch of the sourdoughs."

"I'm old enough," said the driver of the burros. "What's Tom Geary to you?"

"A friend," Tyler answered.

"Well, what kind of a friend?"

"As good as a man would want."

"I guess you know him," said the man on foot.

"I don't know where his claim is, though."

"Maybe I'm doing wrong to tell you," said the driver, "but it's down the trail, there, about a half mile, then you turn left between two hills, and you come to a hollow with a streak of water through it and a patch of trees, and there's his mine. It's a hummer, too, let me tell you."

"Thanks," said Tyler. "I'm sorry I was rough."

"You weren't rough. You was just nacheral," the man said calmly, and continued up the trail.

Tyler rode on through the thickness of the coming night. He found the two hills, turned between them, and saw before him the tall shadows of a grove of poplars, with a glint of starlit water beside them. His mustang waded slowly through the stream, reaching down its eager head and drinking as it walked.

"Hello! Hello!" Tyler called, with a hand to his lips.

"Hello!" shouted a voice close at hand.

The horse gained the farther bank and turned the shoulder of a thousand-ton boulder that had fallen ages since from the side of the cliff above. Then Tyler saw a little lean-to with a low fire gleaming red in front of it. Tending the fire was an unshaven man with a felt hat pushed far back on his head, a man in overalls and with sleeves rolled up to his elbows. He was looking up, squinting into the darkness.

"That you, Mitchell?" he asked.

"No, not Mitchell," Tyler answered.

The man by the fire leaped to his feet. "Tyler?" he shouted, with gladness in his voice. The fire caught him to better advantage now. He was a man of sixty, or nearly that, with a ruffian appearance both of clothes and of features.

"Right!" Tyler said. Coming into the circle of the firelight, he dropped lightly from the saddle to the ground.

Tom Geary hurried up with hand extended. "This is damned good!" he said heartily. "I been expecting you, but never knowing whether you'd get word or not. There wasn't any address, you know."

"I know there was no address. Just west of the Mississippi and north of the Río Grande and south of Canada, was the closest that you could come to my address, Geary," Tyler said.

"Sit down . . . rest your feet. Here, I'll take care of the horse."

"You slice some more bacon," Tyler said. "I'll take care of this broncho." He stripped off saddle and bridle, hobbled the pony, and turned it loose. There was plenty of good grass growing up to the edge of the creek.

His host, in the meantime, fell to work increasing the amount of coffee in the pot, putting some more bacon into the frying pan, and slicing in raw potatoes with the meat.

Tyler came back, sat on a rock, and made himself a cigarette. He was so hungry that he covertly pulled up his belt two notches. For, according to his code of manners, it would not do to express the slightest impatience.

"What gave you the idea of sending Mickey Lawrence after me?" he asked.

"I didn't have that idea," said the miner. "But I reckoned that if I sent a letter to you, it never would get to you before the police. Then I cast around and thought who might be likely to know where you were."

"So you went to the jail?" Tyler said.

Geary laughed. "I went down to the tramp jungle, near the town," he said. "There was nobody there that knew of you. Anyways, they said that they didn't. Then I went and saw a fellow who was just out of the town jail on a vagrancy charge, and he said that he'd heard of you. I gave him fifty dollars and said that, if he could find you and send you here, I'd add a hundred to that, as sure as shooting, the next time he turned up. He seemed to believe what I said, and he allowed that he'd take the job."

"Mickey Lawrence found me, all right," Tyler said. "He gave me the letter." He pulled out the letter and glanced over it again. Written in a clumsy, heavy hand, it said:

Dear Tyler: I need to see you bad . . . real bad. I never needed you before as much as I need you right now. If you can possibly make it, come to see me in Sherman Gulch — I'm working on a mine, there.

Geary had signed his name with a flourish around the last letter. "I'm glad that you came. I'm mighty glad," said Geary.

"What's the trouble?" Tyler asked. "What you into now, Tom?"

The latter shook his head. It seemed that he did not wish to come to that point immediately. "How far'd you come to get here?" he asked curiously, tilting his head to one side as he shook up the meat and potatoes in the big frying pan.

"I took about a three-hundred-mile slant," Tyler said. "Why?"

"I just wanted to know. Something told me that you'd come, if you could. But three hundred miles is a long ways to go for a tramp like me. I appreciate it, Tyler. I appreciate it a mighty lot. It's almost as much to me as what you did before, when you stepped in and took the blame of a killing on your shoulders and so took the rope from around my neck. They'd've got me, and they'd've hung me for killing Tucker Winslow, sure enough."

"They might have hanged you," said the other. "But that's all finished and done with. There's no use worrying about that old affair, partner."

"I don't worry about it, but sometimes I open my eyes at night and lie awake . . . then I wonder and think it over. You didn't know me, Tyler, I

131

was just a stranger. There was no reason for you to take the blame for that killing."

"I told you before," Tyler said, frowning with a touch of impatience, "they'd laid the blame of one killing that I hadn't done on my shoulders before that. It didn't matter if they blamed another on me. And you were a little too old to travel fast enough to get away from the law in this part of the world."

"The law around here is spryer than a jack rabbit," Geary said, nodding his head. "They'd've caught me. I know that."

"And now what trouble are you in?" asked Tyler, obviously controlling his impatience.

"I'm gonna show you," said the miner.

He got up, went into his shack, and came out presently with a handful of crumbling rock that he put into the hands of Tyler.

It was a soft, rotten stone, and it fell apart at the least touch of the fingers, revealing inside of it little glistening streaks of yellow.

Tyler started, raised his hands, turned them to let the firelight strike full upon what he held. "Wire gold!" he said.

"Yeah," muttered the miner, grinning from ear to ear.

"Are you digging this stuff out of the ground?" Tyler asked in amazement.

The other suddenly threw up his hands in the sky and shouted: "Yeah, I'm digging tons of it! D'ye see? That's the trouble that I wanted to tell you about!"

II

"A Review"

Tyler regarded him steadily. "A fellow who's digging fortunes out of the rock every day doesn't need to worry about many things," he said. "What's the matter with you, brother?"

The miner reached across and gripped his arm. "Look at me," he said.

"I'm looking," said Tyler.

"Whatcha see, partner?"

"A hardy old boy about sixty, who's kicked the world in the face a good long while and been kicked himself now and then."

"Eh, you see that, do you?"

"I think so."

"Look again, Tyler."

"I'm still looking."

"See anything like fatherhood in my eyes?"

"Not exactly, Geary. I don't know that things show through with labels like that."

"Don't they? Well, I'll cut it short and tell you that I never been a husband or a father. I got no brother nor sister alive in the world. There's only some sneaking hounds of cousins living back East . . . and that's all that I've got."

"And they don't appear to matter much,"

Tyler suggested.

"No. You think I'm talking like a windy old fool?"

"No. You've got your steam up. That's all."

"Tyler, I want to tell you something. Nobody, so long as I've lived, has ever done much for me. I never had more than a halfway decent break in my life. It's been hard times from the first."

Tyler nodded, rather grave than sympathetic.

"Only once," said Geary. "You know that time?"

"That time when Tucker Winslow got a bullet between the eyes?"

"That time," the miner said gravely. "I told you then and I tell you now that I didn't shoot him."

"All right," Tyler said, "I believe you."

"It was somebody standing behind me, that shot over my shoulder. I saw the head of Tucker fly back. I yelled and jumped up. When I turned, I seen nothing but coat tails running out through the door. That's all I know about it."

"I believe you," said Tyler.

"But nobody else would've believed me. They knew that I hated Winslow. They'd've blamed me. They'd have hanged me. And then you showed up and took his horse in place of yours and rode off on the gelding. That pulled the cry off my trail. That fixed things for me." He groaned, with a sigh at the end of it. "Maybe I ought to've told the story different. I tried to tell the sheriff the right of it. He only swore at me and told me to keep my face out of it. I tried to talk to a reporter for a newspaper, and he thought I was just drunk. Nothing I said could ever make people think that you didn't kill Tucker."

"That's all finished," said Tyler. "I don't regret what I did."

"No," Tom Geary said slowly, "and that's the truth. I reckon that you don't regret it. Anybody else would. But you wouldn't. That's why I thought about you when I made this here strike. The minute that I picked up the stuff . . . the minute that I seen what kind of a strike it was, I thought about you. Believe that?"

"I believe it if you say it."

"And that's why I sent for you. That's my trouble." He broke off in wild laughter and added when he could speak again: "I had more money than I knew what to do with. What good was money to me? A couple of dollars a day would buy all the red-eye that I could drink. And here was thousands and thousands coming out of the mine. You march along with me, will you?"

He snatched up a lantern, lighted it, and led the way to the mouth of the mine that yawned nearby. Once inside, Tyler could see a shaft that slanted easily downward toward the heart of the hill. It was not very deep and presently they stopped before the raw face of the rock. Across it, dark as mud, stretched a wide band of rock quite different from that above and that below.

"Look!" Geary said. "Try it. Try it with your

135

bare hands, will you?"

Tyler leaned over and worked at the rocky formation. He found it wonderfully soft as he broke off a fragment with the tips of his fingers. A golden wire gleamed on one side of the bit of rock, running down and disappearing like a worm into the side of it. "It's rich," he said.

"I never seen anything like it. I been mining forty years," said the miner.

"There may be millions in it," Tyler agreed. "I'm glad that you struck it so rich, man! I'm mighty glad!"

Tyler stretched out his hand. The other seized it and wrung it hard, shouting out, while the shaft rang and thundered with his voice: "It's you that have to be glad, Tyler. It's you, Jim. You get every penny of it!"

Tyler took the lantern from Geary's hand and raised it. His own eyes gleamed. "You haven't been drinking, either," he said.

"But I'm drunk with happiness," said the older man. "Look! Kicked around the world all my life, and then I meet one man with the heart and the soul to take a chance with death, just because that was how decent he was. Life is what I owe you, Tyler. Money is all that I can give you for it. But I'm going to give you the money. I'm going to give you mule trains loaded with it. I'm gonna give you enough to build palaces, if you want to spend it that way. You can go to Europe and marry a duchess, is what you can do. You can be a swell in Paris and London. You can step out with the best of 'em. And me, old Tom Geary, I'm gonna be the man behind you!" He broke off with a change of voice: "Let's get out of here. The ideas that I got in my head, right now, they make me dizzy. I need room around me, or I'll choke."

They went back to the fire. Tyler calmly rescued the contents of the frying pan, which were about to burn, saying as he did so: "Old fellow, this is fine of you. This is in the grand style. I knew there was heart in you that first night I met you, when you stood there with the dead man in the room, beaten, but not done for. But as for taking your mine away from you, I can't do that. Friendship is worth more than hard cash to me. That's all I'll tell you. And I'm as glad to have heard you talk this way as to have you give me a thousand tons of bar gold out of the mine. That's a fact."

Geary shook his head. "You think that I'm a crazy man, eh?" he said. "Well, I'll tell you the other side of it. It ain't the gold that excites me. It's the thinking of what you could do with it. You're a gentleman, is what you are, Jim Tyler. You'll know what to do with a fortune. But me? I'd waste it. I'd throw it away. I'd be swindled out of it, and the coat on my back. That's happened to me before. All that I need is a stake, a burro or two to steer through the mountains, and a hammer to chip the rocks as I go by. That's my pleasure, son, reading the mind of the mountains . . . like these that go waltzing up into the stars all around us." He waved right and left toward the outlines of the big peaks, rising up and shutting out the stars.

"I know," Tyler murmured. "I've heard other prospectors talk in that vein, too. I respect it, Geary, but I. . . ."

"There ain't any buts," insisted the other. "There's only this . . . how you gonna be able to get back inside the law to spend the coin that I can give you?"

"How can I escape from outlawry?" repeated Tyler.

"Yeah. They say that you've killed eleven men, Jim. Eleven is quite a pile, take it first and last."

Jim shook his head as Geary dished out the food onto the two tin plates, and both began to eat. Jim was looking thoughtfully at the fire. Plainly he was rehearsing both his answer and the facts of his life.

"They've even gone and stuck a price on your head," the miner added. When there was still no answer, he said: "Eight thousand dollars, ain't it?"

Finally Tyler said: "This is the way of it, Tom. They don't accuse me of killing eleven men. Not the police, at least. It's just newspaper talk. The newspapers would die pretty fast if they didn't have lies to feed to their readers. But, as a matter of fact, the police accuse me of killing six men."

"Only six, eh? Well, that ain't eleven, but it's considerable."

Tyler went on: "Public opinion has me down as a killer."

"Maybe public opinion is a liar?" said the miner.

"No," answered Tyler hesitantly. "I've killed men. I suppose that I deserve to die for it, too. I've fought with guns for the sake of the fun I thought it was."

"Have you changed your mind about it, maybe?" asked Geary.

Tyler sighed. "Sometimes I think I have . . . till I get into a pinch," he answered. "But here's a point. Of the six men they charge against me, nobody in the world can say that it was not self-defense in four cases. When those two Derrick brothers jumped me in Santa Fé . . . why, that was self-defense. Twenty other men looked on. I was never even arrested for it."

"Go on," said the miner eagerly. "That leaves only four."

"Harry Montrose was number three on the list of the law. But Harry had a price on his own head. He was a gunman, always had been. They wanted him from Mexico City to Ottawa. It was just a case of a friendly bet between us, you might say, and I won the bet . . . his horse against mine. I killed him, all right. I admit it, but it was a fair fight."

"Go on," Geary urged. "I'm eating this up!"

"Slim Joe . . . Joe Wentworth . . . you've heard about him?"

"The gambler?"

"Yes."

"I've heard about Wentworth. Of course, I have. Nobody would ever have to come to trial for the killing of that hound."

"No more did I," said Tyler. "But you can see that by this time I was known as a fellow who reached for his gun when in doubt. And when Dan Sharkey was found dead in the shack that day, people simply took it for granted that I was guilty. I stood for the arrest . . . I thought that I'd get a fair trial. But the very first day in jail, a mob rose up . . . maybe you've heard about it?"

"No. Lynching party, eh?"

"Yes, they wanted a regular necktie party. And I didn't. While they were beating down the front door of the jail, I got out the back way, ducked through the line that was watching for me there, grabbed a horse, and rode off. That was all. I never laid a hand on Dan Sharkey."

"He was a hound, anyway."

"No, Sharkey was all right, except when he was boiled with red-eye. Now that disposes of the whole list of six that's charged against me, except for Tucker Winslow, and you know the truth about how he died."

"I know the truth!" exclaimed the miner. "But then they got nothing ag'in' you, partner. Nothing real."

"Nothing that a smart lawyer couldn't clear me of."

"And why didn't you get one?"

"That would mean a ten thousand dollar fee, about."

"By thunder," Geary shouted, "we'll give him a hundred thousand and tell him to keep the change."

III

"The Shot Across Hills"

They sat by the fire with the miner staring about excitedly, like one who sees new and bright visions of the future, while his taller and younger companion continued to eat with a very good appetite.

"It's as smooth as can be," Geary announced. "There's not gonna be any trouble about it, at all. What you need is money and a smart lawyer, eh?"

"Yes, and an honest town to stand my trial in. I know where I could surrender and where I could be tried."

"Where's that?"

"Digger Creek."

"I thought that that was a pretty wild and woolly place, though?"

"Yes, but it's a town that knew what a pair of thugs the Derrick brothers were, and it's a town that feels kindly to the man that killed the pair, as I happen to know."

"The pair, eh?" murmured the miner. "And how did you do it, Jim?"

"Oh, it was a bar brawl," the tall man answered carelessly. "I was feeling mean. I'd been riding through alkali dust for eighty miles, and the whisky didn't rinse the stuff clean out of my throat in the least. There was a little play of dice, just for the drinks. But Jack Derrick, he couldn't help practicing his dirty, crooked tricks even for a dollar stake. I told him what I thought of him . . . and those two beauties went for me at the same time." He raised his coffee cup to his lips.

"And you got 'em both?"

"Yes, both," Tyler said, putting his cup down and pouring more coffee out of the pot.

"And you weren't hurt a mite?"

"Hurt a mite! Ever have four Forty-Five caliber slugs go plowing through you inside of two seconds? You bet I was hurt. I was lying on my back on the floor before the finish, and I got Bill Derrick by shooting over my head while I was lying there. But you can bet that I was hurt. It hurts still, just thinking about it."

The miner gasped. "You've led a hard life, partner," he murmured, a great respect growing in his eyes. "There ain't been any fear in you. Never a mite."

"Yes, there has," Tyler admitted. "But the fear that makes one fellow sick is what gives spice to life to another one. It's not such a very big difference. Sometimes I may be under pressure long enough to crumble, and then any man will be able to kick me in the face and make me take water. I don't know. I've seen strange things happen to men when their hearts are broken."

The miner caught his breath again. "I believe you, Jim," he said. "I don't want any of those pressures, thank you. But I think that if you got out of this life, you'd go straight, easy enough, don't you?"

"If I got out of outlawry?"

"Yes."

"I think I would," Tyler agreed. "There've been times in the winter, with frostbite in my face and feet, and nothing in my stomach. . . ."

"Hello, Geary!" shouted a voice nearby.

Jim Tyler rose and made a gliding step backward into the darkness. "It's all right," he said, seeing Geary's greatly alarmed face. "Nobody around here is apt to know me, at least, in this light."

"Hello!" Geary answered back, thus reassured.

Out of the darkness came a striding man, his voice arriving before him to explain: "I've got a wagon rutted down in the mud on the trail, not a quarter of a mile from here, Geary. It's Dick Mansfield. Can you give me a pony or two that'll help to pull me out? My mules are balky, and they won't give the buckboard an honest lift." It was a long, loose-jointed fellow who came into the circle of the firelight.

"I'll get you an old hoss that I got here," Geary said. "But he don't pull a rope worth a cent."

"Much of a load on the buckboard?" Tyler asked, stepping out into the firelight.

"Not enough for any one hoss that's got anything in him," Mansfield responded.

"I'll fix that buckboard for you, then," Tyler offered. "That is, if you've got some rope or a chain."

"I've got plenty."

"I've got a pony over there that'll pull the pommel right out of the saddle, or get you on the trail and rolling once more. Wait a moment."

The mustang was quickly saddled, and Tyler rode it at the side of the stranger to the point on the trail, not far off, where the buckboard was bogged down, with two gloomy-headed mules standing before it, their ears flattening as they heard the men approaching. A stout rope was made fast to the wagon at one end and to the horn of Tyler's saddle on the other. Then the mustang squatted like a cat and began to strain. The driver, in the meantime, whooped and cracked his whip. There was a sudden lurch, and the rope turned slack.

"Cast loose! Cast loose!" shouted the driver.

For the mules, having changed their minds suddenly, were now at full gallop up the trail, and Tyler had barely time to cast loose the rope when the wagon went bounding and clattering past him, the thanks of Dick Mansfield roaring dimly back in the ear of the outlaw.

The latter watched the buckboard disappearing into darkness and smiled a little. He was not so sure that he would find, in any other part of the world, exactly the contentment that he found among the free and easy people of the

West. He had been born and bred to their ways and, although his education had taken him to distant parts of Europe, still he was not sure that any other spot would satisfy his hunger for the West and for Western men. As he gathered the reins again on the neck of the pony, he heard, or thought he heard, the sound of a pistol shot beyond the two hills that separated him from the Geary camp. That, however, was not at all unusual. Sometimes a hungry wolf will stalk a campfire with extraordinary boldness, and more than one has been picked off with a snap shot. Or a rabbit might have scampered through the edge of the firelight, or an owl have sailed boldly near to the strange light.

These possible explanations were all in the mind of Tyler, and he did not hurry in making his return to the camp. Yet there was trouble in his mind, in the very darkest corner of his heart, so that he was already frowning when, dismounting by the fire, he had no sight of his friend. The latter might be in the lean-to, of course.

"Hello, Geary!" he called.

There was no answer.

Suddenly he shouted at the top of his lungs: "Geary! Geary!"

There was not a whisper, and yet certainly his voice must have carried as far as Geary could possibly have gone from the fire. He was about to leap on the horse, but in what direction should he ride? Rocks and trees broke up the ground, made ten thousand hiding places all around him. A thousand men might have been lurking within speaking range of the place, all unseen. He looked around him with anxiety and with foreboding. When a man had such a mine as poor old Tom Geary possessed, motives for doing away with him would not be hard to find.

Then, glancing beside the fire, he saw a dark spot, as though coffee had been spilled there. He jumped to the place. Beside it was the clear impression, in the much trodden dust, of the body of a man that had been stretched there not long before. And that dark stain — he lifted a bit of the mud — was blood. Had that one shot been the end of his friend? Staring bleakly down, in his wretchedness, he saw something more — letters scrawled in the wet, red mud with a clumsy and uncertain finger. Leaning down over them, he was able to read — **San Andreas**. Was that the name of the murderer? No, but more likely of the place where the murderer might be found. He could not doubt that the message had been scrawled there by the finger of old Tom Geary.

IV

"Any Port in a Storm"

Nothing but the lightning flashes and the good sense of his cow pony brought Tyler through the storm, for the way was the dimmest of trails, and it hooked and twisted back and forth among the rocks and the hills. When they came up to the throat of the pass, the force of the wind focused upon Tyler, and he felt sure that he would have to give up forcing his way through the pass. But the mustang shook its head and plodded steadily on. When they got beyond the crest of the pass to lower ground, where the ravine widened, there was still less of the gale. Yet it was strong enough to soak Tyler to the skin. He had bound down his slicker to keep out the water, but the whipping force of the storm lifted mere wrinkles and corners here and there and forced jets of water through the small openings. His very boots were filled with water.

He endured this inconvenience fairly well, for it was not the first time in his life that he had been caught out by evil weather. He had been on the range through fully nine of his thirty years, and nine years on the range, in those days, were equal to thirty of them in these degenerate times.

The gale that had been screaming at him now lost a good part of its force, but, in place of the rain, large hail began to beat down on him. It hurt when they struck on the back of his hands, and they delivered a thousand little hammer blows upon his slicker. He knew that it was not likely to do either him or the horse any harm, of course, but they had traveled far, and the cold of the mountain pass was so greatly increased by the hail, that he decided in the course of the next half mile he would have to get to shelter. There were no trees to speak of, but there was plenty of brush and, since he had his hand-axe with him, he determined to dismount and fell a great heap of fuel, which he would then feed into a fire, kindled in a sheltered nook among the rocks. He began to feel that what he had heard was perfect truth that only a madman would attempt to ride the pass at night, particularly on such a night as this.

He was in just this humor when the sky was ripped apart by a long furrow of lightning, and this illumination showed him a big, high-shouldered house that stood back from the pass a little distance. Its windows blinked at him like so many dead eyes. It was not a cheerful-looking spot, but it meant much to a man who had just determined to camp out without food in such weather as this. He turned without a moment's hesitation; the mustang, too, understood that there was shelter for man and beast not far away, and it picked up into a trot, weaving among the rocks toward the house with the uncanny skill that it had been exhibiting all the way through the pass.

By another flash of lightning, Tyler dismounted before the patio gate that was the only entrance visible on that side. When he tried it with his hand, he was surprised to find it locked. He was surprised, because in his part of the world, if the latch is dropped, the latchstring is, nevertheless, left hanging on the outside. Hospitality is not a virtue in the Southwest; it is simply a matter of fact.

He shook the gate until it rattled, and began to feel that the place must be uninhabited. That did not matter so much, because he would be able to force an entrance in one way or another. But now a pair of dogs began to clamor in the distance. They rushed up close to the gate and gave tongue as though they wished to be out and at him. This angered Tyler. In fact, he was a fellow who took offense a little too easily, and now he was ready to curse the master on account of the dogs. It had a very inhospitable flavor, this whole scene; perhaps, he thought, he had ridden so far south that he was in a part of the world where men follow another school of manners. He rattled at the gate again. At this the clamor of the dogs became so violent, he slipped the revolver out of its holster and held it ready.

But presently there was a dull gleam of light through the crack in the gate; someone bearing a lantern was coming out through the wet patio.

"Who's there?" demanded a heavy voice.

"A man," Tyler said, angered more than ever.

"No place for you here," said the man inside the patio.

"Are you turning me out on a night like this?" demanded Tyler.

"Owen's Inn is only five or six miles down the pass," said the other.

"Fifteen or sixteen, more likely," Tyler answered. "I've reached my limit, and so has my horse. I'm coming in here to stay the night."

"Stranger," the man said, "if I go and unbar this here gate, it won't be to let you in, likely."

"Why, damn you," Tyler responded. "If you talk that way, I'll smash the lock of this gate and walk in, and, if those dogs bother me, I'll brain 'em. Now I've told you what I'll do!"

"I hear what you're talkin' about," was the answer. "We'll have a look at you, brother." There was a decidedly threatening growl in his voice, as he said this, then the sound of a bar being drawn.

Lightning again shot across the sky; the thunder boomed from mountain to mountain in the pass. Then the gate swung open. He saw before him a man of middle height and excessive breadth of shoulders, with a great cloak thrown over head and body, a lantern in one hand and a stalwart club in the other. A shadow covered his face, but Tyler saw the gleam of eyes and the shiny teeth behind a snarl. From his side, two big dogs that looked capable of running down wild mountain lions and killing them, sprang out at the stranger.

They did not charge home, however. Tyler, instead of retreating, leveled his gun, and the dogs dodged to one side, as though they were perfectly familiar with the dangers of the weapon.

The man with the club had taken a step forward, also, while making a significant gesture with his club, then he had halted. He saw before him a tall fellow, whose hat brim was weighted down with water, and whose lean, weather-darkened face showed resolution and courage of the highest sort. It was not a handsome face, unless strength is beauty, but it was strong in the best sense of that word. The jaw, the big cheek bones, the arch of the nose, all bespoke mental power. The shoulders of the wanderer, moreover, gave hint of ample power of body to back it up. The man at the patio gate, after a brief instant, called off the dogs, and they slunk back to him, snarling and growling.

"You better go on down the pass to Owen's Inn," said the man of the house. "We ain't fixed here for making people comfortable. You go right on down the valley, and you ain't gonna miss the way. It's clear as the nose on your face."

"I know what this trail is like, because I've been riding it mostly all night," Tyler said. "I told you that I intended to put up here, and that's what I'm going to do."

"Well, all right," said the other gruffly. "It

ain't Christian to turn a man away in weather like this. I hope you'll like what you find inside," he added, with a decided shadowing of a double meaning in his words. With that, he turned his back, and this very blunt action was taken by Tyler as an invitation.

Accordingly, he led in the mustang, and his guide marched across the pavement to the right-hand wing of the building that surrounded the patio on three sides. There he pulled open another big double door, exposing the long, narrow aisles of a commodious stable. There were already half a dozen horses in it.

"Put up your hoss," the man with the lantern said. "There's another lantern hanging from a peg in there. Then come back across the patio. You'll see my light, and I'll see what I can rummage for you in the way of chuck."

V
"The One-Eyed Cook"

With the man traveling back across the patio, Tyler fumbled under his wet slicker, found matches, scratched one after another, and finally found one dry enough to ignite. He found the lantern and, touching the wick of the lantern, saw the fire burn with a dull sparkle across it, and clamped down the chimney again. By that light he cast a look over the stable. It was old, very old, indeed. The floor was stone, furrowed and worn toward the center of the aisle by generations of tramplings. A stone floor was bad for horses, as he very well knew, but he saw that the animals in the stalls were deeply bedded in straw.

He looked at the horses with attention, as he went down the aisle. They had the narrow hindquarters of two-year-olds, it seemed, and a great length of leg under them. Suddenly he stopped and stared at one from the side. The gelding was narrow, to be sure, but deep-quartered, and the lantern light flickered over the sleek ripple of shoulder muscles of the most exquisite sort.

"Thoroughbred, by the jumping thunder," Tyler said to himself. He stepped back a little and looked at the row of hindquarters again.

They were all about the same — seven horses with the lines of hot blood. Those hocks, clean and bony and big, told a story of their own. What were animals of this sort doing tucked away in the middle of a mountain pass that had been long in disuse? A generation before, the railroad had cut through these mountains, and, since that time, it had not paid to pack goods across the upper pass. It was a waste of time, men, and money.

He had tried the old, old way over the summits, and here he was. Not many others would come in the course of a year, and this was a refuge as secure, in fact, from outside surveillance, as though it had been buried in the deepest heart of the mountains. Certain thoughts concerning the horses and the character of the owner made Tyler smile faintly and grimly. He drew out his revolver again, looked at it, and his smile took on a tone of affection and irony, at once.

He put the gun up, led the mustang to a stall where the bedding of straw was already spread, stripped off the saddle and bridle, and tethered the pony by the halter. He forked down enough hay from the mow to fill the manger. It was very good hay, timothy and wild oats, mixed, and had a sweet, pure smell. One could wish for no better bed than a roll of blankets on top of that haymow. But how did timothy and wild oats come to be here in the middle of the rocky pass? It must have been packed in. And to think of packing in horse fodder to this end of the world . . . ?

He remembered a black sheen of water in the patio, standing in a trough just outside the door of the barn. So he found a bucket, filled it at the trough, and watered the mustang. Then he looked about with a vague hope that he might find grain. There in the corner, to be sure, was the feed box, and he found it almost brimming with the finest oats. "Oats," he said aloud, as he fingered the grains. He added his favorite exclamation under his breath: "By the jumping thunder."

These were not wild oats, not these plumply filled kernels. This had been packed in, too, from the distant and expensive outside world. Certainly the man or men who owned those horses were determined that they should have the best. Had they been in the center of the blue-grass hills, they could not have been better fed.

He gave the mustang a liberal measure of this good fodder, and then closed the barn door, after putting out his lantern, and crossed through a beating rain toward a lighted window on the other side of the enclosure.

The two big dogs came and sniffed at his heels as he crossed. But he regarded them not at all. He knew that a dog, having been over-awed once, will not soon forget the lesson and show its teeth.

There was a door beside the window, and, when he opened this, he found himself in a great,

155

old-fashioned kitchen of the Spanish type, with a huge fireplace built into the wall on the inner side of the room — it ran almost the width of the room. A small fire was burning in it, with big, blackened pots hanging from their irons, some in, some out, one directly over the flames.

He who appeared to be the cook had only one leg and one eye, the other eye being covered by a great black patch. He had an apron tied around him, by way of a professional badge, and his hands had flour-marked it liberally here and there. His sleeves were rolled up to the elbows, and, through the hair that covered them, Tyler saw three or four extravagant pieces of tattooing such as sailors love to have marked on their skin, after a barbaric custom of their own.

This man looked up with a squint in his one eye and muttered: "How d'ye, stranger?"

The man who had led Tyler into the patio in such a surly manner was in the kitchen, and his glance was no more friendly now that Tyler was in the house. He sat in a corner, smoking a pipe and reading a newspaper so old and thumbed that it curled over at the corners of the pages. He had thrown off the cloak that had covered him from the downpour, and now he appeared dressed in overalls, a heavy flannel shirt, and thick brogans. His face was as broad as it was long, due to the shortness of his chin and the dimensions of his jowls.

The cook was busily cutting bread, using one flourish of a heavy knife to slice through a thick loaf to the cutting board, and turning off half a dozen slices in as many gestures.

"I'll have something for you in the line of chuck in a minute or two," he said. "Set yourself down and dry by the fire."

"I'll give my clothes a wring, first," Tyler said.

There was a galvanized-iron laundry tub over there in a corner of the room. Tyler stripped off his things and began to wring them out into the tub. It enabled the other two to see the perfect type of athlete in perfect training and at the age of physical perfection. He was a mass of complicated sinews and long muscles that fitted well up around the joints. There was no wastage about his hips or stomach. His weight was where a prize fighter would have liked to have it — in the deep chest and the heavily muscled shoulders — and this working machine was supported on legs like those of a stag, fit for speed and endurance. The inside of the knees were red from the grip he had been maintaining on the sides of the mustang during that long and difficult ride.

The cook with his one eye, openly, and the other man with both eyes, covertly, examined this athletic body with close attention, and with the air of people who knew what was what. Particularly they were interested when, in the action of powerful wringing that made the water burst out from the tightening folds of the heavy cloth, all the strength of the arms started into sight in bulges, ripples, and long, indented lines.

The damp trousers and the shirt he put on

again, and it was noticeable that he got one arm into a sleeve at a time, and ducked his head afterwards quickly through the neck hole of the shirt. There was not half a second when this process of dressing made him helpless. He put on his socks, also. The other dripping garments he placed near the stove, the boots upside down.

This procedure the cook regarded with a favorable interest, and he talked as he heaped on a plate of enameled kitchenware a great mess of mulligan stew, in which the hungry eyes of Tyler distinguished the red of tomatoes, the crystal white of potato wedges, and the wrinkled, brown skin of chickens. With the bread, and with the fragrance of coffee beginning to stream now through the room, it seemed plain that he was to feed well.

Warmth and satisfaction relaxed those inward muscles that had kept his heart taut through so many days and through such terrible dangers — not that he entirely relaxed; not more than a wildcat when it reaches the shelter of a strange den, not more than a hunted wolf when, with the pack off the trail for the moment, it lies down to pant and rest in the sun.

So he sat down to the table and heard the cook saying: "Them that will take the trouble to take care of themselves can see through the worst of bad weather. Many a time I've been in an old hooker that lay off Cape Stiff with her nose pressed against a steady wall of the westerlies. And many a time I've gone weeks and weeks with never a dry bunk to sleep in and with never a dry stitch to my back. And it was up on deck, all hands, every hour or so, and it was tack here and tack there, to try to dodge through under the arm of the devil that guards the Horn.

"And I've seen my shipmates hale and hearty one week, coughing sick the next, and dead after a fortnight . . . them that said, as well be sopping wet as wrung out wet. But me and the ones that knew, we was never too tired to wring out our socks and hang 'em up, and never too spent to do the same by our clothes. If a big one came aboard and walloped us the first minute we was on deck, a-lashing of our oilskins, why we stood it, and knew that the next night, and the next, we'd have better luck. With the water wrung out, your own body heat will steam you dry, if you've got time."

"Followed the sea a long time?" Tyler asked around a mouthful of that delicious stew.

"Followed it, man and boy, twenty years and more. Followed it around the world and seen the lock on Davy Jones's locker once or twice, but here I've wound up like you see, in a warm kitchen and a good job. Davy, he got an eye and a leg off me, but that's better than leaving both legs and both eyes behind you. Try that coffee, will you? Jeff, hand me the coffee pot, will you?"

Tyler lifted his stern head and glanced toward Jeff, but the cook shook his head and winked knowingly.

"Them that have been pinched hard," he said,

"they forget their manners for a time." With his wooden leg, he went stumping to the stove, and presently came back with the coffeepot, from which he refilled the stranger's cup. "Which way you come? Up or down?" asked the cook.

"I came across Dry Creek," Tyler responded.

"From Dry Creek! That's a rough trail," said the cook. "I been that way. Took me a day and a half. How long you been traveling?"

"Less than that. I left Dry Creek last night."

The cook whistled. "That's traveling," he said. "Hear that, Jeff? That's traveling, I say."

Jeff said, still from behind the paper: "There's some that travel fast because it's their pleasure, and there's some that travel fast because they got a whip on their backs."

"Come, come, Jeff," said the cook. "There ain't any sense in holding malice. You wouldn't expect a man to travel on through this kind of weather, would you, when there's a house like this nearby, and the smell of a mulligan stew floating out of the chimney? Listen at that weather."

The howl of the storm came mournfully down the chimney, and the house trembled with the wind.

"Well for you to stand and gabble," Jeff said. "But what'll the chief say when he comes back?"

VI

"The Chief"

From the sudden start of both the cook and Jeff, it was apparent that the last remark had exceeded the limits that Jeff had imposed on his own conversation. Now he bunched his shoulders forward and stared at the guest.

But the latter went calmly on with his meal, merely remarking: "Don't worry about the way that I forced myself into the house, Jeff. I'll tell your boss that you wanted to keep me out and couldn't."

This suggestion pleased Jeff even less than his own last words, but, before he could devise an answer, Tyler had finished swallowing his supper and stood up from the table. "Thanks a lot, doctor," he said to the cook. "That tasted better than anything I ever set my teeth in."

"This kind of weather is the sauce that a cook wants," said the one-legged man, grinning. "Are you turning in?"

"Yes," Tyler said, picking up his damp clothes from the place where they had been spread out beside the heat of the stove. "I've had a long ride, and I make an early start in the morning."

"Show him a room, Jeff, will you?" asked the cook.

"You be damned!" Jeff spit, resolutely taking shelter behind his paper again like one who has submitted to all the indignities that he can endure.

The cook glared at him. "In a barn was where you was raised," he said, "and in a damned drafty barn, too, what I mean to say. Come along, partner, and I'll show you where to bunk." He picked a lantern off a peg on the wall and lighted it, then, with the light in his hand, he led the way out of the kitchen, walking with a peculiar swing, on account of his wooden leg.

Yet he made very good progress in spite of that handicap, and took Tyler across a big dining room, where stood a great table that would accommodate twenty men, at least, and through this to a hall beyond. There they went up a flight of winding stairs to the floor above, where the cook threw open a door and showed Tyler a big room with three beds in it.

"Maybe a couple of these beds will be filled before morning," he explained. "We're expecting some of the hands to come back in the night. But that's all right. You can turn into that bed next to the wall there. Nobody has a claim on it."

"Thanks," Tyler said. "A blanket and a pile of straw would look good to me just now." He dragged off his coat as he spoke and began to hang the still moist garments on empty hooks along the wall. A good many other clothes were hanging up already, and there were at least a dozen pairs of shoes or boots in all stages from shining newness to moldy age and disuse.

There were other things, such as one might expect to find in a house like this — fishing rods in one corner, a shotgun, two rifles, and two pairs of revolvers, all neatly stowed on a home-made rack.

"Don't you mind Jeff," the cook said, lingering. "He's got a grouch on tonight, but he'll come out of it, all right."

"I won't mind Jeff," Tyler assured him.

"That's the way to talk," said the cook, nodding. "You been around the world a little, brother, ain't you?"

"I've stepped about a little," Tyler agreed.

"Travel is mighty widening to a gent," said the cook. He nodded again and winked his one eye. "It shows him what's worthwhile in a lot of places."

"It shows him what not to see in other places, too," Tyler commented, looking straight at the ex-sailor.

The latter squinted narrowly in return. Then, gradually, a twisted grin distorted his face, for he smiled chiefly on the side that had the eye, and the wrinkles thrown up high in his brown cheek reduced his vision to a single gleam of light. "Maybe there's something in that, too," the cook said. "I never had no use for a prying fool."

"Nor I," Tyler stated.

They looked silently at one another for a moment.

"Well, good night," said the cook.

"Good night."

The cook left the room, leaving the lantern behind him and saying that he knew every wrinkle of the house and could find his way anywhere in the dark.

Tyler, once he was alone, stood motionless for a moment, listening to the roar of rain or hail on the roof, and to the howling of the wind. Now that he was under shelter, it seemed incredible that any human beings could be out in such weather as this.

The window of the room opened to the lee of the storm, so he pulled up the sash and looked out. He could not distinguish the exterior very clearly by the light of the lantern, but he could make out that the room did not open on the patio. He was glad of that. In case he had to make a sudden exit during the night, he would want to get clear of a house that might turn out to be a deadly trap for him.

He was fairly confident, whatever the occupation of the inhabitants of this place, it could hardly be a legal one. Tucked away in these mountains, there had always been robber nests from the earliest Mexican and Indian days. The refuge was too distant and secure not to tempt the lawless, and he was reasonably certain that he had settled down for the night in a den of them. Luckily most of them were away; perhaps they would not be able to make their expected return before morning, considering the state of the weather. However, even if they came, he felt that they would not look upon him with too critical an eye. There was a certain piratical cut about his own appearance that would not make them too hostile, he was sure.

At any rate, now that he had found shelter, he intended to stay with them until daylight. Having made up his mind to that, he straightway finished his undressing, rolled up in a blanket that would have been considered very meager warmth to a man of less iron body, and had hardly put his head on the pillow before he was asleep.

He slept soundly, dreamlessly, as a man will do when the body is thoroughly exhausted, but after a scant hour the neighing of a horse wakened him. He sat up in the bed and listened.

The storm had fallen somewhat, but it still maintained such a roaring that he was unable to make out any new sounds. However, the whinny of the horse assured him that the travelers had probably returned, as expected. He lay back in the darkness, merely thrusting a hand under his pillow to make sure that the revolver was in place there.

Presently sounds of voices and of trampling feet came dimly up to him. Somebody began to thunder out a song, the last of which was shut off by the closing of a door, apparently. The whole house was quivering with life. And Tyler smiled

165

a little, as he stared above him into the darkness. He had known enough wildness in his life to sense the thrill of it, in that vibrating gloom.

Then a step came down the hall, and the door of his room opened. A man carrying a lantern entered, a tall man, whose enormous shadow covered most of the ceiling and the wall behind him. He came straight to the bed and raised the lantern a little.

"Hello, stranger," he said.

Tyler remained flat on his back, but he raised a hand in salute. "Hello," he said.

He saw a man who in build might have been his twin brother. But he was perhaps five or six years older, and he wore a mustache in a vain effort to disguise a great scar across his upper lip, on the right side. The effort was vain because the mustache, although it grew thick and strong, continually parted above the scar when the man spoke. It was, aside from the scar, a rather handsome face of Tyler's own predatory type, but the jaw was a trifle too long and heavy. One would have said, at the first glance, that here was an excess of strength that naturally suggested cruelty.

"Gotta ask you some questions," the man with the lantern said.

"Blaze away," Tyler answered. "I like a lot of things better than questions, though."

"People that like to answer questions ain't apt to be riding down this here pass," said the other.

"Nor to be living in it, either," suggested Tyler.

The man of the house nodded. "That might be true, too. You might even think that we don't raise cows on this ranch."

"I even had that thought myself," Tyler said.

"What else do you think?" asked the man of the place.

"I thought," Tyler went on, "that it would be a good house to stop thinking in, and to forget as soon as I hit the trail once more."

"Did you?"

"Yes, I did."

For it appeared to Tyler that to have pretended total ignorance and innocence in such a place would have been a folly more likely to excite suspicion than a certain degree of frankness. Moreover, he already had spoken quite openly with the cook.

"Well," said the man of the scarred lip, "any gent that has eyes is pretty sure to use them. But how am I to know that you'll be able to forget as fast as you think you can?"

"You look me over," Tyler suggested. "I'm no eagle that lives on what the fishhawks catch, if that's what you mean."

The other smiled a very little. "You've got a brain in your head and a tongue," he said, "but maybe you were wrong to crowd in here where you weren't wanted."

"Maybe I was wrong," Tyler agreed calmly.

"I'm going to ask you questions. Will you talk back?"

"I might," Tyler said, "up to a point."

"You'll talk right on past that point, too," the other said, "if you know what's good for you."

VII

"A Bargain"

The answer of the man in bed to this question was rather odd. "How far from here is San Andreas?"

"Fifty miles . . . about," said the other. "What the devil has that to do with what I'm saying?"

"I'm wondering," Tyler said, "whether I can tell you the truth."

"Maybe that's worth wondering about, too," answered the questioner. He kicked a stool nearer and sat down. His grim, bright eyes were always fixed immovably upon the face of the other.

At last, Tyler said: "Well, I'll try the truth for once, and see how that does." He chuckled a little. Then, stretching his arms above his head, he yawned. He drew down the arms slowly, looking thoughtfully up toward the ceiling. His left arm continued to come down until it was lying on his breast. His right was lost beneath his pillow.

"Truth is always easy," said the man of the house.

"Yes, unless it gets you a slug of lead between the eyes," Tyler answered. "I'm Jim Tyler."

The other lifted his brows. "It's a long time, but finally we've met up," he said.

"Whom have I met with?" asked Tyler.

"Why, I'm Carter. Ray Carter."

"Oh, you're Carter, are you?"

"Yeah, that's me."

"You're the fellow who stuck up the Q. and T.O., are you?" Tyler asked.

"They say that I did that little job."

"You killed Warren and Smythe and Doc Gillespie."

"People talk a lot," said the man with the scarred lip. "They say that you killed the two Derricks, and Slim Joe Wentworth, Dan Sharkey, Harry Montrose, and a lot of others."

"You know what there is behind talk," Tyler responded.

"Yeah, I know," the other outlaw said, without smiling.

"And now I'm on my way to San Andreas. You're not in the picture, as far as I'm concerned, and I don't suppose that I'm in your picture. I don't want the money that's on your head, and I don't suppose that you want the money that's on my head, either."

"You're to the point," remarked Carter. "Why are you driving at San Andreas? It's not much of a town."

"No?"

"No, it's not."

"There's something in it that I'm interested in."

"I don't believe that," Carter said.

"Don't you?"

"You better come clean," Carter threatened. "There's nothing in San Andreas for a high-flyer like you, partner."

"I'll come clean. A friend of mine disappeared, and I take it that San Andreas is his new address."

"Do you? Why?"

"Where he was lying, where the sign of him was marked on the ground, he'd written that name in the mud that his blood made."

"It's a blood trail, then?"

"I suppose there'll be more blood, if I reach the right spot and find the right man," admitted Tyler. "I've told you the story, though."

"What's the name of your friend?"

"It seems to me that you're asking a lot of questions."

"That's the way I am."

"My friend's name is Tom Geary. Miner in the ravine across the pass."

"*Humph,*" Carter sighed.

"Well?" murmured Tyler.

"I'm thinking," said the other. "Maybe you're telling the truth, but maybe you're only a damned spy who. . . ." His right hand moved in a sudden flash.

There was another flash straight before his eyes, as the right hand of Tyler appeared from beneath the pillow, bearing with it the sleek and oily length of a Colt .45.

171

The hand of Carter was arrested. "All right," he said calmly.

"All right," Tyler echoed.

He sat up in the bed very slowly. The strain on his stomach muscles of that gradual change in position must have been great, but he showed nothing of it in his face, and it was plain that his right hand was under no pressure whatever. He could have fired the gun at any moment.

"This doesn't change things much," Carter remarked.

"It changes them a little," Tyler answered.

"The house is all behind me," Carter reminded Tyler. "I've got two men out there in the hall."

"The window doesn't open into the hall."

"It's a hundred and fifty feet of cliff to the ground under that window," said Carter.

Tyler squinted his eyes. Then he remembered that his outlook had been dimmed by the down rush of the rain. It might, after all, be just a distance to the ground. "I'm a housefly," he said. "I walk up the walls and across the ceiling."

"You'll land on your head, if you try to walk down that wall."

"This don't lead to much," Tyler answered, resting his revolver on his knee as he sat up finally, and faced the other.

"Not so very much," Carter agreed, and said nothing more for a moment.

"I may lose the game," Tyler said, "but it looks as though you can't win it."

"You worked on a wrong idea," Carter said very calmly. "You really thought that I meant a gun play."

"Yes, I think you meant a gun play."

"You're wrong. I was simply going to declare trumps."

"And trumps are what I hold a handful of."

"Just now you do, but you're only playing for fun."

"How do you make this out?"

"You can't get shut of the house, Tyler. You're a smart fellow, and you're a game fellow. But you can't kill me without the sound of a gun-shot from a Colt. And when you make that noise, things are going to start moving inside of this place."

"You talk sense," Tyler said. "Anyway, I don't want to hurt you, Carter. I've nothing against you . . . and you keep a good cook."

"Suppose that we agree about something, then?"

"I'm ready to agree, all right."

"You and I could do business, Tyler."

"I can see that, if we could agree about the business."

"Begin with San Andreas," said Carter.

"That's a good starting place."

"San Andreas starts right here."

"I thought you said that it was fifty miles away?"

"It is," Carter answered, "but I own San Andreas. It's in my pocket."

"That interests me a lot."

"I'm glad it does, because you interest me."

"Do I?"

"Yes."

"Then maybe we could make a bargain."

"Maybe we could," said the man with the scar. "I have a lot of good men with me, here, but I never have had anybody as good as you are, Tyler. You and I could split the thing up. There has to be a double lead to almost any job, of the sort I work on. Maybe you could play the other lead with me."

"Maybe I could," Tyler answered, "but I don't play any lead until I've been to San Andreas."

Carter nodded. "This here Geary, he was a friend of yours?"

"Yes," Tyler said, "he was a bunkie."

"That goes," replied Carter. "You want to go to San Andreas. You think, when you get there, you can spot the people that killed Geary, eh?"

"They didn't kill him, I think. At least, not till they got something out of him."

"What?"

"I've done a lot of talking already," Tyler stated.

"That's right. You've done a lot of talking. I can go down and find out what any of the boys know about Geary. Shall I do that?"

"I'd take it kindly."

"And afterward?"

"Afterward I'd work for you on one job, free of charge."

"No commission, even?"

"Not even a commission."

"You got me all wrong," Carter said, smiling faintly, so that the mustache bristled aside and showed the silver gleam of the scar on the upper lip. "I ain't a cheapskate. I pay for my fancy, and I'd pay big to have a fellow like you along with me, brother."

"Thanks," Tyler said. "We don't have to squabble about that. San Andreas is the next thing on the program, I guess."

"It is," answered Carter. He rose and walked hastily up and down the room, with a face darkened by the most intense thought. "Maybe I'm taking some big chances here," he said.

"Maybe you are," Tyler suggested.

"But let 'em come or let 'em go, chances are what I've taken all my life," Carter snapped suddenly. He stepped straight up to Tyler. "Suppose we shake, man to man?" he said.

"On what?" Tyler asked.

"That no harm comes to you inside this here house . . . and that you work with me on the next big job that I ask you in on."

"You have to understand one thing."

"What?"

"That the only violence I understand is self-defense," Tyler said.

The other suddenly smiled. "I won't ask you to go out and rap anybody on the head," he affirmed. "I guess we can shake, Tyler."

175

VIII

"Introspection"

Their hands met in a long, firm grasp, and during that contact they stared deeply into the eyes of one another. Then Carter nodded briefly.

"My word goes," he said. "Nothing can happen to you in this house."

"My word goes," Tyler echoed even more deliberately. "The next job you call me on, I'm with you."

"Go back to sleep," said the leader, and immediately left the room.

After he had gone, Tyler reflected for a moment. Going over to the window, he looked out of it at the diminishing might of the storm, for the cloud wreckage was beginning to stream down the west in dark masses and a moon from some quarter of the heavens illumined the great shapes with misty light.

By that same illumination, he was able to look down to the ground and verify what the leader had said. There was, in fact, a steep bluff continuing down beyond the wall of the house, and the total descent was apparently a full fifty yards, straight down, most of the way over masonry as smooth as ever a wall was laid. He nodded, when he saw this, but still he was frowning when he turned back into the room and sat down once more on the bed.

All might be well, but he realized that there was between him and certain death no more than the personal integrity of a professional bandit. Once more, however, he shrugged his shoulders, risked all upon the chance, and, lying down in the bed, he was instantly asleep.

Ray Carter strode from the room and down the hall. His lantern struck in waves against the ominous form of a Mexican half-breed, who leaned on his rifle at a corner of the hall, a broad-faced man who never had been known to hold back from any deed, no matter of what brutal violence.

The leader hesitated an instant, then nodded and said: "All right, Pedro. No watch on him."

"No watch?" Pedro said, opening his little brown eyes until they were quite round. "Ah," he added, "he'll never need watching again, eh?"

Carter turned on his follower, and a quizzical smile lighted his face. It was only from time to time that the extent of his descent in the world became apparent to him. Flashes, blinding flashes of light, now and again, showed him the road on which he had set out, but none more clearly than this remark of Pedro's that implied very clearly that he thought his master had put the stranger out of the way with a knife thrust. Carter merely shook his head, then he went on.

But his thoughts were busy as he passed down the stairs. There was little kindness or gentleness in him, but he had always felt in himself a certain degree of integrity that he would have found it hard to put into words. He was, to be sure, a thief, but he told himself that men must do what they can to make a living in this world. There was Robin Hood, for example. If there were instances of cruelty and even of savagery that could be called up against him, there were other instances of generosity, courage, and good faith.

But that opening of the eyes of Pedro surprised him into a more profound understanding of the pit he had dug for himself. As he went down the stairs, he was telling himself that he must be careful. He was growing older. It was time for him to secure one respectable stake, and then to retire from the wild life. That had, from the first, been at the back of his mind.

He tried to conceive of himself going to a foreign country — France, say — and settling down in some pleasant villa, marrying a charming wife, living as a man with an indistinct past. But always, when it came to visualizing himself as simply the proprietor of an estate, with no one to take his orders except a house servant or two and a gardener, his heart failed him. The very breath of his existence, it seemed to Ray Carter, was wrapped up in these fire-souled daredevils who were under him, following as wolves follow a leader, only so long as that leader brings them to many kills, or so long as that leader keeps his sharpness of brain, his sharpness of tooth. One day they would sink a knife in his back, or part his brainpan with a slug of lead. But that would have to be when he was much older, much more stupid. So he said to himself, setting his teeth, resolving himself grimly.

But he was still in a confusion of ideas when he came into the long dining room, where his men were finishing their supper, some already leaning back to smoke their cigarettes, some taking second or third helpings of that nourishing stew that had been provided by the cook.

Jeff, with his usual sullen face, was waiting on the others or clearing away emptied plates. It mattered not how easy or how hard the work was, Jeff presented to the world only one expression at all times.

As for the chief, he thought less of Jeff on this night than ever before. The man had allowed a stranger to intrude. To be sure, that stranger was no less a celebrity than Tyler, but all the better to have kept such a man away. There were few persons in his world against whom Carter would have feared to measure himself, but he felt, after his talk with Jim Tyler, that he had been at least equaled. The thought made him grim. Jeff could have got round it somehow, if he had been a better man.

So Carter sat down at the end of the table, signaled for another cup of coffee, and then said: "Jeff, you take a stack of these here dishes and stay out in the kitchen. I've some talking to do."

Letting his surliness suddenly get the best of him, Jeff replied: "Ain't I a man same as the rest of 'em? Why can't I hear what you gotta say?"

"You ain't a man," Carter said in a voice of ice and poison. "You're only a damn' bottle washer. You're not even a cook. You're overpaid and under worked. Get out of here and get fast." He knew, as he spoke, that he had, of course, given an offense that would never be forgotten. Such words as these, spoken before witnesses, could never be retracted, except in blood. But he was careless of that fact.

He saw Jeff, with a white face and a black brow, trudge out of the room to the kitchen, while the other men looked after him with cruel smiles of pleasure in the shaming of the servant. A hard lot, but, then, he was a hard master. Realizing it, a hot pang of joy shot through him.

IX

"Tales of a Sleepy Bird"

He said calmly: "Who knows Jim Tyler?"

Of the seven men came seven voices, saying: "I know Tyler."

"Who knows him best?" asked Carter.

"I do," said Sid Shaw, Bud Wynne, and Chuck Lavigne.

"What makes you think you know him best?" the leader asked the three men.

"I was in a million-dollar game, once," Sid Shaw said, looking far off and shaking his head at the visions that he saw in that distance. "It was over in the Philippines."

"Aw, cut out the islands, will you?" growled a voice.

"It was the sort of a game that every man sits in once in his life, if he follows his cards," Shaw explained, paying no attention to the interruption. "There was a big contractor for the Army in that game, and there was a multimillionaire from Pittsburgh that didn't know how much money he had in the bank . . . and the heir of I don't know how much from Virginia, and there was a Lord Mount-Something from England. There was six of us, altogether. Me, I figured on being

181

the gent that collected . . . I could make the cards talk my way, all right. The sixth man was a long, leathery, wide-shouldered gent, not saying much, and looking sort of sleepy around the eyes. I figgered that I'd freeze him out about the second or third hand. But he didn't squeeze, brother. I won't tell you how long that card game lasted. We raised the stakes, and then we threw off the limit at the Englishman's suggestion and made it the sky. I never seen an Englishman yet that wasn't dead game. But still the sleepy gent was in the game. And pretty soon the other four were writing checks and IOUs. That was all right, too. I seen that sleepy bird was a fox, and I passed him the wink to work together and split the pot, but he didn't seem to understand what I meant, though I could see pretty clear that he was a shark, and that he was stacking that pack.

"How much there was on the table, finally, I won't say. You wouldn't believe me. But, if I'd had even half of it, I wouldn't be here now. I'd be up in Scotland shooting grouse or some fool thing like that to pass the time. Anyways, as I was saying, the whole damn' boodles of notes and checks, cash and chips was heaped up almost entire in front of me and the sleepy-looking gent, except that he wasn't sleepy no more. He was wide awake, and there was red rims to his eyes. It was about six in the morning. There'd been Scotch and sodas all night long. You know how the booze soaks up in you like in a blotter in that kind of weather, and I'd been fighting shy, and drinking mostly soda and no booze.

"That sleepy bird, he'd been drinking one or two ahead of anybody else. So I thought that his head was groggy, and finally I got my big hand. Four queens! Four honest queens. And I played 'em. I pushed in my stack, and he pushed in his. There was a cartload of money there in the middle of the table. I called him with my last five thousand. And he laid down four aces, four little aces, side by side!"

He paused, made a cigarette, and lighted it, while various exclamations resounded around the table. They wanted, and they wanted badly, to know what had been the final outcome, and had that other fellow been, veritably, the celebrated Jim Tyler.

"Wait a minute," the speaker said, resuming his tale, "that wasn't Jim. But the next play was him. He pushed back his chair and give a little look around the table. There was something to see, too. That fellow from Virginia must have overdrawn his checking account, and he meant business . . . suicide, I mean. Well, that was his affair, I would have said, but not Tyler. The others were all hard hit, too. It had been a crazy evening. A million-dollar game I called it, and that's what I mean. But Tyler, he said . . . 'Well, gentlemen, it was a grand game. Now let me get all those checks and IOUs together.'

"He held that paper in the air till it was flaming — the best part of a million dissolving into smoke. Then he let it flutter down to the floor and stamped out the fire right there on the rug. After that, he said . . . 'We'll just split the table stakes four ways, I think, and call it quits.' Says the Englishman, Lord Something-Or-Other . . . 'Mister Tyler, I wish to know what this means. Isn't our money good enough for you?' And Tyler said . . . 'Your money is perfect, but I'm not perfect, and neither is my friend Shaw yonder. We're both card experts, and we have only been sitting in on this session to teach you fellows that you don't belong at a table when serious poker is played. Because serious poker, you see, is a matter for experts only.' Now, as he says that, he shuffles the money on the table into six stacks, and gives it back to the six players, including himself.

" 'Even so,' he says, 'I'm five thousand dollars richer than I was when I sat in at this game, but I'm going to call that a fair commission. One last drink on me, and then we'll all go down and have a plunge in the bay. And that is why I say that I know Tyler better than any of the rest of you," Sid Shaw concluded. "Beat that, you fellows, if you can."

"I can beat it," Bud Wynne said instantly. "Yours is a good yarn, all right, and I guess Tyler would do just such a thing as that. There ain't anything this side of hell that he can't do. But I'll tell you what I seen, and what I know, and it sure knocks your yarn into a cocked hat."

"Go on," Sid said. "Go right on and make a

fool of yourself. You can't put a million dollars on the table like I done, unless you out-lie yourself with a running start, brother!"

"I can't put a million dollars on the table," Bud responded, "but I'll tell you that there's some things that beat money, or am I wrong?"

"Maybe you ain't wrong," broke in Ray Carter, nodding his head. "Get along, will you?"

"It was like this," Bud Wynne began. "It was down in a rotten little town in Mexico that was full of ponds and pools, water lilies and hell-fire, a little town that I ain't gonna give a name to, like Shaw done, but you can take my word for it. Down in that there town, there was a little slip of a girl about five foot three, by name of Anita Gonzalez, and she was gonna be married to Don Pedro. He was the cream of the cream, but he gets interested in a revolution and is throwed into the hoosegow . . . which a greaser hoosegow, in revolutionary times, is one foot in the grave, and that foot up to the knee, if you know what I mean."

"I know what you mean," one of the men said with a sigh. "I been there."

"Shut your face and don't take none of the bloom off my story, which is true, and yours is a lie," Bud said. "But I mean to say that this here queen of the greaser world, this here Anita, when she heard that her boyfriend was grabbed by the *rurales*, she sat down and had a think, and she turned around in her head what she would do, and then she thought it all over, and she come to a conclusion that what she needed was a real man."

"So she come to you, maybe, brother Wynne?" suggested someone softly.

Wynne ignored the thrust. "I been interrupted twice," he said calmly, "and I won't be interrupted a third time." With that, he laid a Colt .45 on the table, and, running his eyes deliberately over the faces before him, he went on slowly, choosing his words: "Well, the upshot of it all was that Jim Tyler and me and three other gents, we goes up the greaser prison in that there little town. We goes one moonlit night, and Tyler, he gets to doubting two of the fellows, and he makes 'em stay behind and hold our horses. That leaves two of us.

"We gets to the prison, which it had a moat around it, and we swims across that moat where there was a black shadow from the wall. We crawls to the top of that there wall, which we couldn't've done if it hadn't've sloped sort of. We puts one over on the guard at the top, and then, with what we got out of him, we finds our way down to the cell where Pedro is chained, passing gents on the way down that never paid no 'tention to us because we acted nacheral, having no hats or socks or shoes on. And Jim Tyler, he gets Pedro out. That's what he done. I reckon it shows I know that gent, don't it?"

"It shows you know him," agreed everyone.

"He's kind of peppery, now, ain't he?" asked

the cook, who was listening in from the doorway to the kitchen.

"Beat it if you can!" Wynne challenged triumphantly.

"Hold on," Chuck Lavigne said. "You fellows have done a lot of talking, but talking don't amount to much. Look at this!" Suddenly he ripped off coat and shirt and stood with his swarthy, powerful body naked to the hips. Half a dozen round, silver-tinted scars showed up distinctly on his dark skin.

"Tyler done that to me," Lavigne said. "Now say who knows him best!"

X

"The Chief Speaks"

The character of Jim Tyler seemed to have been brought out quite clearly from the three speeches that had been made about him, but the stories of the first two speakers had less weight than the mute evidence of Lavigne's scarred body. At any rate, Carter said: "Well, Lavigne, I'm going to ask if you think that he can be trusted."

"Yeah," Lavigne answered. "I'd trust him to do this to me all over again." Hard-faced, grim-eyed, friendless, and savage in his nature, it was strange to them all to hear Lavigne so readily admit the superior strength of an adversary.

"Suppose that he gave his word?" asked the leader.

"He won't," Lavigne said, "but if you could get him to, he'd keep to it, I guess, until hell split the world in two parts."

"That's all that I want to know," Carter stated. Lavigne was putting on shirt and coat again, as Carter added: "I wanted to find out because he's here in this house."

Lavigne burst out with: "Here? Here in this house? Come on, fellows, two or three of you, any of you that ever called me friend before, and we'll put an end to him."

Carter held up his hand, smiling faintly. "Nothing happens to him in this house," he said.

Lavigne, in the act of struggling into his coat and drawing his revolver, suddenly paused and cursed — one long, hissing syllable. Then he fixed his eyes upon the chief and said through his teeth: "What d'you mean?"

Ray Carter was a man capable of playing autocrat in the fiercest and most absolute sense of the term, but he was also one who knew how to value his men, and he had no one about him better than Lavigne. Therefore, he now condescended to explain, saying: "I want you to understand, Lavigne, that I'm not throwin' away chances like a drunken fool. I've got reasons behind what I'm doing, which I mean to say . . . why should I throw away dynamite like this fellow Tyler, when I've got ways of using him for all our sakes? Just stop and think it over a minute. Tyler's given his word that he'll try his hand at one big job for us. Any objections to that?"

Lavigne folded his arms across his breast, but even his wrath, after a moment, subsided greatly. Finally he said: "Well, if you can get him into your hand, he's a sharper tool than any you've ever grabbed before."

"I tell you fellows the plan because it's a beauty," went on Carter. "Take it, by and large, our lay-out here is pretty good, isn't it?" There was a general murmur of assent, while the leader went on: "We bunk in here, safe and warm . . .

189

we're too far for posses to chase us . . . and if one or two agents or marshals come up here, they're walking into more trouble than they'll ever walk out of again!"

A growl of agreement followed this.

"There's hardly a better position that we could have," the great Carter continued. "We have to do some tall riding to get at our game, but the game is worth the riding, and we've got plenty of first-rate horseflesh to burn up on the job. We're as safe here as a nest of hawks under the eyebrows of a five-thousand-foot cliff. And there's only one big drawback that makes us uncomfortable. I don't need to tell you what that drawback is."

"Miguel Cambista," blurted out Bud Wynne.

"Hold on," Shaw warned. "It's true that Cambista runs San Andreas, but he's signed up as a friend of ours. We're to leave him alone, and he and his gang are to leave us alone, likewise."

"Maybe it looks that way to you," broke in Lavigne, "but Cambista and Carter are too big to live even fifty miles apart. We've had trouble with those greasers before, and we'll have trouble again."

"We'll have trouble again," Carter agreed. "I ain't the man to let a Miguel Cambista split up the range with me. I'll have it all, or he'll have it all. And that brings me back to Tyler." They waited, while Carter looked around the table with his hard-lipped smile that they all knew so well. "I'm going to use Tyler as the bomb that'll blast Cambista, or else Tyler himself will be destroyed by the greasers, and no loss to us, either way."

"You mean that you expect Tyler to go down there to San Andreas and tackle the place with his single pair of hands?" asked one of the riders.

"What Tyler can do with his single pair of hands would make you a little dizzy, brother, if you was ever to see him work," Wynne declared.

The leader continued: "I send Tyler down, and Tyler has this to gain . . . he wants to get a partner of his out of trouble, and there ain't much doubt that the man he wants is in the hands of Cambista. Well, then I give him a note to Cambista, and in the note I tell Cambista that Tyler is a friend of mine, a great friend, and that it will be a help to me if Cambista can help Tyler find his friend. You see? Tyler goes to San Andreas and sends the note to Cambista, and Cambista asks him in for a talk. While they talk, Cambista makes his excuses . . . he'll do that, of course, because, though he'll want to keep friendly, he's too much of a pawnbroker to give up anything he has his yellow fingers sunk into.

"Well, as they say, while they chatter together, Tyler will be using his eyes. It may be that they'll be talking in Cambista's office, and in Cambista's office there's a safe, and in that safe, as you all know, there's the top cream that he's skimmed off the face of the world for fifteen or twenty lucky years. So you all see how the thing works?

"I go down there with a few of the boys, and wait around like a hawk. But the probability is that we'll simply send Tyler in there to do his best, make a fool of himself, and be lost in the mire. At the best, he may sink a slug in the heart of Cambista. When that's done, his gang will blow away like smoke. At any rate, the way I look at it, we'll probably wipe Tyler out of the picture this way, which will please Lavigne, here, and we may sink a knife into Cambista's back." When Carter had finished this explanation of his deep, complicated treachery, he leaned back in his chair to gather applause, and he received it at once.

Some of the men admitted that he was a clever fox, others that they would hate to have him for an enemy in their path.

Carter, listening to these compliments, quite forgot those nobler stirrings of the soul that had troubled him as he came down from the room of his guest-prisoner above.

XI

"Down the Pass"

In the course of the night, the storm blew itself out, and Jim Tyler rode through brilliant sunshine down the pass. On either hand, the rivulets were still running full, the water leaping and singing in the brilliant morning light. His mustang, too, was rested and revived by the good food it had enjoyed. In the breast pocket of Tyler's coat was the letter that had been written out for him by Ray Carter. In the mind of Jim Tyler there was a doubt that would have needed for its expression far more words than were written on the paper that he carried. He had little actual faith in the note that ran:

Dear Miguel: This introduces an old friend of mine, Jim Tyler, who is looking for a partner of his, Tom Geary. He has some reasons for thinking that Tom may be in San Andreas. If Geary is there, I told Tyler that you would do everything you can to find him, and whatever trouble you take, I'm thanking you for in advance.

Always yours,
Raymond Carter

193

In addition, Carter had said: "I told you that San Andreas was in my pocket. It is, because it belongs to my friend, Cambista. He's no more a friend of the law than you and I are, Jim, and you can talk to him straight from the shoulder. Probably one of his boys picked up Tom Geary, but Cambista will turn him back to you. I've no doubt of that. Anyway, this letter will get you in to see him and, while you're there, look around. You'll see something worthwhile if you see the safe in the corner of his office . . . that safe has a fortune in it. And whatever you spot, you could work on later."

"After he gives me back Geary?" Tyler had asked coldly.

Carter had waved a brown hand in the air. "I don't mean any double-crossing," he had said. "I simply mean, suppose that he don't come across with Geary? Then you're free to play your hand against him. Am I right?"

"You're right," Tyler had answered slowly.

"If you bump up against a bad trail with Cambista," Carter had gone on, "you can leave him and come back up the trail . . . you'll probably find me and some of my boys waiting for you where the two creeks run together."

"Hold on," Tyler had said. "I thought that this Cambista was a friend of yours?"

"He's a friend so long as he acts the friend," the other had said, "but if he can't oblige me in a little thing like your man Geary, then he's no friend of mine."

"I see," Tyler had said.

Shortly after that, he had started down the trail, but he was not at all satisfied. Treachery was so apparent in the proposed dealings of Carter with Miguel Cambista that he could hardly expect that the Mexican would be amenable to persuasion about Geary, especially since Cambista knew, no doubt, what Carter did not — the quality of the ore in the Geary mine.

Tyler came to a point where two creeks rushed together, swift brown currents that dashed themselves into a white frenzy in meeting. They joined on his right, and, passing beyond them, he saw the ravine opening suddenly before him and showing a little valley in which stood the whitewashed village of San Andreas, with the river flashing beside it. There might be a thousand people in that huddle of adobe houses, arranged around a central plaza, and all of those people were, as Carter had said, in the hands of Miguel Cambista. Tyler shrugged his shoulders and shook his head. He knew well the wonderful strength of a Mexican leader who has established himself as overlord. If there were dangerous work ahead of him, he could not have chosen a worse setting, he was sure.

As he rode down toward the town, he took note of the rolling hills on either side, where herds of sheep and goats and some few cattle were pasturing, with brown, half-naked little boys guarding them. He regarded the little narrow strips of corn growing here and there on

195

flats or easy slopes. And it seemed to him that the very soul of old Mexico breathed up out of the soil.

In one of those patches of cultivated ground, he saw a *peon* toiling with a massive iron-headed hoe, bending almost double as he swung it; there seemed to be tireless springs set in the small of his back. His soiled trousers were rolled up to his knees, sandals were on his feet, a straw hat was on his head. Attached to the hatband, he saw hand-made cigarettes tied up with narrow bits of colored ribbons.

Yes, it was old Mexico all over again, breathing up at him. A sense half of drowsy content and half of tingling danger passed through him. All his days south of the Río Grande had not been entirely peaceful.

When he came into the town, it was not hard to find the house of Cambista. There was one two-story structure in the place and that, he was assured, must be the dwelling of the bandit. So he went leisurely on toward his goal. It had been a long, hard trail that they had followed, and, as the mustang jogged through the heat of the late afternoon, Tyler looked over the rooftops on either side of the plaza and saw how the white-headed mountains clustered about, very much like waves of a sea, blown up with ragged tops, about to plunge down and fill up the suction hole of a great whirlpool.

He dismounted in front of a big gateway. It was in the middle of the street wall of the two-storied house. Across the patio inside, he could see chickens and a duck straying. A dog slept there in the sun, twitching its skin frantically and vainly to scare away the flies. In the shadow of the doorway, a *mozo* was seated playing a game of solitaire with greasy, crumpled cards. A rifle leaned against the wall at his right hand.

Jim Tyler came forward on foot, his mustang following at his heels, and offered the letter. "That's for Miguel Cambista," he said in correct Spanish.

The *peon* looked at both sides and the edges of the letter with a mild curiosity. Then he paused to yawn, gathered up his cards one by one, and, thrusting them into his coat pocket, he picked up the rifle and sauntered off toward the house without a word to the *gringo,* either to bid him wait or to follow.

Jim Tyler set his teeth, very hard. His temper was fairly well under control, but the hot surge of it was as hasty as the fury of a wildcat. However, he waited where he was. He knew Mexicans fairly well, and yet he was sure that there were always ceremonious instincts in the race that he could never fathom. If he were wanted inside the house, this insolence of the guard would be apologized for; if he were not wanted, it would simply be a preliminary to still greater insults.

Presently a long-striding fellow in a metal-braided jacket and with long-spurred boots came hurrying across the patio. The boots and the jacket indicated a great expenditure of money. The trousers between the two extremities were as soiled as those of the laborer in the field. Once more, Tyler felt that he was in the center of old Mexico.

This emissary received the stranger with much bowing and led him straightway across the sunny patio and up an outer stone stairway to the second story of the building. Here he rapped at a door that was opened by a *caballero* with a short-cropped mustache and a superior air. He gave Tyler a bloodless smile, a word of greeting, and conducted him down a dark corridor to a room in which sat a man whose body seemed to be swollen with equal portions of muscle and of fat. He had a wedge-shaped face, very thick in the jowls and narrow in the forehead, but something about the yellow-stained eyes, something in the air of this fellow, told Tyler that he was facing Miguel Cambista.

The latter waved the escort out of the room; the door closed softly. Tyler, waiting with acute senses, felt certain that there had been no retreating footfall down the hall. Yonder, cutthroat of the cropped mustaches was waiting outside the door like a panther, ready to spring in again at the first suspicious sound.

Cambista, in the meantime, had risen from behind a table on which there was a litter of papers. He came forward, a man of middle height, broad, stepping lightly in spite of his bulk. His smile was ingratiating; his handclasp was firm and quick. Now, waving his visitor into a chair, he retreated again to the place behind his official table.

It was the room about which Carter had spoken. Here were the many big white goatskins on the floor, the couch draped with them, the photographs of Mexican revolutionary generals on the wall, and, above all, the little safe in the corner, with the gilded name of the maker across the top. There was an air of consequence about this place, as though events that mattered had taken place in it. Jim Tyler settled himself in his chair with every nerve on the alert.

Cambista pushed aside some of the papers on the table and spread out his hand before him in a frank manner. "Now, Tyler, what can I do?" he said, speaking in English.

"Carter wrote it down in the letter," Tyler responded.

"Carter wrote down that you were coming to get a friend of yours, Tom Geary. But what makes you think that he is here?"

"My friend was shot," Tyler said, "and how badly he was wounded, I don't know. But he spilled enough blood to make a wet spot on the ground, and in that mud he wrote the name San Andreas." He waited.

The Mexican nodded. "So you came here?"
"Yes."

"You are a friend worth having, Tyler," Cambista stated with that same air of frankness. "You took the trail at once."

"I took the trail," said the American.

"And how far away was this?"

"Two days' hard riding. Across the mountains."

"Suppose that your friend died from the effects of the gunshot wound?"

"He could have died," Tyler admitted. "I've told you everything that I know."

"Do you know why he should have been attacked?"

"Because he had a mine, I suppose."

"What sort of a mine?"

"Gold."

"A good one, eh?"

"I don't know. I'd not been with him more than an hour, I suppose, before I was called away. He was shot in the half hour that I was gone." He had felt that it was necessary to cover up his knowledge of the richness of the ore in that new mine. The other details he had stated with perfect openness.

"It is a long distance to bring a man," the Mexican said. "But it may be that he's here in San Andreas. I don't know everything that goes on in it."

He looked away, shaking his head and pursing his lips. Tyler had instantly drawn two deductions — Geary was, in fact, in San Andreas, and Cambista knew all about the affair.

Cambista drummed softly on the top of the table with his plump, strong fingers. He was still looking out of the window, seeing his own thoughts, as it seemed, when he said: "Carter is a good friend of mine. There's nothing that I wouldn't do to please him. And I can have inquiries made through the town about this Tom Geary. Would you be bringing the law on the kidnappers if, in fact, he was kidnapped?"

The other smiled a little. "I want my friend back, Cambista," he said. "I don't care a rap about how he was taken, or who did it. That's his business later on. I simply want to see him safely back where I first found him."

"Good!" Cambista announced. "I see that you're a practical man."

"I hope so," Tyler said.

"Gregorio!" Cambista shouted suddenly.

A second door, which Tyler had not noticed before, opened at his back. Instinct made him whirl out of his chair and come to his feet, but he regretted that movement an instant later. He saw to the side a fellow with a brutally fierce face who had just entered the room.

"Gregorio," Cambista said, "I want you go out and ask a few questions. Find out if there is an American in San Andreas. A man wounded two or three days ago, and perhaps brought up here. Be back here as soon as you have found out. Have the name of the man who's holding the American."

"Yes," Gregorio said, and then started to retreat. But as his eyes fastened on the face of Tyler, suddenly the features of Gregorio contorted. *Hai!* he suddenly said with a snarl. "Don Miguel, look! That is the man!"

XII
"Rawhide"

Cambista was admirably free from excitement. He raised his hand and shook his head gently, although there was a quiver of his fat cheeks. Then he asked: "What man, Gregorio?"

"That! That!" said the other. "I saw him on the night Don Ramón died. That is the man who killed him! I saw him shoot!"

"Everything softly, Gregorio," Cambista said. "Now, then, what is it?"

The excitement of Gregorio would not down. He advanced a little, with his right arm extending, pointing it at Tyler like a spear. "You, *Señor* Tyler!" he shouted. "You shot Don Ramón Díaz! In the prison at Santa Anna you shot him that night! You and other *gringo* scoundrels broke into the prison and took away Pedro Salvatore from the death he should have suffered!"

Tyler turned his back on the ruffian and faced Cambista with a question in his eyes, and Cambista answered: "Ramón Díaz was a half-brother of mine and very dear to me. But have no fear, *señor*. The hospitality of a Mexican gentleman is never disturbed by a blood feud. Hate stops at the door of the house."

"Does he deny it?" Gregorio shouted. "I tell you, I saw the bullet fired! It was in the corridor, before the light went out from the explosions of the guns. And there in the corridor, I saw this man. Look! He is smiling now, and he was smiling then! Don Ramón and I were at the other end of the corridor. Don Ramón had a shotgun, and I had two revolvers. I was a little behind him. I saw *Señor* Tyler fire quickly from the hip, and Don Ramón fell back against me. I lost my footing and dropped with him. And this man ran over us, and with him was that cursed Pedro Salvatore. I heard the jangling of his chains that had not been unlocked. By the time I got up, they were through the door at the end of the corridor and had slammed it. It had a spring lock. I stood there, beating against the door and screaming to the other guards, but the *gringo* was gone!"

He gripped at his throat with one hand as he reached the end of his narrative, but Cambista said calmly: "That is all, Gregorio. Go, now."

Gregorio made a mute gesture of despair with both hands. It was plain that he would have preferred to hurl himself at the throat of the white man, but discipline seemed exact and powerful in the gang of Cambista, and Gregorio ended by turning on his heel and leaving the room.

Then Cambista said to Tyler on whose face a slight perspiration was glistening: "Ramón Díaz was of my blood, but, when brave men meet in fighting, one of them must fall. You had the good fortune that day. Why should I hate you for it?"

"Why, Cambista," Tyler said, "you talk like a man. Not many people in the world would be as generous as this. I appreciate it."

"I want you to appreciate me more later on," Cambista responded. "Perhaps there are qualities in both of us that we'll only understand when we've spent more time together. But, first, we must learn about your friend, the *Señor* Geary. Come into another room with me, and we'll have something to drink."

He stood up and went to the door, which he opened, and then stepped back and waved the American through before him. Tyler, as he nodded politely over his shoulder in acknowledgment of the courtesy, stepped into a dim corridor and saw a shadow standing on either side and heard the whispering of something that rushed about his head. He leaped back with the speed of a startled cat, but the nooses of the lariats already had dropped over his shoulders. A hard pull came from either side and jerked him to a standstill. His arms were lashed tightly, helplessly against his sides. There was nothing in the world that he could do against such force. And he made out, in the dark of the hallway, that the face of the man on his right was Gregorio's. What subtle sign had the leader made to his follower, what signal that told him what was to follow?

Behind him, the voice of Cambista said: "As I

pointed out before, there may be many things which we should have to learn about one another through a longer acquaintance, *Señor* Tyler. Now I hope that we shall have time, much time. I am one who dislikes being hurried, and no doubt you are the same, though most of you Americans are just a little hasty, just a little sudden with your hate or with your trust." He laughed. There was an oily, bubbling sound in the hollow of his throat.

"It's all right, Cambista," Tyler answered. "This may be the finish of me, but, as a matter of fact, you're a smart enough fox to catch bigger game than I'll ever be."

Cambista laughed again. "Ah, Tyler," he said, "what a pity that we could not have known one another under different circumstances. What a pity! You and I are men who would have done much, if we had become friends earlier. But now there is between us the little matter of Ramón Díaz, for whose death the lives of ten *gringos*, of course, could never pay. And there is the matter of Tom Geary. You did not know about the value of his mine, then, my friend? That's a pity. You would have seen wire gold in the black of the rotten rock. You would have seen a million or two that could almost be broken out with the tips of your fingers." Again he laughed, and said abruptly to his men: "Take him and put him with the other *gringo*. But tie him hand and foot. With fresh rawhide, you understand? With fresh rawhide!"

There was a brutal snarl from Gregorio. And the heart of Tyler turned to stone. To be tied with fresh rawhide — he knew what that meant. As the hide dried, it would begin to contract, with a force like the shrinking of red-hot iron. His mind was busy with that thought, as he was dragged down the hallway. Then he was being drawn down steep flights of steps, one after another. Vague ideas came to his mind. Suppose, for one thing, that he were to bribe the men who were guarding him, or if, by some device, he could loosen for an instant the nooses that bound his arms.

But there was no time. He was taken into a damp cellar filled with the stench of hides. In a moment a third servant, working there, was cutting a fresh hide in long, thin strips. Like sword blades, they would cut through flesh to the bone, when they began to shrink and harden.

Quickly and thoroughly the Mexicans did their work with the air of men who had done it before. His legs were bound together at the ankles and at the knees. His hands were lashed before him, wrist to wrist, and a fresh layer of the hide was wound about his hips, and the hands bound to this belt. Next, and most cunning device of all, a strong noose of the hide was wound about his head — when it contracted, how the eyes would thrust out from their sockets. Long thongs were then fastened from the back of this bandage to his hip belt, and thence down to the lashing on his knees. As the rawhide contracted, of course, the head would be drawn back and the throat muscles would vainly struggle in agony against the strain of the leather, until they gave way and either he strangled or else the neck was broken. One by one, Tyler thought out these results while he was being bound.

Gregorio, in the meantime, was in a laughing frenzy, repeatedly exclaiming that now the *gringo* would see the judgment that comes upon dogs that show their teeth to Mexican gentlemen. He fairly danced about the room. He shook his fist and then his long hunting knife in the face of the captive. But Tyler knew better than to waste breath by answering back.

His fate was sealed — that was the only word for it. He merely asked: "How many have gone this way before me, through the cutting of the hides, I mean, as they contract and kill the prisoner? How many has your friend Cambista bumped off like this?"

"How many?" Gregorio repeated. "I only know of seven or eight. But perhaps there were more before my time. Enough to howl at you when you go down to hell from this place. The road there is short from here, brother, but before you start on it, you will screech and yowl like a cat."

"Very soon," the prisoner agreed. "I know how fast the hide works."

"Yes, very soon, when it is bound as tight as this." And he laughed again in a half-insane manner.

Tyler looked quietly at the ceiling above him. "In my time," he said, "I've thought that killing was a brutal thing, but now I can understand perfectly how you and Cambista enjoy this, because I think of the joy it will be to me to have the ending of the pair of you, and more, perhaps, many more in this house. *Hai*, Gregorio. I hope that I shall have the leisure to deal with you slowly, adequately, one by one."

"You?" said Gregorio. "You?" He put back his head and howled loudly with fiendish laughter again.

XIII

"The Rat Hole"

They carried Tyler across the hall and already, as they walked, jesting with one another, he could feel the first sting of the bonds where the hide began to pull at the hair on his wrists. Soon the pull would settle deeper and deeper, working under the flesh toward the bone. They opened a door, carried him down more steps. A faint but foul odor filled the air. It was cold and damp as a rainy day in autumn. Presently he was laid down on a damp, moldy floor.

"There's company for you," Gregorio announced. And with his companions, who still laughed, he left the room.

There was only one movement possible to the prisoner, and that was to roll himself by violently twitching and turning his entire body. But there was nothing to be gained by moving until he found a better spot to lie on. The rank, half sweet smell of the mold on the floor and walls of the cellar sickened him, and he could see very little for there was only a dull ray or two of light coming from a single peephole at the side of the ceiling.

He twitched himself on his left side. There was

only the wall there, close before him. What was that speech about company? He realized suddenly what might be meant, for there was a scampering of light feet and a great gray rat, faintly seen, came up and boldly sniffed at his face, wriggling its long whiskers, its bead-black eyes shining. Tyler snorted in disgust and horror. It leaped back, but only a short distance, and then sat up on its hind legs, like a squirrel, and sniffed at the air. In this posture, he could see its ribs, pinched and worn with famine.

A piece of iron rattled across the room. "Who are you?" a husky voice asked in very bad Mexican.

"My name is Tyler," he answered in English.

"Jim Tyler?" cried the unmistakable voice of Geary. "In the name of the saints!"

"I'm Tyler," Jim answered, "but in this place it looks as though you'd better say, in the devil's name. How are you, Geary?" He twisted over, as he spoke, and made out, very dimly, the form of his older friend, seated way over against the wall on the farther side of the room.

Geary was exclaiming: "Jim, you followed the trail for me, and you've wound up in the same hole! A curse on the day that ever I wrote the name I heard them speak in the mud there by the fire. I thought you might locate it. I never had an idea that it would bring you to a hole like this."

"Stop, Tom," Tyler ordered. "This is the sort of black broth that a lot of people have to live on for years." Then he added: "How did it happen to you?"

"I was sitting by the fire, waiting for you to come back. That's all I know. Then I heard a step and jumped up and pulled a gun, because it was a sneaking step, coming out of the brush. As I turned, I got a bullet through me."

"Through you!" exclaimed Tyler.

"I thought it was through me. It hit me hard enough to knock me down, but I guess it glanced off the ribs and came around and out my back. But I thought that it went straight through my innards. Then they confabbed a minute, while they looked at the wound, and they wondered whether it would be better to kill me then and there, or try to get me all the way back to San Andreas. Another gent swore at the fellow who did the shooting, blaming him for not clubbing me down instead of using a gun, and the gent that did the shooting, Gregorio, he allowed that *gringos* was too fast and straight with guns, and chances couldn't be took with 'em."

"Gregorio," Tyler hissed. "Something tells me that I'm going to have my hands free and his throat inside 'em, one of these days. What happened to you next?"

"Why, they dumped me onto a hoss and rode me off, and a while up the trail . . . but I've forgot to tell how, while I lay by the fire, I wrote the word I'd heard 'em speak in the wet spot that the leaking of my blood had made."

"I know that. Go on, old son."

211

"They took me off the hoss and wrapped a hard bandage around me, and then they started again, and they never stopped riding. And a fever worked in me. And the pain near killed me. I dunno how many times I fainted. They had to lash me to the back of the hoss. When I sagged over too far to the side, they used their quirts to wake me up again. I've got welts all over me. Finally, they fetched me here and. . . ."

The door opened with a slight scraping sound, footfalls came down the steps, and the voice of Cambista was heard, saying: "You see, Tyler? I've been as good as my word and actually found Geary for you. You give me credit for that, I hope?"

"I give you all the credit in the world for a bright fellow," Tyler said. "I'll never forget you, old son."

"Never forget me," Cambista urged. "But then, you won't have much time left to do the forgetting. Rawhide does little tricks of its own. It has a will of its own, you know."

"I know," muttered Tyler. "I know all about it. It takes the Mexican brain to think of that sort of a thing, eh?"

"It takes imagination, brother. Now, then, Geary, you see that there's no hope left for you. You had a bet or two left on your friend, Tyler. But now he's gone. Any man would hope while such a friend as Tyler was loose to help him, but now Tyler is here, and you may as well give up. Give me your word, and that instant you're a free man. You understand? There's only a little writing to do, first."

Geary groaned as he spoke: "Tyler, he wants me to make out a deed of sale to my mine. He gives me a dollar, and I give him the mine, damn him!"

"Not a dollar! Not a dollar," Cambista said with his bubbling, deep-throated laughter. "No, no, *amigo!* I give you a thousand dollars. Enough to make an excellent stake for you when you start out to find another mine better than the first one. Why, Geary, the mountains are full of gold, and it only needs a clever fellow like you to find the right places. What you've done before, you can do again."

"Tell him to go to the devil, Geary!" Tyler exclaimed.

Stronger language than that flowed from the throat of Geary, as he took his friend's advice.

Cambista came to his second prisoner and stood over him.

"You can give advice like that now," he said, "but in another hour your screaming time will come, Tyler. Then I shall return to listen . . . promptly, in an hour. If the rats are not at you before that, the rawhide will be doing its work. While you're yelling, perhaps your friend Geary will change his mind, eh?"

"Cambista," Tyler said, "I think so much of you that I have to tell you something. Will you listen?"

"Oh, with the greatest of pleasure. Of course, I

shall listen, *amigo!* What is it that you have to say?"

"It's a sort of intuition, Cambista, that I'm not to die here. I'm going to live. Satan himself is on my side, now that my mind is so filled with black things that need doing."

"Ah, the black things that you want to do to me and my men! Is that it?"

"A genius like you, Cambista," Tyler said grimly, "can read the mind like a book."

"We shall see," Cambista murmured. "In the meantime, you have an hour before I come back. I know just how long it will be before the thongs begin to bite. And they're stronger in the jaw than wolves, eh?"

"Did you ever feel them yourself?" asked Tyler.

"Once, years ago, when I was a boy," said the other, "I was caught by some Moquis. Rough people, eh?"

"Rough fellows," agreed Tyler. "Did they tie you up like this?"

"Yes. Just like this. I lay as you're lying. And in an hour came the screaming time. I set my teeth against it. I would not give them the pleasure of hearing me screech. But when the hour had passed, I could not help it. My jaws yawned open of their own free will. *Hai*, how I screeched, until my throat ached. My eyes popped, and the Indians stood around and laughed. It was a pleasant song for them. It would last a long time, too. The chief, during a pause in the screaming fit, gave me water to drink. He wanted to keep my throat clear as long as possible." Cambista chuckled.

"And then you had a touch of luck?" the prisoner pursued.

"Well, a man never knows what will happen," said the other. "Some *rurales* came over the hill. They were not hunting for me, but, when the Moquis saw them, they started to run like rabbits, and the *rurales* simply started chasing because they saw the Indians running. Like rabbits they killed them, too. And then they came back and looked at me. I knew that I was safe, then, but just the same, I could not keep from yelling.

"Those *rurales* were hardy men. Most of them had been sentenced to long terms in prison, and let out only on condition of doing duty as *rurales*. They stood about me, and they listened, and they struck attitudes, as though they were hearing violins. It was quite a time before they would cut me loose. And they were still laughing and pleased, when I got staggering to my feet."

"And how many Moquis, how many *rurales*, did you kill afterward, to make up for that hour?" asked Tyler.

"How many? I never kept strict accounts," Cambista responded. "It's always come easy, go easy, with me, whether money or men. Sometimes I have them, and sometimes they're spent. Does that answer you?"

"That's a good answer," Tyler agreed. "And now, brother Cambista, let me tell you that I'm as sure of living and walking and spending a Cambista, as I'm now sure that I'm lying here in the rawhide lashings. You understand?"

"It is the hope that always lives in the breast of very sick or very brave men," Cambista stated. "I shall soon return, *amigo!*" He laughed again as he left the cellar prison.

XIV

"The Blessed Bacon"

"Lemme tell you something, Jimmy, will you?" leathery old Tom Geary said. And when Jim replied — "Go ahead." — Geary started in with his reminiscence.

"I used to have an old Maltese cat that spent the most part out of every day in hunting lizards. The more lizards that he ate, the sicker and the thinner he got, and he never ate anything but the tails. He used to get nearly crying mad, pretty nigh onto every day, because, when he'd finished eating the tail of a lizard, he couldn't make up his mind to eat the rest of the lizard and get more indigestion, or keep on throwing the lizard around like a dead mouse, and risking the chance of that critter getting away from him. He'd lie there and lash his sides with his tail like a tiger, and champ his teeth together, and tell that lizard as plain as day that he was going to eat him, and that he didn't have no use for him, but he'd give him one more toss into the air.

"And after giving the lizard a throw, that cat, he'd lie there and suffer a regular hell for a whole half second or so, blinking his eyes real tight. Then he'd leap up and go for the lizard again. A

217

lot of them lizards died, and a lot of 'em lived, and them that were alive, they were only half lizards, as you might say, and they weren't no good at climbing up walls and such things, and they seemed to stay in the corners and sort of pine away, like they were ashamed to get out into the light of the sun without having no tails on. Now, then, brother Tyler, it looks to me like you and me are gonna die right here in the cat's den, meaning Cambista, or, if we manage to live through it, we're gonna be marked for life."

"That may be true," Jim agreed.

At this point a great rat, evidently one of the patriarchs of the tribe, returned to examine him at closer range, so very close, in fact, that its horrible odor aroused in Tyler an inexpressible revulsion. He snorted and jerked back as well as he could. But the rat, merely wincing at this gesticulation, began to steal still closer, and a man of duller sight than Tyler's could have noted the thin rim of red fire around those staring eyes.

What was he, Jim Tyler, to that creature? Merely so much meat, and, if he lived, it was just that much better than dead meat which would hold less juice. That thought sickened Tyler, and he remembered what Cambista had said about the rats starting in on him. What scenes had been enacted here in other days? He forgot his dread of the rawhide thongs. He shouted, and still the rat only retreated an inch or so, then came yet closer. A gaunt cousin of that monarch ran up the body of Tyler and stood on his shoulder, wriggling its nose and working its long, silver whiskers. Vast things they were, it seemed to the terrified brain of Jim Tyler. For he was truly terrified now. There might even be a sort of grim satisfaction in matching the dauntless iron of his will against the excruciating pressure of his bonds, when the mortal moment came, but that would be as nothing, compared with the horror of being nibbled away by vermin.

"Listen to me, Tom!" he cried.

"What is it, son?" asked the miner in an alarmed voice.

"How d'you keep the rats away?"

"I don't. They never give me a peaceful minute. They was tryin' to eat the rind of bacon that's left to me now, and, if I dare to drop off into a sleep, they come and get what they can. They've eaten off the ends of both my boots, and my toes are stickin' through. They'll be at the toes next with their poison teeth!" He added: "Rattle your chains at 'em! Kick at 'em!"

"How can I rattle chains and kick, when I'm wrapped up like a mummy in a swathing of rawhide, Tom?"

"Is it really rawhide?" Geary asked.

"That's what they've put on me . . . green rawhide!"

"Can you roll over here, Jim? I'll kick the devils away from you. I can't come to you. I'm chained ag'in' the wall!"

"I'll come if I can," said the prisoner.

Straightway, Tyler began to make a wretched

progress across the floor, turning over and over on his shoulders and hitching his legs about to keep the line of his movement to where his friend sat. It was slow work, and it seemed that the rats understood these movements as those of a dead or of a dying creature, for a dozen of them gathered and retreated only little by little as he flopped across the floor.

So, panting heavily, he came near Tom Geary, and the miner brandished his chained hands. With slight dodging motions, the vermin avoided the blows that threatened them.

"Bold, ain't they, Jimmy?" commented the miner. Then he added, leaning forward and staring at the bonds of his younger friend: "Forgive me, Jimmy, for draggin' you into this kind of a mix-up."

He brandished his chained hands again, and the rats withdrew, but only a little. Then the miner picked up a morsel of bacon, saying: "I saved this here meat. They gave it to me the last meal, but maybe they'll change their minds about feedin' me again with such good stuff. How these rats want it. How the smell of it ravens in 'em. Think of what their hunger must be when they'll eat the soles off my boots."

Already the tightening rawhide was burning Tyler's flesh and bruising his very bones. But now he started, as an idea came to him. "Look here, man," he said.

"What?"

"Reach over here and rub that bacon hard

against the rawhide where it covers my wrists, will you?" Tyler instructed.

"What's the matter with you, Jim? Out of your head?"

"Will you do what I tell you, you old moss back, and stop wasting time?"

"Well, you see that I'm doing it," Geary said, obeying the request of his friend. Leaning forward as well as he could, he rubbed the half-fried rind of bacon hard against the thongs that crossed and re-crossed the wrists of Tyler.

"That's it," Jim prodded. "And now we'll see if I'm crazy. Let me be, and let the rats swarm on me, if they've a mind to." He made a turn away from Geary and lay still.

Certainly Tom Geary was right. As soldiers rush forward when the trumpet sounds, those rats came hurrying to the scent of the bacon. The gray monarch of the lot instantly had his long front teeth sunk in the tough leather. And what teeth they were, chisel-like, able to slip through the toughest wood. Far more easily, they cut through the green hide. Others came, and still others.

Now and then, one turned and bit the next jealously. There were squeals and scamperings. Now and again, a sharp pang struck through the nerves of the prisoner, as he felt those fangs, poisonous, perhaps, as his friend had suggested, miss the leather and slice through his own flesh. More than all the rest, it was the faint but distinct odor that revolted him.

Tom Geary was saying in a muffled voice: "Great saints, man, what are you doin'? Makin' friends of the reptiles? Makin' pets of 'em for company? Little company you'll be needin', poor lad, when those thongs get to eating into you. I recollect once when. . . ."

There was a sudden, loud, snapping sound. The rats scurried away, and the hands of the prisoner parted. The hide had been sufficiently eaten through for him to snap the remaining tough shreds.

Free hands! But there was still work to be done. He set about instantly. Thrusting up with such force that it seemed he was about to tear the scalp from his head, he worked off the circlet about his head. It was gone. It hung down behind him, and now he could sit up. After that, the work still dragged out through long minutes, and, as he worked, he talked softly to his friend.

"Tom," he said, "there's a half hour gone, and at the end of an hour that demon, Cambista, the greasy, smiling, snarling swine, will be back here to enjoy the screaming time, as he called it. Ah, man, if only I can have the use of myself when he steps in through that door."

"What good would it do you, son?" asked the other. "He won't be coming alone. There'll be others with him, make sure. And they'll kill you out of hand."

"They won't kill me, I think, but, if they do, I'll die fighting. There's something in me, Tom, that says that I'm not meant to die in the dark of

222

a cellar but in the open sun somewhere, or under the stars, with clean air in my face. Dying that way is nothing, but to be buried alive, like this, with the worms eating you, as you might say, before the breath is out of your body is another matter."

The last of the bonds gave way under the working of his dexterous hands, and he leaped to his feet. He paid a penalty for that. For the rawhide had worked in so close to the bone about his ankles, that there was no sensation in his feet, and he promptly fell down on his hands again. Time would take care of that, however, what little time was left to him. He crawled to Tom Geary and examined his bonds.

"Where are they fastened?" he asked.

"To the staple ag'in' the wall," Geary responded.

"It's half loose," said Tyler. "Rust has rotted the iron or time has rotted the stone. Let me see."

One hard wrench, delivered with all of his force, yanked the staple from the stone. There were still irons on hands and feet, but some limited movement was now possible. At this moment the door to the cellar room opened with a dull, grating noise.

XV
"Daylight"

Never did a cat move more softly, more swiftly, than did Jim Tyler across the floor of the room. Two men were at the door, one of them carrying a lantern. The second man was just behind him.

The one outside the door was saying: "Never mind the old fellow, Gregorio. Just see how the young one is, the *gringo*. It's strange that he's not yelling or at least groaning already. He'll groan soon enough, though. I'm closing the door, while you look. I can't stand the stench of the rats." He closed the door, in fact, while Gregorio, merely muttering vague sounds in answer, pushed up the chimney of the lantern, scratched a match, and lighted the wick.

How could he guess that a figure was stealing up behind him? He would as soon have expected to find a ghost walking in that chamber of horrors. But now, from the holster at his thigh, a swift hand plucked the revolver. He turned about, throttled with fear, not of men, but of spirits, since he believed that no human being could be moving in that dungeon. Yet, there, before him, he saw Tyler with the lantern shedding a soft light on the blue-steel barrel of the Colt.

"Softly, softly, Gregorio," Tyler warned. "Not a sound, not a whisper. Walk down here with the lantern. Walk slowly."

Gregorio obeyed. He was unnerved, for the bravest men have little resource of courage when the totally unexpected happens.

"You have the keys, you dog of a jailer," Tyler said, through his teeth. "So, unlock these chains."

It was done. The lantern was laid upon the floor, and Gregorio immediately unlocked the chains that held Geary.

Old Tom stood up, groaning a little and pinched to one side by the pain of his wound.

"Can you move, Tom?" asked his friend.

"I can move, all right. I could run . . . to get away from this hole."

"Thanks for that," Tyler muttered. "Now, Tom, go through him and fan him for any more guns."

There was another gun, of a smaller caliber, a .38 worn inside the coat of Gregorio. There was also a long hunting knife, capable of taking the hide off a deer or cutting the animal's throat to the bone at a single slash.

"Take that gun and stand at his back," Tyler said.

It was done, as the other guard began to push the door open, calling out: "Well, Gregorio, you're taking your time."

"Tell him to come in," Tyler ordered.

"Come in, Manuelo," Gregorio said, throwing

himself into the treasonable part with a strange spirit. "Come in and see what I've found here for a show."

Manuelo came down the steps. It was this man who had played number two in the capture of Tyler. He suddenly threw his hands over his head with a groan of terror, for by the lantern light he saw the leveled gun in the hand of Tyler and, worse than that, the face of the man behind it, like white iron.

"We'll tie 'em face to face, and gag 'em," Geary suggested. "Men can't move, when they're tied face to face, because all the moves go backward."

"Good," said the other. "And here are the rawhide thongs to use on 'em."

They made the pair lie down, face to face.

Manuelo began to moan. "In the name of the kind saints, good gentlemen, don't tie me with the rawhide. Look at the scars on my wrists, where *Señor* Cambista. . . ."

"Be still, you fool," cautioned Gregorio. "Why they don't cut their work short and our throats, too, I don't know. Be still, or take a knife in between your ribs."

So Manuelo was still, while Tyler's cunning hands rapidly gagged them, and they were bound swiftly together by twistings and retwistings of the long rawhide thongs.

Faintly groaning, they were left lying a helpless bundle, face to face.

"Now?" Geary asked.

"What do you want?"

"A chance to get away, of course."

"More than a chance at Cambista?"

"He can wait. I want my hide safe on my back, first."

"Take your own way out, then," Tyler said. "But I'm going at Cambista. It means more to me than life to say a few things to him before I even try to leave the house."

"I'll stay with you, Jim," the other responded. "Of course, I stick with you . . . only there's poison in the air of this place."

"You're wrong," Tyler stated. "It's the finest, sweetest fragrance in the world that I have in my nostrils. D'you hear, Tom? A chance to be even with Cambista! To do something to him that won't take as long as slow death in the rawhide, but that'll hurt him more. The beauty of it. I just begin to enjoy the prospect."

Then, turning up the steps, he passed, with Tom Geary behind him, into the corridor above, and so on down through the dim windings of the halls. It was as easy for him to untangle the maze of many passages as it would have been for a fine hound working by scent, so thoroughly had every turning point been printed upon his brain by the horror he felt when he was first taken through the house on the lead, like a wretched dog dragged to the pound. But now he went freely, with a gun in his right hand and a very sharp knife concealed inside his coat. He had trusted Cambista enough to enter his house freely. He had met only villainy within. He would repay Cambista, and in such coin as the bandit had never expected.

Now, as he went stealthily down the hallway, he glanced ahead, and thanked his good fortune that the way was clear before him. Blinding white appeared the arch of the open doorway at the farther end of the passage, but no watcher was there. It seemed strange to see the daylight. It seemed as though he had spent at least a round of the clock down there in the cellar. But this — this beside him — was the door to the room of Cambista. He laid his hand softly on the knob, then thrust it suddenly open and stepped in.

Cambista sat at his table, bending low, his brow furrowed by an intense concentration, his head well to one side, as he wrote rapidly on a large sheet of paper, the pen making a loud, scratching noise. "Well?" he said, picking up a piece of blotting paper, and pressing it down on what he had just written. "Well, Gregorio? What did you find?" He got no answer, and, looking up, at length, he saw that two men were before him. Tom Geary was in the act of softly closing the door.

XVI

"The Robber Robbed"

The ruddy face of Cambista turned sallow. It might have been the color of death. He sat frozen in his chair. "Fan him, Tom," Tyler ordered.

Geary, grinning with a nervous joy, stepped behind the bandit and went rapidly through his clothes. A bulging wallet, a short-nosed revolver, a stiletto, and two or three odds and ends were taken from him. That was all.

"The safe next, Cambista," Tyler announced.

Cambista raised his brows. "The safe?" he muttered.

"Open it, brother," Tyler barked.

"I have to die anyway," Cambista said with remarkable calmness. "I'll not open it."

"Open the safe," Tyler ordered again, "and I give you my word that neither of us will lay a hand on you, unless you try to prevent us from getting safely away."

"You promise that?" Cambista stated slowly.

"I promise it."

"You swear it?"

"I'd even swear it, though I don't know what good oaths should be in this house, Cambista. However, I'll swear it."

"Then . . . ," Cambista began. He paused, in the act of turning toward the safe. Suddenly his head went back, and his shoulders turned rigid. But this pang of shame and of rage was only momentary. Presently he could be heard muttering: "It's the only way." He leaned before the safe and manipulated the combination. As he worked, again in a calm voice, he murmured: "And the curs, Manuelo and Gregorio? What became of them?"

"They are lying tied up in the rawhide thongs, Cambista, *amigo!*" Tyler answered.

"Good," Cambista said. "Very good, indeed!" There was a purr in his voice. Plainly he would see to his two failing servitors later on. The door of the safe opened.

"Take out the stuff, Tom," advised Tyler. "That's it. Wrap it in that coat that's on the chair, yonder. Good! How much value in that stuff, Cambista?"

"Thirty or forty thousand," Cambista murmured.

"And the shame, Cambista?" Tyler asked.

The bandit turned on him with a complexion bronzed over with the greenish tint of rage.

"Now you walk before us through the door and down the hall, Cambista. There are horses in the patio, standing at the rack. We'll take three of 'em and ride off."

"You break your oath, eh?" Cambista asked.

"I told you that we'd not lay a hand on you unless you hindered us from getting safely off,"

Tyler reminded. "And you are our only means of getting safely off. Furthermore, I repeat, once we're safely away, we will never touch you or harm you."

Cambista raised his clenched fists above his head. "I lead you safely out of the house," he said. "I take you to the horses. I ride with you through the gate of my own house, and my own money is in your hands! *¡Dios, Dios!*" He ended with a groan.

"We want safety, Cambista," Tyler repeated. "As for revenge, the money is a small part of it. The shame will be another part."

The Mexican suddenly drew himself up and took a quick breath. "What must be done, must be done," he said. "I, like a fool, argue when words are useless. Perhaps I may live to another time." He shrugged his thick shoulders, and then marched straight out of the room and down the hall, like a free agent.

Only the quiet voice of Tyler, walking behind, was at his ear. "Not too fast, friend Cambista. Remember that Geary is not altogether fit. And then there's the danger if you make a sudden move of any sort. You have little signs and signals with which you pass messages to your men, as you did to Gregorio a while ago in your study. And the moment that I see any sort of a sign, and the moment that I see one of your men on guard make the least movement, I shoot you, Cambista, with your own good little bulldog revolver that I carry snugly here in my pocket. You understand?"

Cambista cursed, speaking under his breath, however, and so they came out in the hall into the glare of the afternoon sun.

The patio, for the moment, was empty. They could not look, from this angle, through the deep casement of the gateway. Off to the side were half a dozen horses, among them Tyler's mustang. Luck was still with the fugitives.

"So," Tyler said, as they climbed into the saddles — Geary painfully stifling a groan; Tyler like a cat, leaping, Cambista stolidly, with a heave of his strong shoulder muscles.

The guard in the gateway, as they approached, was sitting down, but now he leaped up and threw his rifle to his shoulder, staring wildly at the two *gringos*.

"Down with that gun, you fool, you rat's food!" Cambista snapped. "Do you dare to raise a rifle when I am in front of it."

The other backed up. He was so staggered by what he saw that he stood there, shaking his head and gasping, as they passed him and turned into the street. There they struck a soft dog-trot that raised the white dust in clouds behind them.

In the heart of Jim Tyler there was a riot of joy that bloomed suddenly in his heart, under the white heat of the sun.

There were no more than two or three children in the street, who stood up silently and stared, as the familiar and forbidding figure of Cambista rode by them with the Americans apparently attendant upon him, for they rode scrupulously half a length behind.

They were well clear of the village when Cambista said: "How much farther do I ride to make your safety sure, *Señor* Tyler?"

"To the place where the two creeks meet. It's not so very far away . . . you can see for yourself," was Tyler's response.

"Good," Cambista said. "At that place, you don't end your promises with a murder?"

"I told you, that whatever happens to you, we would not touch you . . . today." He added to Geary: "Close up on him on that side, Tom. We don't want the wildcat to run screeching home before we're ready."

And so, as they climbed the easy trail, they came through the brush and through the nest of rocks, suddenly into the presence of six armed men, riding fine horses.

"Carter!" shouted Cambista, raising his arms as though at the sight of salvation. "Take this pair of robbers and murderers! Take them. Thank the saints! I've come to friends!"

"Steady, brother," Carter snarled. "You've come to friends, but what's brought you out here alone on the trail with a pair of fellows you don't like?"

"It's treason!" Cambista yelled. "Treason, and. . . ."

Tyler cut in with: "Cambista, you've come to the screaming time, you fat-faced dog. Now howl, and see what good it does you! Carter, I've brought this man out to you. You think that he's a good friend of yours, but, if you still think it, you're a fool. Here's my friend Geary, who was rotting in the dark cellar of his house. And here am I. I gave him your letter, and he straightway shoved me into the same hole and tied me in rawhide. You can see the marks where the thongs cut into my forehead and my wrists, if you like. It was torture, Carter. And that was the way he received a man with a letter from you!"

"Listen!" screeched Cambista. "In the name of the saints, Carter, listen to me, while I tell you that this savage dog killed a gentleman at Santa Anna, a gentleman of my blood, Ramón Díaz."

"The swine that commanded at the prison," Wynne butted in with a quick violence. "And he needed killing."

"Carter!" shouted the Mexican. "Do you hear me?"

"Cambista, Cambista," Carter said with an affected gravity, "I'm pretty badly saddened by this here. You know I wanted to make a deal with you that would split up this territory between us. You know how you hung onto San Andreas like a hog and shut us out. And now you won't even listen to little requests that I send you, as one friend to another? I'm afraid that something ought to be done about it. I'm afraid that this is as good a time as any, this bright day." And he laughed in the face of the Mexican.

"Screaming time, Cambista," said the voice of Tyler. "I told you it was coming. And mind you, you dog, I've kept my promise. Whatever happens to you, I haven't laid a hand on you. Neither has Tom Geary, though we both have reasons enough for forgetting our promises and cutting your throat without giving you a chance."

One yellow-eyed glance of hatred was cast by Cambista toward Tyler, then he said: "Carter, they got thirty, even forty thousand dollars out of my safe! Do you let them take that?"

"You wanted one big job done for you, Carter," Tyler said. "Isn't it a big enough job, the day that I bring you this Gila monster, or do you want a split of the money, as well? He opened his safe for us, Carter."

The latter laughed long and loudly. "He opened his own safe for you? Tyler, keep the cash and a long welcome to it. What does it matter to me, a little pin money like that? It's worth half a million to have this wildcat out of the way, because now we'll have the whole pass in our hands. Give me half a day to clean the Cambista tribe out of San Andreas, and then we'll settle down in it as snug as bugs in a rug. Oh, Cambista, if you only knew how glad I am to see you, you lying, throat-cutting, promise-breaking sneak. Now I have my hands on you. Close in around him, boys! Wynne, put a rope on that horse of Cambista's. You can have the horse for your trouble, afterward.

"And you, Tyler, if ever you lose your way again, don't forget to knock at my door. One thing more. Watch your way up the valley because Lavigne is somewhere, and he doesn't like you particularly. *¡Adiós, amigos!*"

Up the valley rode the gang, shouting, laughing, while Cambista, bowing his head, gripped the pommel of his saddle with both hands and submitted to fate.

Jim Tyler looked around and then stretched out his hands to the sky. "Maybe gold is a wonderful thing, Tom," he said. "But after an hour in Cambista's cellar, getting nearer and nearer to screaming time, why, man, there's nothing in the world equal to a double handful of sunshine!"

The Trail of Death

I

"Windings"

The main street of the town was winding, so was the gait of old Tom Geary. The only trouble was that the bends did not coincide. In fact, the street seemed too narrow for him, for he was continually shouldering through a pair of swinging doors on one side of the street, only to glance off to the other side a few moments later and bump open a similar pair. There were plenty of those pairs of doors in the main street. It was not the first time that people celebrating had decided to enter them all, but usually the system was to go up one side of the way and walk, or be carried, down the other side. Tom Geary preferred to go in a zigzag that would embrace everything as he went along.

Tom was in late middle age, a stocky fellow, with a head bald in front and a scalp as red as the sunny side of an apple. He was wearing the clothes that he wore in his mine and that served him for all occasions, but in spite of the roughness of his appearance he had a following and a big one.

The point was that Tom Geary could make the party last as long as he pleased, call for as many drinks as he pleased in any of the saloons without fear of being refused credit, and treat the entire town as though it were his own. That was why the crowd followed him, enjoying the free drinks, enjoying, also, a sense that this man had tapped a fountain of almost inexhaustible wealth.

They had seen, almost every one of them, samples of the ore from that wide, black vein that he had uncovered. In the meantime, his claim was shouldered on either side by other claims, but no one else had uncovered such a treasure as lay under the drills of Tom Geary's hired men. It was for that reason that he could go as he pleased and do as he pleased. No matter what he called for, he would pay for it the next day, blindly, even though the charges were excessive. Besides, he enjoyed an immense popularity in the town. Since he had struck it rich, the gold rush had become a wild panic. It was because of him that this main street, for instance, had doubled its length in a single month.

When he entered the Golden Hour Saloon and stood before its gilded mirrors, he could see, imaged beside him and over his shoulders, a perfect sea of faces — most of these big Westerners towered above him. Three bartenders began to spin glasses and bottles down the long length of the bar; a roar of many voices, speaking together, made the thin walls of the room vibrate.

Through this roar came the voice of the proprietor, who asked, with a broad grin: "Say, Geary, why don't you tell us the straight up-and-up of how you got out of the hands of Miguel Cambista?"

Geary laid his hand on his side. "I don't wants do no thinkin' about him," he declared. "I've hardly got the bandage off the wound, and it still annoys me. Besides, you gents all know it was that long-geared friend of mine . . . that Jim Tyler."

"Him that the Mexicans call The Wolf?" asked the saloon owner.

"Sure, it was him. What am I gonna tell you fellows that you don't know?"

"Any part of that yarn is worth hearing, though it takes a pile of believing. What did Miguel Cambista want out of you?"

"He didn't want nothing," he said, "except a little paper signed by me, stating that I'd sold the mine to a friend of his. That was all he wanted. And that was what he'd've had, too, before long. There was too many rats in his cellar to suit me. After they'd ate the toes out of both my boots, I was ready to quit. That was where Jim Tyler come in. He trailed me, and they grabbed him, lashed him in green rawhide, and put him down there in the cellar to let the rawhide draw. Cambista himself, he was comin' down there to enjoy the yells of Tyler, when the rawhide got to drawin' good. But the rest of it nobody believes, and so I ain't gonna tell it again."

"What rest?" asked a man at the shoulder of the miner. "I'm new to the town, partner."

"You wouldn't believe it, so it's no go."

"You give me a try."

"Why, Tyler got me to rub bacon rind on the rawhide thongs that was eating into his wrists, and he let the rats eat through the thongs. And in a minute or two, after that, he had himself free."

"That's a tall one," said the questioner, and laughed loudly.

"So's Jim Tyler tall, and you wouldn't be laughing if he was around here," Tom Geary said, growing angry. "But fill 'em up, boys, put 'em down, and drink hearty, all of you. We've only started to crack this little old town open, and, before we get through, we're gonna see the inside of the nut, and no mistake. Here's another round coming up. My credit good, Dan?"

"Good to the end of time, Geary," said the owner, glancing with gratification down the bar at the multitudinous flashing of the glasses as they were raised and lowered.

"We'll have one last round, then, and try a new kind of air farther down the street," Geary announced, whose eyes were beginning to redden.

The man at his shoulder, a powerful fellow with a brutally heavy jaw, said sneeringly: "About this gent that the rats ate loose, Geary, what did he do when . . . ?"

"Hold on. Here's Tyler now," said someone.

"Come to take Daddy Geary home, eh?" asked another gloomily.

"Why should he let Geary waste money that's gonna be his one of these days," muttered another. "He's made Tyler his heir, ain't he?"

Tall, active, the broad shoulders of Jim Tyler worked sinuously through the crowd. "Tom," he said, "aren't you getting just a little heated up?"

"Me?" Geary questioned, looking mournfully up into the lean, hawk-like face of his younger friend. "Why, I ain't hardly started to get warm, Jimmy. You wouldn't want me to stop before. . . ."

"Why not stop now?" Tyler asked. "You've had enough already to keep you groaning all to-morrow. If you go on, you'll be in bed for three days."

"Come on, Jim," said Geary, "and have a couple drinks with me, and then you'll see things different."

"I don't want to see things differently," Tyler assured Geary. He picked up one of the glasses and sniffed curiously at the aroma. A few drops of the liquor remained in the glass. "This stuff is enough to eat the lining out of your stomach," Tyler stated.

"Are you aiming to break up my business?" asked the saloon owner, glowering.

Tyler put down the glass and looked the other in the face with his singularly cold and direct glance. "Is that honest whisky?" he asked.

"It's as honest as goes over pretty near every bar in town," declared the proprietor.

"It's honest enough for the town, perhaps, but it's not honest enough for me," Tyler answered.

241

"Maybe it's honest enough for rats," said the big fellow of the jaw and the well-developed jaw muscles.

Tyler turned his head calmly toward the speaker. Every face in the barroom was ominously clouded, regarding Tyler. But he seemed unaware of their attitude, or curiously indifferent to it. "What's that about rats?" he asked.

"Why, you're the rat man, ain't you?" said the other.

"I've never been called the rat man before," Tyler said gently.

"You're being called that now, though," the man of the jaw said, thrusting it forward.

"Very well," Tyler stated. "Bad names don't hurt me until they bruise the skin or break it." He turned back to Geary. "Hadn't you better come along with me, Tom?"

"Jim, leave me be, will you?" complained the miner. "I ain't had a party since. . . ."

"Since Saturday," Tyler interjected, "and you were down and out last Sunday and Monday on account of it. Tom, every party like this is a shot between wind and water for you, and one of these days you'll sink. Hadn't you better come?"

"Well, damn it, I'll come," mumbled the older man. "Confound you, Jim, you certainly know how to spoil things. G'night, boys. G'night, Murphy."

"What's the bill?" Tyler asked of the saloonkeeper.

"That's all right," answered the man, blacker

of face than before. "I'll send over the bill in the morning."

Tyler's glance swept over the faces.

"There are fifty people here. How many rounds?" he asked.

"Three, I guess," muttered the other.

"At fifty cents a shot, that makes seventy-five dollars," Tyler calculated. "Here's the money." He slid onto the bar three golden double eagles, a ten-dollar and a five-dollar piece. There were no thanks expected and none offered because it appeared perfectly clear that a bill of twice this size would have been sent over to Geary in the morning.

"We'll go on home to the hotel, Tom," Tyler said. Taking the arm of the other under his, he drew Geary resolutely from the barroom.

The man of the bulging jaw watched this performance with increasing rage, his eyes growing smaller, shining more brightly from instant to instant. Now, as the doors swung shut behind the departing pair, he exclaimed: "That yaller dog takes water, and he's gonna take some more from me for breakin' up this here party!"

He started with a lunge. The way cleared with odd suddenness before him, and he was almost at the door before the voice of the bartender said coldly: "You tackle Jim Tyler, and you're steppin' into a hospital. Likely he won't kill you, but he'll put you in bed for a few weeks." The calmness of this voice carried conviction with it, and the man of the jaw halted suddenly, his hand on the door.

"You mean he's a gunman?" he asked, turning an amazed face over his shoulder.

"Him?" said a bystander. "He's poison, brother. Don't fill your hand while he's sitting in at the game."

II

"Sally"

It was the middle of the next morning when Sally Champion drove down that same winding main street in her buckboard, and brought her two mustangs to a stop at the watering trough in front of the hotel. She sprang to the ground, a cloud of dust flying from the folds of her dress and the bandanna around her neck, and in a moment she had the bits out of the mouths of the mustangs. Then she stood by, watching them drink with their muzzles plunged deep, their eyes half closed. With a twist here and a shake or a brush there, evidence of the long drive began to disappear.

"Somebody here to put up my team?" she asked.

A boy came out, a barefooted, brown-legged, steely-eyed youngster, chewing a straw. "Whacha want, ma'am?" he asked.

"A good feed of grain for them," said the girl. "Oats, if you have 'em . . . barley if you haven't. Give them a currying and brushing, too, if you please. I may have to start on again in a few hours, and they've put a lot of ground behind them already."

For answer he glanced over the familiar tough-

245

ness of those mustang lines, and then, with a jerk of the head, led them off down the alley toward the stable behind the hotel.

Sally Champion went up on the verandah, where the eyes of three or four loungers rested curiously upon her, with that shy deference that even the most brazen of true Westerners pay to a woman. She put them at ease, at once, by saluting them with a wave of her hand and a smile. Her face was red with sun and wind, but the smile showed the blue of her eyes and suddenly made them all see that she was very pretty, indeed. But she took no advantage of her good looks to keep them at a distance. She slipped into the nearest chair beside a gaunt fellow with a cadaverous face and a snarling look about the mouth.

"Hot," she said.

"Mighty hot," agreed the man beside her. Envious looks were cast at him by the others. He was aware keenly of those looks.

"I'm looking for a man here in town," she said. "I suppose everybody knows him. I imagine he's the most popular fellow here. Jim Tyler, I mean."

"Him? Yeah, I know him," said the man. He was suddenly silent, although it was clear that he could say more.

She went on: "I understand that he's done a lot for the town by smashing the Miguel Cambista gang. Isn't that true? Weren't they a pest before?"

"They were a pest, all right, but, with Cambista out of the way," said the man, "the Carter gang has a free hand. And I dunno that they're much better than the Mexicans were." He shook his head. "They're a hard lot," he added.

"At any rate," she said, "I hope that I'll be able to get Jim Tyler to work for me."

"Him!" exclaimed the man.

There was a general scraping of chairs as the others on the verandah hitched forward and then leaned so that they could see the girl more clearly. She met their gaze calmly, her eyes flicking from one face to another.

"Why, yes," she said. "And why not? He does odd bits of work, doesn't he?"

Her nearest companion looked askance. One of the others ventured: "Yeah, most of the work he does is kind of odd, all right. But you couldn't hire him now."

"Why not?"

"Why, he's gonna get Tom Geary's mine. It's the richest you ever seen. By reason of him saving old Tom's life a couple times, Tom is makin' him his heir."

"Well, that's proper enough, I suppose," Sally responded.

"Yeah, sure, it's all right. Only, you couldn't be hiring him, I guess. Not unless your job was what it ain't likely to be."

"I don't understand that," she replied.

"Aw, you know how it is," said the man who

neighbored her. "Tyler, he don't care much about money, or anything like that. It's trouble that he lives on. These here peaceful times, they don't mean nothing to him."

Another offered: "I've seen him sit out here with his head down and his chin on his chest for hours at a time, looking like he was ready to die. There ain't anything in the world for Tyler, except trouble. And he ain't got no trouble now, except to keep Tom Geary sober. That ain't any life for Jim Tyler."

"What does he want to do, then?" asked the girl.

"He wants to have trouble on his hands, trouble up to the elbows. That's what he likes. Just plain work, and just plain folks, they don't mean nothing to him. He won't have a hoss that ain't got kinks that need straightening out every time you climb onto its back. He won't take no interest in nothing, except there's knives and guns around the corner or some such thing."

"Ah," Sally mused.

"I seen him last night," said one of the group, "looking over a crowd in a saloon with a sort of a cold, dead eye, waiting for somebody to start trouble. There was almost some trouble started, too, but the fool that wanted to jump Tyler was called off. A man might as well jump a stick of dynamite."

The girl, however, was not over-awed by what she heard. She merely shrugged her shoulders and laughed a little. "I want to see Tyler. Where can I find him?" she asked. "Is he in town?"

"He's upstairs now, takin' care of old Tom Geary, I guess," said one of the others. "I'll go up and tell him you wanna see him, shall I?"

"Thanks a lot," Sally said.

The man who made the proffer, a leather-skinned cowpuncher, wearing overalls patched at the knees and the finest of shop-made boots, arose and stumped his bowlegs across the verandah floor, disappearing into the hotel. He climbed to the second story and knocked at a door.

"Stay out," said a hard voice.

Another voice groaned. "Gimme another wet towel on the head, Jim, will you?"

The cowpuncher grinned. Then he knocked again. "Hello, Tyler," he said.

"Who's there?" came from inside the room, in the same iron voice.

"Me, Sim Wilkins."

"Wilkins? I don't know you, and, besides, I'm busy."

Sim Wilkins colored with anger. He was about to strike on the door again with his balled fist, but changed his mind and thought better of that. He had turned away, when he remembered that he had come on behalf of a woman. He hesitated, scratched his head, and finally called again. "They's a lady that wants you, Tyler, not me."

A step crossed the floor of the room, and the door was jerked open. The keen, grim eyes of

249

Tyler fixed on the smaller man. "Wilkins," he said, "if that's your name, will you go tell the lady that I'm busy and can't see her."

"All right, all right," Wilkins grumbled, with a shrug of his shoulders. "Only she was kind of in a jam. That's all."

The door had begun to close, but was arrested in this movement, while the other demanded: "What sort of jam?"

"Oh, I dunno. Just something that brought her all the way from nowhere."

"She'd better go back to nowhere, then," Tyler said.

He had almost shut the door, when Wilkins said: "Just a matter of life or death, I reckon."

The door was pulled suddenly open. "What you say?" asked Tyler. He stepped out into the hall, towering over the other man.

"Life or death, I guess," Wilkins said, delighted with this sudden response.

"Hey, Jim, Jim," groaned the voice of Tom Geary from inside the room.

"Wait a minute," Tyler said. He closed the door from the hall, adding: "Maybe I was a little short, Wilkins. I'm sorry for that, too. You see, Geary has been a little trying this morning."

"Yeah, I know," agreed the other. "When they get boiled at his age, it takes a lot of time unboiling 'em again." He chuckled.

"Where's the lady?" asked Tyler.

"Down on the verandah."

"I'll go down and see her," Tyler announced.

He hurried down the stairs, and Wilkins declared, afterward, that he heard the tall fellow humming softly to himself as he ran down the steps. Such was the mere prospect of danger to this man.

Stepping out on the porch, his grave face was directed at once toward the girl. Unsmiling, he faced his keen eyes upon her, and never a hawk stared down at a quarry with more intensity than this man, fixing his glance upon the girl.

She got up from her chair and smiled a little at him. But her smile went out as she extended her hand. "I'm Sally Champion," she said. "Harry Champion's sister."

He took the hand with a light touch and abandoned it again at once. "Harry Champion?" he said. "I don't seem to remember."

At this, she gasped, amazed. "You don't remember?" she said.

"No, I don't remember."

"The man you saved from that Mexican scoundrel, El Tigre, with his cat-face, and his gang of cutthroats?"

"Oh, I remember now," Tyler answered. "The boy with the horse that was too good for him."

"Too good for him?" she queried, frowning.

"I mean," he said, "the horse that looked as though it wouldn't stay in those hands for very long. That was why I followed him. But I remember everything, now. Will you come inside with me, Miss Champion?"

III

"The Ten Days"

She looked up for a moment with a doubtful hesitation toward that grim, unrelenting face, then, with a nod of the head, she passed in through the doorway of the hotel, and he followed.

Wilkins stood on the verandah and detailed his account of the little difficulty he had had in inducing the tall man to come downstairs. "I'll tell you what it is," he said. "There ain't anything in the world that means nothing to him, unless there's a scent of death in it. Death trails is the only ones that bloodhound will run on. Nothin' that I said budged him. I could've stood there and told about the pretty face of that girl a hundred times, and it wouldn't've meant anything to him. Not a damned thing. It was only when I said it was life or death. That fetched him. Lemme tell you what I think."

"Aw," said another, "we all think the same way. Why does he gamble? To win money? No, but just to get the thrill out of putting up all of his coin and giving it a ride, and a hard ride. I seen him bet a thousand dollars with a crazy miner by name of Tuck Walters the other day. There was two birds sitting on the rail, yonder. 'That right-hand bird is gonna fly first,' Walters says to him-self.

" 'A hundred dollars that the left-hand bird flies first,' Tyler says as quick as a wink.

" 'Yeah, or two hundred,' says Walters, that don't take water from nobody.

" 'Make it a real bet. Make it a thousand,' Tyler says.

"And they made that fool bet, I tell you! And there they stood, and Tyler, he pulled out the makings and rolled him a cigarette without looking at what his hands were doing, and he just stared at them two birds, and there was a grin in the corners of his mouth, too, like it done him good to have a minute like that to live through. Me? I'd've had nerves, I would've. But not him. Walters got sort of pinched, with all that money in the bank, too. Pretty soon, the right-hand bird gives a flutter of the wings.

" 'You win, Walters,' " Tyler says, chuckling.

"But the right-hand bird didn't fly, after all. He was just letting the sun and the air soak into his skin when he raised the feathers, I suppose. Then the left-hand bird, without no prepara-tions, just dropped off that post a foot, opened his wings, and went skimming. Walters paid his bet, all right.

" 'That left-hand bird was a good one,' Tyler says, grinning at him. 'I'd back that bird against the world.' He meant it, too. He's that way."

The men listened to Wilkins with interest.

One of the group said: "You heard what he did

253

with Budge Swanson's hoss the other day?"

"No. What was that?"

"Budge, he had a runt of a no-good buckskin mustang that had piled him a coupla times, and he asked Tyler to try to ride him. And Tyler got into the saddle and rode that mustang around the corral, and then he made him jump the bars where they was low, and the mustang tripped on the top bar and fell down. Tyler rolled a mile, but he got up like a cat and was in the saddle and spurring that mustang to its feet before you could say Jack Robinson. It had been bucking pretty good before, but now it brought out everything that I ever seen a horse do, and twice Tyler lost a stirrup, but he caught it again on the swing, and he rode that hoss to a lather and rode it quiet ag'in.

"Then he comes back, and there's a trickle of blood running down from his nose, and another trickle running down out of his right ear. But he don't seem to mind it, he gets off and smiles, and shakes his head to get the buzzing out of it. And he says . . . 'I almost gave up that buckskin, but just when I was through, it came to life. You never can tell where you'll get the best shock, boys.' And that's what he's after . . . the shocks!"

While this grave conversation was being carried on in the front of the hotel, Jim Tyler was sitting with the girl in an inner room, his long hands folded around his knees, his head thrust forward, his lean, iron-hard jaw locked fast. Never once did his eyes leave the face of the girl.

She said: "Harry never should have gone back south across the Río Grande, of course."

"Why not?" Tyler asked.

"Well, because of El Tigre, and all of those rascals. That's enough of a reason, I suppose."

"He might find Mexico a mighty amusing place just now, Miss Champion," Tyler said.

"He might find it a good place to die in!" exclaimed the girl.

"Well," Tyler said, "everybody dies once. But what was he hunting when he went south of the Río Grande? Can you tell me that?"

"There's a town called Santa Anna . . . ," she began. Tyler nodded. "You know it," she went on. "Harry has told me about the wonderful thing you did there, when you entered the prison and brought out Pedro Salvatore. And it was in that same town that Harry saw a girl so pretty that her face haunted him after he had left Mexico."

"They catch quick," the tall man stated gravely. "Those Mexican girls catch faster than a fire."

Sally Champion continued: "After Harry had come home, he was never contented, no matter what was being done. Nothing seemed to amuse him. Finally he went to Father and told him that he wanted to go south and find that girl and marry her."

Tyler nodded. "Your brother's a fellow," he said, "that usually acts on the first idea, isn't he?"

"Yes," Sally said, "he's that sort." She added: "Father told him that he could do as he pleased, but that, if he married a Mexican woman, he'd not get a penny of the estate. Of course, that determined Harry. He's too proud to be run with a strong hand."

"I discovered that," Jim Tyler said, sighing.

"So Harry said good bye to us all," said the girl, "and rode south."

"Not on the stallion, I hope," Tyler put in.

"Yes. He said that stallion, Spring of the Year, was good luck."

"If getting his throat cut is good luck to him, yes. Spring of the Year nearly did that for him!" exclaimed Tyler. "He rode into Mexico on that same horse, did he?"

"The same one."

"Good," Tyler said, and nodded his head. "There will be some excitement, then." He thrust out his lean jaw still farther, and a strange, cruel smile twisted the corners of his mouth.

The girl, staring at him, grew rather pale for a moment. Then she shook her head. "I don't understand you," she said.

"Go on with the story," he insisted.

"He went to Santa Anna," she continued, "and found that Ines Flores had gone with her father's family to another town, farther south. He followed her there. He saw her and was well received. He wrote me a letter about her beauty and her grace and all that. The next letter was not so cheerful. He had told her father that he would not have a penny. *Señor* Flores did not like the idea of having his daughter marry no hard cash."

"Is Flores rich?" broke in Tyler.

"No. Just comfortably well off."

"Go on," Tyler urged.

"The first two letters were what you might expect to hear from Harry," said the girl. "He was being well received everywhere. Everybody knew his name, because of you. That is to say, everybody in Mexico seems to know how you've handled that man-eater, El Tigre. And they remember that Harry Champion is one of the men you've helped. So his way was smoothed for him, he said, a great deal. People might have wanted to steal the great stallion again, but they remembered that you were a friend to Harry before, and they were afraid that you might be his friend again. But the first two letters hardly count. It's the third letter that matters. Here it is." She took an envelope from her pocket, drew out the letter, and handed it to Tyler.

He read:

Dear Sally:

The thing has come to a showdown. I'm to see Ines and have the thing talked out.

Something else is in the wind, and I can't tell you what. All I can say is that I'm walking on quicksand, and that I may make a wrong step and go down at any time. I don't like to write to you in an alarming manner like this, but the fact is, if you don't get a letter or a wire, at least, from me, inside of ten days, you'll know that you'll never see me again. In that case, this is good bye.

I don't think that I'll go under. I'm ready and on the alert because I have a pretty good idea of what the danger will be like. But one can never tell. If you don't hear from me, *adiós*. My love to you and to Father, also. There'll be no use making inquiries in this part of the world. If you don't hear from me, just forget me as fast as you can.

Harry

Jim Tyler looked up from his reading and saw that the face of the girl had lost all its color. But she was brave enough, with her fear. She kept her eyes steadily on him.

"And the ten days?" he asked. "Have they elapsed?" His voice was very gentle as he asked the question.

"Two days ago," she said. "I waited for one day, then I started out to find the only man in the world who could possibly help me. I came straight to you."

IV

"To Mexico"

He turned the letter over and looked at the post-mark. "Patos del Oro," he murmured. "Patos del Oro is far south." He shook his head, looking down at the floor.

"You won't go?" she whispered.

He drew in a breath. "I didn't say that," he answered. "I simply said that Patos del Oro is pretty far south, meaning that it will take a long time for me to get there . . . and your brother seems to be in pretty bad need of quick help."

She nodded. Her eyes clung eagerly to his face. "Do you think there's nothing to be done?" she asked him.

"I don't know," he said. His voice was harsh and dry. He got up from his chair and began to walk the floor with long, swinging, noiseless strides. She watched the forward thrust of the face, and the compression of the lips. His face shone with moisture, and it was plain that every nerve in that body was strung taut.

"I've asked too much," she said. "But I wanted to tell you, as far as the money goes, my father will pay every penny that he has in the world. It was only an explosion of temper when he told Harry that he'd be cut off without a cent, if he married against my father's wishes. It was only a matter of temperament. Father's as explosive as Harry is. As a matter of fact, he would give you hundreds of thousands, if Harry could be brought back safe."

An expression of indifference, even disdain, crossed the face of Tyler. He made a gesture with the flat of his hand. "We're not talking about money. We're talking about Harry Champion," he said. "There's blood on this trail. I know it. I smell it. And I take no blood money."

She watched him with awe. It seemed that nothing she could say would have any effect upon this engine of a man.

"Tell me," he said, "if in the other two letters, the first two he wrote back, he suggested anything about this danger that he referred to in the last one."

"Not one word. After this third letter came, I went over the first two with Father, very carefully, step by step, but I could make nothing of them. There was no hint of anything mysterious. There was only a great deal of raving about this beautiful and perfect Mexican girl."

"Did he send you her picture?"

"Yes, he sent a picture," she said. She took out a pigskin wallet, opened it, and drew out a snapshot. Tyler took it and examined it with care, his brows contracted, while the girl watched him with much curiosity, expecting that silly expression that usually comes over any man's face, no matter how old, when he is looking at a woman who is both young and beautiful. Instead, his features grew only more grim.

"Soft," he said. "No physical exercise. Vain. Spends most of her time on clothes. Proud, by the way she holds up her chin, because people who are not self-conscious face the camera as they hope to face the rest of the world. Vain, proud, and soft. That's not a good combination." He gave back the picture with a jerk of his hand.

"But lovely," said the American girl.

"Eh?" he said.

"Don't you think that she's beautiful?" she asked.

He took the photograph again and stared at it. "Oh, I suppose so," he said. "I suppose so." He snapped his fingers as though this were the slightest matter in the world and worth no consideration at all. He resumed his pacing while Sally Champion, staring at him confusedly, replaced the photograph in the wallet. Was it true that she had found a man to whom women meant nothing? Her own face was not so flushed and hot with travel now. She reached up and pushed her hair into place, settled her hat at a more careful angle, and regarded him once more.

"Whatever she is," she said, "she has run poor Harry almost demented. If you want to see the first two letters. . . ." She offered them with a tentative hand, but an expression of disgust came over his face.

"I don't want to see them," he said. "They don't offer anything. Just a young puppy barking up the wrong tree. That's all. Bah!"

It angered her a little, not what he said about her brother, but an imputation not too deftly covered over that women were of no essential importance. However, her wits were quickly back at the crux of the matter. It was simply what this man could do for her brother. She remembered, now, the many times when Harry Champion had spoken of Tyler — the limitless resource, the iron nerve, the terrible love of danger, and the irresistible attraction of the impossible for this man. It seemed to her that she could have guessed at these same qualities in him without any previous knowledge.

Suddenly she stood up. "If we cannot reward you," she said, "we have no right to come to you like beggars and ask for your help." She held out her hand.

He disregarded it. Or, rather, he looked first at it, and then quickly up to her face. "Don't play the fool," he said.

It shocked her more than a blow in the face. Before she could respond, he had resumed his pacing.

"I'm going down to Patos del Oro to see what I can do about Harry. That's settled. The jackass had to take the stallion with him again. Good luck! Luck enough to get a knife buried in his back, I suppose. Spring of the Year for luck." He snapped his long, hard fingers in an ecstasy of impatience.

"Mister Tyler," she said, "the matter is closed, as far as my father and I are concerned. This would be too dangerous a mission, I suppose, and I. . . ."

"What have your father and yourself to do with it?" he snapped, scowling at her. As she was absorbing this second shock, he continued: "Harry is my friend. Whatever I can do for him, I'll try. That's all. I want you to help me with information as far as you can. That's all. Tell me, is he one of the young calves who is always falling in love in the spring of the year?" She shook her head, angrily. "Think again," he said.

She looked gloomily back over the past. It was true that she could remember certain names and faces that, from time to time, had been the center of all interest for her brother, as it seemed. Then she said: "He's lost his head, now and then."

"Usually in the spring of the year?"

"I suppose so." She admitted that with reluctance.

"No wonder he called his horse by that name," Tyler said savagely. "Women, they're the root of most trouble. Soft and clinging, or hard and brittle . . . small, mean, and detestable, or big, gross, and revolting."

She stiffened, and her teeth clicked.

He added: "I don't mean you. Of course, I don't. I'm only wondering what rotten mess this girl with the beautiful face has brought your brother into. Where is he now? Dead? Chained in a cellar? Held somewhere in the hills for ransom? What's happened to him? I've got to find out." He exclaimed finally: "I might have known that he would ride into trouble again on the back of that brute of a stallion!"

"I wish you'd taken the horse when he offered it to you," broke out Sally.

"What would I do with a long-legged picture horse like that?" he demanded roughly. "A picture horse and a picture girl . . . it's a mess, and that's all there is to it." She was silenced, but her face burned. Then he said: "Well, there's nothing more that you can do for me. Good bye. I'll send you word when I learn something. I know your address, unless you've moved since the old days."

Suddenly he had shaken hands, merely touching her fingers with his, and was gone from the room and striding up the stairs.

She sat down, stupefied. A hubbub of voices broke out in the story above her. But she could not make out the words.

Then a middle-aged man in overalls and a flannel shirt, open at the throat, came rushing into the room, his hair tousled, his eyes reddened and staring.

"Where is she?" he was muttering. "Here you are!" He planted himself before her with a violence that made her jump up as though prepared for flight.

"You're the one that sent Tyler south of the Río Grande, are you?" he demanded.

"I sent him nowhere," she replied.

"You came with a cock-and-bull story," cried Tom Geary, "about trouble in old Mexico, and you got him to go! You know you did!"

"Who are you?" she exclaimed.

"I'm his friend!" Geary shouted. "And I know what would happen to him south of the river. They're hungry to get their hands on him . . . the police and a thousand crooks that he's beat and made fools of in the past. But you sent him down there to die on a wild-goose chase."

"He hasn't left. He's still here!" she cried in protest.

"Then make him stay," Geary groaned. "Go and stop him before he leaves the stable."

"I'll do what I can," she cried.

"This way," he urged, and hurried out onto the verandah. "Too late!" he gasped. "There he goes. Nothing can stop him now." He pointed, and she saw a tall, wide-shouldered horseman swinging down the street on a mustang, already half obscured in the dust cloud of his own raising.

V

"A Long Shot"

Three miles from the town of Patos del Oro, there was a buzzard that had newly lighted in a field, and in the neighboring field a *peon* stopped his work to lean on his hoe and stare toward the bird of ill omen. He was wondering what could have caused the wanderer to drop out of the hot blue sky to the ground. Was it the body of a sick rabbit? Was it some ground squirrel that had fallen over, dead of old age or from wounds received in some intercommunal broil?

Suddenly the buzzard stretched its horrible, naked neck, flapped its great wings heavily, clumsily, and rose from the ground. Then, having risen, it made a single quick dip downward, almost as though it would have fallen to the earth, having lost balance. Instead, it came out of the dive in a long, soaring motion in which it seemed hardly to need the thrusting of the wings to help it upward. It was the sign that it had returned to the deep sky of its native element, where it could wander for days and weeks, unresting on the wing. What could have startled it?

Over the brow of the hill came the reason — a

tall rider who made his mustang seem small, a man riding in very long stirrups, a man with wide shoulders and a very erect, light bearing in the saddle. He saw the buzzard rising, shooting off now toward one side in a mighty whirl. Suddenly there was a flash of steel in his hand, the explosion of a gun shattering the air, and that drawn weapon disappeared instantly into the clothes of the rider.

The buzzard sailed on, unperturbed, and it seemed to the *peon* that not a feather of it had been disturbed. A foolish thing to shoot with a revolver at that distance, at such a swiftly sailing target! The *peon* shook his head, and, noting that the rider had continued unperturbed on his way, never breaking the steady dog-trot of the mustang, the laborer was about to turn back to his hoe, shaking his head at this useless waste of ammunition, when he saw a thing that he never had observed before, even in the midst of a hurricane — a buzzard wavering in its flight. It seemed too heavy on one side, heavier and heavier still, and presently it turned over like a boat sinking at sea and dropped straight down through the thin blue of the sky. So hard did it strike that it rebounded again a little, and a fluff of feathers went sailing off down the wind. The *peon*'s lower jaw dropped against his chest. That bullet, then, had not been wasted, after all. Who under the wide heaven could shoot like this, so terribly certain of striking home, that he would ride on, never turning his head to make sure of the result?

The whole soul of the *peon* stood in his eyes, as he stared after the rider. "Not The Wolf himself could shoot like that," he muttered to himself. "No, not El Tigre, or Miguel Cambista, either, no matter how great they are." Who then was this? Was it simply a lucky shot? No, because the speed and the surety of that shot indicated absolute self-confidence. That rider had known what he could do with his gun. Marvelous, indeed, that he did not once turn his head.

Now he was disappearing into the hollow, now he was rising again. Silhouetted against the horizon, the *peon* saw again the outline of the wide-shouldered man and the width of the sombrero's flopping brim. "All the kind saints!" he gasped, as the thought came home to him. He blinked his eyes, for they burned in his head, they had been thrusting out for so many seconds, unwinking.

But there was the description that rang in his brain, the words beating home like the clapper of a bell. "There ain't anything in the world that means nothing to him, unless there's a scent of death in it. Death trails is the only ones that bloodhound will run on. Those were the words with which that terrible man from the Northern land was described — The Wolf. And he shouted suddenly, throwing his hands to the sky to hear him witness: "The Wolf! I have seen him!"

He stared again in the direction in which the figure had disappeared, and he saw before him the whitewashed walls of the town of Patos del Oro with the shadowy fringes and clouds of the big trees, here and there, the great cypresses that arched beside the river, and the huge, sheer walls of the church rising aloft above the rest of the place, and holding its gilded cross like a gleam of yellow flame in the heart of the sky.

"He is descending on the town," said the *peon*. "And now . . . may my wife and my poor children forgive me if it slipped out of my fool's head . . . there is money to be had for him, thousands and thousands of *pesos!* The state will pay much. He who informs against that terrible one, is it not whispered about that forever and forever El Tigre and his men will never harm him or touch his lands so long as he lives? His horses and his cattle go unhurt. No, more than that, El Tigre will give help and is he not rich and strong, great and wise enough to help?" As he finished speaking, the *peon* stepped out of his sandals, cast aside his hoe, flung down upon the ground his wide-brimmed hat, and headed straight over the hills for the town.

He was not yet arrived at middle age. He had been a good runner in his youth, and those wiry Indian legs of his had not lost their strength. If they were not quite as fleet as of old, they had more stamina, and, indeed, they were fast enough to keep the hair blowing straight back from his head all the three miles to the town of Patos del Oro.

He was glad when his bare, bleeding feet

found the soft dust of the streets that puffed up into his face and settled on his sweating body, there blackening to mud through which new streams of sweat kept breaking out in rivulets. He was fairly masked and encased in mud and dust of this sort when at last he reached the headquarters of the gendarmerie.

He was so excited that he would have burst in through the high, arched doorway, except that two gendarmes, standing there, received him on the butts of their rifles and threatened to smash in his ribs and his head for him, unless he straightway gave them room.

He was so exhausted from his running that his gasping voice could hardly be heard as he wheezed out: "To the *capitán*. Quickly, quickly. I have terrible news. I have wonderful news!"

"Here's the captain coming now. You can tell him your wonderful news yourself."

They looked at one another, the two gendarmes, with faintly superior smiles. They had been *peones* themselves once, before the great good fortune came to them, but now they were dressed in metal braid and closely fitted jackets, and the eyes of women softened, looking upon the beauty of that uniform, those eyes that never condescended to glance down toward cheap, wrinkled, cotton trousers, or ragged shoes. From the hips up they were generals. From the hips down, they were beggars.

The captain, though, was dressed gloriously to the heels of his shining boots. He paused, twirled

270

his mustache and frowned.

The *peon* threw up his hands. "Heaven be my witness!" he cried.

"You didn't do the murder, eh?" the captain of the gendarmes said, for he was a hardened man.

"Murder? Was it murder to shoot a buzzard?" asked the *peon*.

"What's the fool talking about?" the captain asked of his two men.

"Listen," broke out the messenger again, for he was recovering his breath and dancing in hot-footed excitement as he thought of the reward that would surely soon come to him. "I have seen with my own eyes The Wolf himself!" If he had declared that he had seen Satan in person, he could hardly have shocked the three before him more thoroughly.

The captain suddenly strode out toward him and pointed a forefinger like a pistol at the messenger's heart.

"Where?"

"Over the hills there, three miles from town, riding straight toward it. He passed close. I saw him shoot with a revolver a buzzard that was then half a mile from him."

"You fool!" said the captain. "How could a revolver kill at a thousand yards?"

"It was a distance that you would not believe. It was The Wolf. I knew him by what I had heard. I knew him by his shooting. By the way he stands in his stirrups. By the breadth of his shoulders. By a coldness that leaped suddenly through my heart, as though the devil from an icy hell suddenly had gone by me."

The captain snorted with satisfaction. "He says the truth. The fool has ventured into the midst of Mexico again . . . and this time he is ours!"

Ten minutes later, a gendarme hurried into a room where half a dozen villainous-looking fellows were lounging, taking their ease in the drinking room of the *fonda,* paying no bills, regardless of money. The land was theirs, for they were the *rurales,* hardest-riding, most desperate-minded policemen that ever wandered over the face of a wild land in the name of law and order.

They looked with a good deal of mild contempt upon the excited gendarme, until he cried out: "The Wolf! He has come!"

"The Wolf!" cried out every voice, and they leaped to their feet, and reached for their weapons as though Tyler at that very moment were about to break through the door and rush upon them, breathing sulphurous fires.

"The Wolf!" they repeated, staring at one another.

"No, *amigos,*" their officer said, "we shall see. He has made fools of the gendarmes many and many a time before this day, but, if our good luck has brought him actually to Patos del Oro, I tell you that this is a golden time, indeed, for all of us. For there are tens of thousands of *pesos* to be had for his head. *Amigos,* it is our fortune that you have heard."

VI

"A Garden"

Just on the edge of the town of Patos del Oro, there was a big house that turned its back to the road. It had a broad, high-shouldered back, but its front was quite pleasant with its heavily pillared arcade that opened upon a garden, running down to the river. In the center of that garden was a water lily canal that went down, step by step, to the verge of the river. Here was built a strong but open fence, the posts of which were sharpened at the top to keep intruders from climbing over. The garden had much privacy; there was the glimmer of the flowing river beyond the fence, and on either hand were walls fifteen feet high, built ponderously of the sun-dried bricks of adobe.

In the midst of this garden sat Miguel Cambista, his face more swollen and reddened than usual, and El Tigre himself, who was now brushing the tips of his fingers across his short mustache and smiling as though the hairs of the mustache were tickling his skin. But very little of the smile got up into his round cat-like eyes, the pupils of which were continually enlarging and dwindling, not so much because the light of the day softened toward evening, as with the changes in his own thoughts.

"This is about the right time," Cambista said.

"We can wait a while longer," said El Tigre.

Cambista grunted. He was accustomed to speaking and having his word accepted as law by those about him, but he realized that his host was a greater man than he had ever been. The fortunes of El Tigre were comparatively low, to be sure, but they were not nearly so low as those of Miguel Cambista. El Tigre was still a household word through a great part of Mexico and, although his fame had been dimmed to such a point that he actually dared to take a house in town like Patos del Oro, still he had not fallen into the obscurity that had overtaken Cambista. The latter, therefore, lighted another cigar, grunted once more, and settled more deeply into his chair.

"How do you feel now, Miguel?" El Tigre asked, watching the other with a slow turning of his bright eyes. "Now that the time has come? Now that he is going to be ours?"

"Tyler?"

"D'you think that I'm talking of the man in the moon?"

"As for Tyler, I'll believe that he's ours, when I see the knife blade go through his heart and the blood jump out for one beat, then stop pulsing!" Cambista struck his plump hand on the garden table to emphasize the point that he had made.

"He is ours," El Tigre assured the other, "as nearly as any trap can make a wild beast a captive before it actually has closed upon him. Consider this . . . the gendarmes are searching for him . . . and those madmen, the *rurales,* are watching for him, too. We don't need to lift our hands, for a while, because the others will surely be on the look-out."

"The whole town is roused, and that's bad," said Cambista. "You can't expect a crowd like that to catch Tyler. He'll only be all the more warned."

"That may be," El Tigre agreed, "but many hands make light work."

"Too many cooks spoil the broth," said Cambista.

"You'll see," El Tigre stated, veiling those keen eyes of his for a moment, as he looked down at his slender hands.

"Oh, I know that everything has been done that can be done," agreed Cambista. "Only, I mean to say that my own confidence is pretty well seasoned with doubt. I had him in my hands as you never did, El Tigre."

"You did," El Tigre remarked. "But he dared to come into the same room where I was with my men. I tell you, Cambista, when I think of that my heart stops. I choke with anger!"

"Don't speak of anger," Cambista warned. "If you had seen San Andreas asleep in the sun, a pretty village with good pasture all about it for the horses, and the people working like slaves for me . . . if you could have seen the strength of that position, and how I could work from it, descending out of the mountains, here and there, to strike where I pleased . . . and then to think that one man came, as he did, and took me out of my own house, from the crowd of my own fighting men, and carried me away and gave me over to my worst enemy!" He groaned, and struck the knuckles of his fist against his forehead.

"I understand," El Tigre said. He laughed a little, the sound being a mere mirthless whisper. "How did you get away from Tyler?" he asked.

"He promised, if I guided him out of the house, he would not touch me. And he kept the promise."

"He wants no blood," El Tigre said, slowly nodding his head over his words. "You would think that a man like that would have fifty dead men behind him. But not Tyler. He prefers, it seems, to break a man's great name, and then let him live to think of what he used to be and is no more." He gritted his sharp teeth together. Then, jumping up from the table, he exclaimed: "This is time enough! I'll bring him out!"

He passed into the house and left Cambista to walk up and down, chewing his cigar.

Presently Cambista heard a slow, dragging step, and saw El Tigre come out of the house, walking a little behind a tall young man with a pale face, his hands held together with handcuffs before his body, the length of his stride limited by a chain hobble. Cambista turned and regarded the latter with an almost fatherly eye of pleasure. They came nearer.

"This is my friend, Cambista, whom I told you of," said El Tigre. "Cambista, this is Harry Champion. *Señor* Champion, you know, is that so dear friend of Jim Tyler."

Cambista grinned. "Very happy to see you, *señor*," he said, shifting his cigar across his wide, thick-lipped mouth. "Very pleased. Sit down, *Señor* Champion."

The young man sat in the third chair. He rested his chained hands on the edge of the table and looked undauntedly from one face to the other. Evil as was the expression of Cambista, it was nothing compared to the feline cruelty of El Tigre.

"We have news for you, Champion," El Tigre announced.

"Thanks," answered Harry Champion. He closed his eyes, as one wearied of torments, and leaned back in his chair. The corner of his mouth sagged. Physically he was sick, and clearly he was sick at heart, also.

"Leon!" El Tigre cried loudly.

A voice answered, and approached, panting with haste. Before them appeared a broad-faced butcher of a man with the scarred look of a pirate who has seen service on every sea. He gave to the prisoner a leer of hatred and malice.

"Tell me, Leon," said the master of the house, "what the last news is in the town?"

"They have held a meeting of the chief men of the town," Leon answered, grinning. "And they have raised a purse of five thousand *pesos* more for a reward for the capture of *Señor* Tyler." He laughed and suddenly paused in his laughter, his face going savage. "Perhaps I shall have a part of that reward, one of these days," he said with a snarl.

Harry Champion rose slowly to his feet and stood entranced. "Tyler! Who says that Tyler is here?"

El Tigre drew in his breath and made a sound as though he were drinking delicious wine noisily. "Oh, yes! He is here, Champion. He is here to save you, *señor!* He has come down here from his own country all on your account, my dear young friend."

"He wouldn't!" protested Champion. "He knows that the whole country would turn out to capture him. It can't be that Jim Tyler is fool enough to come."

"You'll see for yourself," El Tigre assured. "We are keeping a close watch on *Señorita* Flores's house." Champion swore, but El Tigre merely laughed. "Better and better. Of course, she is the final bait," he added. "You are the chief bait, my dear young friend. I told you in the beginning that you were nothing to us, except that we do not like to see Mexico disgraced by the marriage of one of her beauties to a *gringo* dog. But you, Champion, are little or nothing to us, as I said before. You are only part of the bait to draw your famous friend down into our waiting arms."

Cambista broke in: "The *rurales* and the gendarmes are already hunting, Champion. Your friend has been seen almost at the edge of the town."

"He'll turn back," Champion insisted, "when he sees that everybody is roused and ready for him."

"Are you such a fool as that?" El Tigre asked, curiously rather than passionately. "Do you actually believe that once he has put his hand to any work, he'll draw back because it's dangerous? Don't you realize what he is?"

"He's not a madman!" exclaimed Champion.

El Tigre thrust forward his head a little. "That is what he is," he said, speaking with such deliberation that his teeth glistened. "He is a madman, and his mania is danger. The greater the danger, the better he likes it. The more certain he becomes that the town is prepared against him, the more determined he will be to take you safely out of Patos del Oro. But before he manages that, if we cannot trap him either at the house of Flores or at this house, then Cambista and I, with the *rurales* and the gendarmes to assist us . . . what fools are we, *amigo?* I tell you this . . . go back to your cellar room and taste the pleasure of it. Your friend is about to die for you, *señor.* Perhaps, if we are very kind, we may let you die together."

VII

"The Old Convent"

Tyler went down the river with short, easy strokes of the paddle. It was not in this fashion that he had learned to give power to a boat up there in the wilds of Canada, where men know white water and how to knife into it with arrow-like speed. But he was not in Canada, now, and well he knew it.

He was in Mexico, old Mexico, and nearing the town of Patos del Oro, just in the midst of it, and sliding slowly under the thick shadows of its bridges. He must not act other than as one of the regular watermen who paddled up and down that river, taking the central current as they went down and tugging at their paddles in the shore shallows as they worked their way up the stream. He, being now on his way down the current of the Río Patos, steered well out in the middle of the stream. It was better there because he was farther from curious eyes along the shore, and well he knew that all eyes would be curious, on this night. Not for nothing had he lain in covert all that afternoon, moving hardly more than a snake moves and in the same manner. He had heard enough, and he knew that his coming was announced.

How, he could not tell. His keen memory could unravel, one by one, all of the events of the afternoon, but still he could not find the point at which he had betrayed himself. It was very strange, very mysterious. Still, this was pre-eminently the land of mystery. He loved it for that very quality, and the poison in its beauty was the thing that made his head go higher and that brightened his eyes.

They would have a hard time, now, picking him out as a stranger, particularly as a *gringo,* as he made his way down the stream, handling the canoe perfectly, never removing the paddle from the water in his strokes. He was stripped to the waist. His body was darkened with walnut stain until it was solid brown-black above the hips. And his hair, that he wore rather long, was pulled down over his eyes, in the exact fashion of the boatmen of Patos del Oro who prided themselves upon their ruffian appearance.

It was the time of day that he loved the most, for it was the very death of the sun's light. There was only a trace of color in the sky, only a shimmer of gold in the flats of the river. It was the time when owls come out to hunt, when creeping beasts of prey slide out from their dens and study the air, intent on the work of the night and the call of hunger. A cry was going up from his own soul, the cry for action, great heart-filling action, peril that would embrace and thrill all his nerves.

As he gave his powerful, sinewy shoulder to

the forward thrust, leaning his weight against the handle of the paddle with a fine and rhythmic sway, it seemed to Jim Tyler that this was one of the most perfect moments of his existence. He had on the cotton trousers of a *peon*, rolled up to the knees. His feet and legs were also bare, and also deeply stained with the walnut juice. There was only one adornment, and that was a heavy sash of deep yellow and black that he wore knotted about his waist. The boatmen wore just such a garment, partly for show, partly because it keeps the stomach warm when the river mist turned cold on the wings of a rising wind. Inside of that sash, he wore a single Colt revolver, carried at a slant among the folds, and necessarily so because its barrel was a full three inches longer than the standard size. He had, also, a good knife that was of his own invention — that is to say, it had once been a Bowie knife, but he had with his own hands filed out the curve of the back and converted it into a straight blade a good bit shorter than the beautifully curving original, but perfectly straight and sharp and a razor on both sides. It was literally as sharp, because he himself had honed and ground it, so that he could actually shave with the instrument. It was a treasure that he seldom used, but, when he needed it, it would be able to melt through flesh and bone as through tallow. There was a .45 caliber bullet buried in the butt of it, to give it just the perfect balance for throwing.

These two weapons were all that he carried

with him, and all that he expected to need. Arrayed against him now, as he well knew, were all the rifles and the revolvers, the knives and the stilettos of that fighting body of townsmen. It was well that it should be so. He felt that the odds were not too great. They knew that he was here, but perhaps they did not know where he expected to spring. He must count upon that.

Down the river, on the left hand, was the house of Flores, the father of the girl who had taken the heart of Harry Champion. He must see that girl, if possible, and, therefore, he must break into her father's house. That should not be altogether too difficult, unless the place were watched. He would take nothing for granted.

That afternoon, studying his map of the town with the greatest care, he had been able to distinguish the Flores house. It had been a convent in the old days. Now it was taken over as a private dwelling, and perhaps an air of sanctity clung to the Flores family because of the nature of the building that they were occupying. He smiled a little as he thought of this. He had his own judgment of the Flores girl, at least.

He saw the rising of a dark finger on the left bank, a finger that cast from the west a dim shadow out upon the flat of the river near the bend. That should be the bell tower of the church of the old convent. He regarded the place more closely, then nodded his head, content. That was the house of Flores beyond any doubt. So, with a swerve of his paddle, he slid the canoe out of the central current and cut it across toward the shore.

He looked straight before him, paddling smoothly, lazily. But all the while, from the corner of his eyes, he was studying the shore with the keenest interest and noting how the wall stood a little short of the water; how the base of the wall was crowded with shrubs; and how there was a flight of landing steps that went down into the river, with rusted iron rings at the sides of it to which boat lines could be tied. It was a big wall, breathing its age, irregular of surface, the sort of wall that his bare hands and feet could climb, he told himself.

When he was close, a dark shadow of a man was distinguishable in the brush, just as he had checked his canoe with a backstroke of the paddle.

"Who is there?" asked a gruff voice.

Ah, how much that diminished his chances, if they were waiting and on guard for him at the house of Flores? He saw the long, dull gleam of the increasing moonlight on the barrel of a rifle.

"She has sent you, Bernardo, eh?" Tyler shouted. "She has sent you to badger me, eh? Then go home and tell her that I've done with her. I'll never make another appointment. I'll first see her. . . ." He stopped short in this speech, growled out in guttural Mexican, and, putting his strength into the stroke, as though in furious vexation, he made the canoe jump ahead like a restless horse. In a moment he was around the point.

"Someone was looking for his sweetheart," he heard a voice say from the brush, and two men chuckled. But Jim Tyler was not in a laughing mood. Around the corner of the bend he drifted ahead, letting a canoe strongly paddled by three pairs of hands shoot past him, upstream, cutting with a whisper through the flat of the shallows. When it was around the curve, he scanned the surface of the water, saw that there was no other craft in sight, and ducked the prow of his canoe in against the bank. He was out of it instantly and stepped in under the shadows of the great, round-headed cypresses. Low brush grew under them. In that brush he buried the canoe, and sat down on the top of it to get his breath back completely and to think matters over.

The house of Flores was guarded. This indicated that such active brains were pitted against him that, the moment his presence near the town was known, it was guessed why he had come — for Champion. He snapped his fingers, but made no sound in doing so. Yes, they must know that he had come for Champion, and that he might try to pick up the trail of the missing man by getting in touch with the daughter of the house of Flores. Clever and quick brains were these. He nodded a silent acknowledgment of their deftness.

Then he stood up, and, passing along a few steps under the big trees, he looked up at the walls of the church side of the Flores house. It was not really a church, merely a chapel. The wall was far less imposing than was the garden wall. Suppose that he were to climb to the top, and cross the roof ridge — well, then he would be seen by the increasing moonlight that was gleaming brighter and brighter.

He might go farther up the side of the house and try to climb to one of the small, high windows. But, when he looked more closely, he saw that the window was secured on the outside by bars. Also, a man with a rifle slung in his hand strolled down the alley beside the house, reached the riverbank, paused to look around him, then slowly turned and went back again. Halfway down the wall of the old convent, he paused, and looked over his shoulder for a moment. Then he went on again.

Jim Tyler shook his head. If there were such precautions taken in the guarding of the Flores girl, what precautions were being taken in the guarding of Harry Champion, if, indeed, that poor fellow were still alive? He could wish, now, that he really had some of the qualities that the Mexicans attributed to him. Then another thought came to him and made his heart leap. If they were so particular in guarding the girl, then it meant that they feared he might learn something if he came in contact with her. They could not actually suspect him of cutting her throat, after all? Yes, it must be that they dreaded what she would say, once he spoke with her.

The instant he conceived this thought, his long, lean jaw thrust out, and a smile of iron determination curved the corners of his mouth. Enter that house he would, if he had to tunnel under the ancient foundations.

VIII

"The Moving Hand"

But, far faster than digging under the foundations, there was another way to the interior of the house of Flores. There was a bastion descending to the ground at the side of the church, a pillar that came down in several steps, the least of which was perhaps three feet and the highest eight. But that was as nothing to Jim Tyler.

He crouched there in the dark of the shadows under the tree, eager, hungry, his eyes fixed like those of a runner on the mark. When the sentinel on this side of the building had again completed his round and turned at the river and started back down the lane, Tyler began to climb. He went in such a fashion that he might well have been called a cat. If the guard, this round, turned and looked back, he could hardly fail to see the swift form that clambered up the bastion, bounding over the lower steps, taking the higher ones with hands and feet like a very cat, indeed, and so climbing, swinging, and leaping toward the top.

But the guard did not turn, and, in a few seconds, Jim Tyler lay on the flat top of the bastion, where it sank into the curve of the dome of the little chapel. Lying there, quite safe from the espial of any man on the ground, he got his breath again and, peeking over, saw that the sentinel had come to the end of the lane and was turning back. Down he came through the alley, turned back from the riverbank, reached the chapel, the very bastion on which the fugitive lay, and then turned his eye directly upward.

Jim Tyler shrank out of sight. With every nerve twitching, he heard in prospect the alarm sounded. What had the man found? A naked footprint in the road, leading toward the bastion? No, there was no call, and now the sentinel, as Tyler dared look over the edge of the stone again, was marching on down the way toward the farther street again.

Tyler shrugged his shoulders, and was instantly at his work, which was following the outer ledge that ran around the dome of the little chapel, until he came to the top of the river wall. The house was not immediately behind that wall, as he could have guessed beforehand, from his map of the town. It was simply a naked wall of stone to secure the privacy of the garden. And it was of such ample dimensions that it was three feet wide at the top. What spendthrifts were the *conquistadores* in the matter of the labor of masons. Jim Tyler laughed silently to himself with relief. It would be very hard if he could not use this both as a walk and a screen for concealment, as his desire dictated.

There was only one danger — that a guard

might have been placed to walk up and down the wall itself. One glance into the garden, however, dispelled this fear. There were stiff little evergreen hedges, making certain plots of the garden into a stiff pattern. In the centerpiece, there was the round pool of a fountain from which a tall column of spray shot up, gleaming like tarnished silver in the shadow and flashing like burnished metal in the moonlight. On a bench near this fountain pool sat two women, one old and one young. When Jim Tyler looked at the young woman with his critical eye at this distance, even the moonlight could not shield her.

"Ines Flores," he murmured.

Straightway he was down the inner side of the wall. Lurking from bush to bush, he was soon lying behind a kind of flowering cactus. The shadow from the plant striped his body with bands of darkness. The grass was cold and dank against his skin, but, by merely lifting his head, he could see the two speakers, and he could hear their every whisper.

The older one was apparently the *duenna;* she was huddled into what looked like the dark robe and hood of a monk of another age, a squat, shapeless figure against the sheen of the fountain pool. She was occupied now in smoking a cigarette, which she held like a Chinaman holding his opium pipe, between thumb and forefinger, with the palm of the hand turned inward. She inhaled the draft of the smoke deeply, and blew it forth luxuriously, in three or four puffs, into the brilliant moonlight. She was saying: "A woman may be young several times, but she can afford to be foolish, only once."

Jim Tyler listened, raising his eyebrows. This was the pure Castilian, not the ordinary tongue of Mexico.

The girl turned her head, and Jim Tyler told himself that all photographs are foolish liars. The camera could show the perfection of the features, but it never could describe in any way the pride in the carriage of the head and the bright flash of the eyes. He revised his previous opinion of her in an instant. She was worthy of a second thought and of a long one.

"How can a woman be young several times?" the girl asked.

"She is young," said the *duenna,* "in the first place, when she is a green girl and knows nothing. She is young, in the second place, when she has been in love once and recovered from the foolish fancy. She is young again when she has buried a husband and mourned through the appointed time. She may be young still later on, but she can be foolish only once. You, Ines, have already been foolish once. Most certainly there is no room in your life to be foolish again."

"When was I so foolish?" Ines Flores asked.

"There was the young American. Not that I reproach you with that," said the *duenna*. "If a girl is young enough, any creature that can be called a man will take a woman's eye, and, after her eye has been taken, it is only a step before her heart is captured, also. I suppose that you're over the infatuation, though, by now?"

"Quite," said the girl. "I was simply a silly young fool. I know that. After all, though, he was a little different. He was bold, and he talked well. But now I hardly ever think of him."

If she had said no, and left it at that, the listener thought to himself, *I would have believed her. But she protests too much, as the play says. I put my money that she still is mad about Harry Champion. And that means that the game is not all lost.*

Puffing at her cigarette and half closing her eyes, because the heat of the coal was rapidly approaching to her face and sending up its strong fumes, the old woman spoke: "I could have guessed that before. You would have to be a very deep girl to keep your face so calm and your eyes so steady, after his disappearance, if you cared about him, at all."

"Cared about him?" Ines Flores said. And then she laughed softly. It tingled in the ears of the eavesdropper, that laughter. "If I'd cared about him," continued the girl, "do you think that I would be sitting here, laughing? Oh, no, I'm ready to forget him. I was ready the second or third time that I saw him because, after all, I realized that he was not one of our people."

"True," said the other. "I think that I have a part in that answer, Ines."

"Of course, you have," said the girl. "I never would have had such thoughts, except that I've had you about me, María, and so I could see what it was to have the true, old Castilian blood."

The *duenna* puffed out her chest with a deep breath. "Perhaps I have meant something in this house," she said.

"Something? You have given me a new mind, and that's the truth," Ines said.

There was a growing excitement in the heart of Jim Tyler. He half lifted himself to one knee and stared through the fronds of the big cactus plant at Ines Flores. For it seemed to him, suddenly, that he was hearing lying of such an expertness as he rarely before had listened to in his life.

"My dear girl, my dear child," María said. There she paused, but her breast was still heaving with pleasure.

Her charge now turned to pick up an end of her shawl and pull it over her shoulder, to guard against the chill of the night air. At that moment, her glance lifted from the ground behind her and was fixed beyond it on the big cactus. Behind that plant, her glance was arrested. She saw a hand moving. Plainly it was a signal. She gave a hardly perceptible start. Then she turned back toward the older woman.

Jim Tyler was thinking to himself: *She is true, honest, brave, and quick of wit. I was a fool to judge her as I did.*

Presently she was saying: "I'll go to get you another cup of coffee, María."

"Stay here, child, and I'll get it for myself."

"No, let me go."

"We had better both go in," said the other. "The air is filling with the river damp."

"Oh, you go in if you please," said the girl. "But I'll walk here for a moment, if you don't mind. Because I've had no exercise at all today."

"True," María said. "I'll go in, then, and mind that you're not long, my dear?"

"No, I won't be long."

"Otherwise, the American wolf may come and fly away with you."

"I've heard a great deal about him," said the girl, "but I don't suppose that *Señor* Tyler could jump over the river wall, could he?"

María laughed. "I suppose not," she said. "I'll go in and get the coffee, then. If you wish, my dear, you may stay out her for just a few moments. You may walk up and down, as you say, and fill your lungs with air. Of course, there's no harm in that. Are you sure that you're wrapped warmly enough?"

"Oh, quite."

"Very well, then. I'll call you in a little while." And down the path swayed and shuffled the form of the robed old woman.

IX

"Again the Cat"

The girl rose at the same time, and, as the *duenna* disappeared, she began to pace up and down beside the fountain. Passing the cactus bush the second time, she said, in a low voice, but perfectly audible to the man concealed behind it: "The house is guarded in every part. How have you dared to come here, *Señor* Tyler?"

A chill went through his flesh and blood.

"What makes you think that I am *Señor* Tyler?" he demanded in flawless Spanish.

"Because," she said, "nobody else under the sun would dare to come in this place at this time. I know it well."

He rose to his knees, and, coming closer to the fronds of the cactus, he was able to look through to see her more clearly; and she could see, in turn, as she moved back and forth, the moonlight on that hawk-like face of his, so grim and so eager.

"You could be seen from the wall," she said, moving back from the fountain, never raising her voice or altering her pace.

"There are always some chances to be taken," he said.

"This is a strange and wonderful thing," she said.

"It is," he answered. "Because I never dreamed that I would ever find a woman so much the master of herself."

"I am not master of myself," she answered. "I am shaking with fear."

"So much the better," he said. "Because you keep yourself in hand. How long have we to talk before the old dragon comes back?"

"She? About ten minutes. Perhaps a little less. She is like a new mother bird on a nest and she won't leave me long."

"You hate her," Tyler said with satisfaction.

"The spying, wretched, mouthing hypocrite," the girl said, keeping her voice as calm as smoothly running water. "Of course, I hate her, and, therefore, I lie to her. *Señor* Tyler, you have not come to talk to me about her."

"I come for Harry Champion's sake," he admitted.

She faltered for one step, and her face went up so that the moonlight flowed in a steep, bright tide over it. Then she went on. "For Harry Champion's sake," she said, and nodded her head.

"I've come to ask you questions."

"About him?"

"Yes."

"Ask them, *señor*."

"Will you answer?"

"Since you have dared to come at such a time,

to such a place, for such a purpose, I shall answer if I had to write the words in blood."

"Good," Tyler said, staring at her narrowly. "I almost believe what you say. In the first place, what has become of him?"

"He lost some money at the roulette wheel, and he's disappeared to get money to pay his debt. He'll be back soon."

"He's gone clear to the States to get money?"

"No, I suppose that he's written, but he's ashamed to show himself until he's paid off the debt."

"How much is that debt?"

"Three thousand *pesos.*"

"Do you think that would make him disappear?"

"Well, he's very proud."

"How long ago did you hear from him last?"

"Fifteen days ago." She said it instantly, as swiftly as a mother is able to give the day of her child's birth.

"For fifteen days you've not heard a word from him?"

"Not one word."

"Before that you heard from him every day, I suppose?"

"Yes, every day." She said it readily, but in her accent he could detect the suppressed excitement.

"Then tell me, *señorita,* if he warned you before he left?"

"No, *señor.*"

"Not one word that he was going away?"

"Not one word."

"And still you think that he disappeared only until he could get money to pay a gambling debt?"

"He was very proud!"

"He *was* very proud? Then you fear that he's dead."

She kept on walking up and down, but he saw the swift contraction of her hand to a small fist that gleamed as white as stone in the pallid moonlight.

"God forgive me," she whispered. "I fear that he is dead."

"By foul play, *Señorita* Flores?"

"How can I tell?"

"Through whose foul play?"

"I don't know."

"Someone that you know, then?"

She was silent.

"You are afraid," Tyler persisted, "that someone in your family put young Harry Champion out of the way. Confess that."

"I cannot confess a thing that I don't know," she said.

"Confess it," he urged. "Have you any brothers living?"

"No, I never have had any brothers."

"An uncle?"

"He is old and keeps to his house."

"Your father is living?"

"Yes."

"Then you think that your father has caused Harry Champion to disappear?"

"I've not said that," she answered.

"But you think it," he insisted.

A moan came from her throat, and her head went back again a little. He said rapidly: "*Señorita,* I am here to help you. You love my friend Champion. I love him, also. I am here to save him, if he is still alive. I must know whatever you know. What makes you think that there is a finger of suspicion pointing toward your father?"

She shook her head. "How could I talk of such a thing?" she demanded.

"You forget," he said, "that every minute I spend inside of this garden adds to his danger."

"It is true," said the girl. "I know it, and I am ungrateful if I don't tell everything that I know. I shall tell you, then, no matter what it costs."

"Good," he said. "This is the way that I expected to hear you talk."

"It was in this way," she said. "*Señor* Champion had seen me several times. He came one day to ask my father if he might pay his addresses to me. My father was in a fury. He was polite, but enraged. He does not like the men of your country, *Señor* Tyler."

"No more than I like the men of his . . . most of 'em," Tyler said calmly. "Go on. There are no feelings that can be wounded in this, *señorita.*"

"My father was polite," she insisted, "but he asked *Señor* Champion not to come again. That very night, he called under my window."

"That's all right," said Tyler. "But did you answer him?"

She was trembling. "I tried not to," she said. "But I had to speak. Yes, I went and answered him from behind the bars of my window."

"You have the barred window that looks out on the lane?"

"How did you know that?"

"No matter. Go on."

"The next morning, my father's face was white iron, and I knew that he had been told how I had spoken with *Señor* Champion during the night. He said nothing of it to me. But that same day he brought home that dragon of a *duenna* whom you saw with me. This is the first moment she has left me alone."

"Go on," Tyler persuaded.

"It was two days later. I had seen Harry from the window, but that was all. I dared not do more than make a sign to him, because there was always the woman with me, the spy. Then, I went out riding one day with her. She had stopped a moment with her horse at a runlet of water, for fear of splashing herself with mud. I rode on. We were near the edge of the town. A door opened, and I saw two men on the threshold of a house. They saw me, also, and suddenly drew back, and the door closed. One of them was my father." She stood still, not speaking for several moments. It was plain that she had recalled a frightful moment. Then she continued: "I felt that there was death in the very air I breathed, as I rode on."

The voice of María called very loudly: "Now, my love. Now, my child, Ines!"

"I am coming! One more turn," said the girl.

And the hidden man asked eagerly: "You saw your father. Who was the second man?"

"I never saw him before. He was not very tall. But he looked light and quick and terrible."

"How did he look terrible?"

"I don't know. I can't describe him. Only, he seemed terrible to me."

"At least, where did he live?"

"On the edge of the town, down the river, on this same bank. I think that it's the last house of all. I'm not quite sure."

"Ines! Ines!" the *duenna* called impatiently.

"Only while I take one more breath, dear María!" Ines called in answer.

"Try once more," Tyler encouraged. "What did the man look like who was with your father?"

"I don't know. There are no words for him. He looked like a cat."

"Like what?"

"I know it sounds absurd. But I mean it. His face was round, but not soft. His eyes were round, too, but they were bright with a beastly intelligence."

"Did he have a short cropped mustache?"

"I don't know. Yes, there was, I thought, a slight shadow on his upper lip."

"Ah," murmured Jim Tyler. "I know where Harry Champion is to be found, then, dead or alive. And I know the name of his keeper."

X

"The Password"

"There is one more question I must ask," he said. "If I manage to find Champion, if he's alive, and if I get him free from whatever trouble he's in, what does that mean to you?"

"Ines!" called the old woman at the door.

"Yes, María."

"Quickly, though!" came the angry call.

"It means," Ines said, answering his question, "more than the whole world, my people, my fortune, and all!"

"*Adiós,* then," Tyler said, satisfied.

She turned straightway toward the house, and Jim Tyler heard María scolding her charge and the calm voice of the girl saying something about the pure, fresh air of the night, never had she seen a night half so lovely. Then she disappeared. An instant later, as María closed the door, Tyler heard her exclaiming something, over loudly, about romantic young fools.

Well, she was young, she was romantic, perhaps, but she was certainly not a fool. As he lay there for another moment, considering his plans, the sense of exultation again swept through him. For he saw that these two people were worth a great effort. As for the danger, that in itself was the intoxicating wine that he loved for its own sake. Now speed, speed, speed.

He slunk back as he had come, from bush to bush, moving as carefully as though every one of the lighted or darkened windows of the big house shielded eyes that were staring out at him.

When he came to the wall again, he considered it for an instant and then saw that he had a difficult feat of climbing before him. It had been not hard to descend, but it would be very difficult, indeed, to get up. However, there was the angle between the garden wall and the chapel. He braced his back against the latter, and then began to worm his way up. Half a dozen times he paused, wedging himself with knees and elbows, his shoulders flattened against the chapel wall. Eyes closed, lungs heaving, he drew in enough of the pure oxygen to refresh him, and on he went again.

When he got to the top of the wall, however, he lay flat on his back, with his arms stretched above his head. A wind was rising, and the chill of the river mist was blowing with it, but this was of slight moment to him. His muscles were free and relaxed from all aching weariness. That was the important thing. He would have need of everything that he possessed in the way of agility and strength before the long night was finally over, perhaps.

When he started moving forward again, he had recovered from the immense effort of climbing the wall, although he was shuddering from head to foot with cold. He went along the top of the wall as before, rounded the side of the chapel, and lay stretched out again on top of the buttress that had given him shelter and a spy's position before this.

The sentinel was still at his post, walking up and down the alley, more dimly seen now, through the fog that rolled in from the river, and the night was turning weird as the moonlight made the upper fog luminous as pearl, with the tops of the big trees thrusting up in black tangles toward the sky. He waited for the guard to turn at the riverbank and pass up toward the alley, then he began his descent.

He was halfway down when an edge of stone coping, broken through and loosened by the work of winter cold and summer heat, suddenly gave way under his left hand. He swung by the right hand only, dangling perilously out over the ground, while the fragment hurtled down, rebounded from a lower step, and struck the alley with a thud.

Instantly the voice of the guard called out: "Who's there? What's that?"

It was too late to start climbing up again; there was no shelter behind which he could hide; and, therefore, Tyler began to go down as fast as he could manage the descent. Like a great monkey, he went leaping and sliding to the ground. As he swung outward for the last leap, a rifle rang at his very ear, as it seemed to him, and a bullet hissed in the air.

But there he was on the ground, and the guard, leaping back to get to a little safer distance, was jerking the rifle to his shoulder for a finishing shot. Tyler drew and fired, aiming low, and saw the other topple sidewise with a yell. Not one yell only, but scream on scream for help.

Tyler leaped for the trees from which he had come, changed his mind, dashed down the alley a little distance, then turned sharply off to the side down a path that went between brush on the one hand and garden wall on the other.

Behind him, it seemed that Patos del Oro awoke like an army at a signal from a trumpet. Still that trumpet was pealing, as the hurt man in the alley screeched for help, in fear of his life. He had a bullet through his right thigh — that was all. Nothing would happen to him of any serious import so long as the wound was looked to before he bled to death, but it was sheer terror that inspired those screams, and they roused scores of answers.

Doors slammed here and there behind the vague mistiness of the white fog. Men shouted. A gun exploded in some rash hand. There were rapid footfalls everywhere.

But Tyler no longer cared. Instead, he went forward with a long and steady stride.

Two men leaped forward, and seemed to be rushing straight at him. Instead, they swerved aside from this tall, gaunt, half-naked form and hurried on toward the tumult that was closing in

305

behind Tyler, drawing to a point very rapidly. From that gathering point of danger and noise, the search would begin and spread outward for him through every corner of Patos del Oro.

They would spot him, he could guess, and he groaned with disappointment to think that his excellent disguise was so quickly wasted. They would surely guess, of course, that the tall, wide-shouldered, shaggy-haired man descending from the chapel was, in fact, himself. They would look inside the garden of the house of Flores, and there they were sure to see the imprint of his naked foot at least once or twice in the soft loam. And all because luck had been against him in taking a hold on what had seemed a perfectly sound and massively strong stone.

Where could he go now to find shelter from the search? Half naked as he was, he was sure to be more easily spotted than if he had worn almost any sort of clothes. After all, his build was not that of the average Indian. They might be as tall, but they were not likely to have such width of shoulders, such spindling hips. He must get, as rapidly as possible, to that place in town where he would be least expected. And what could that place be, when he might be expected anywhere?

He could give thanks for one thing, at least, and that was for the river fog that thickened now under the moon and was rolling all through the streets of Patos del Oro. Running forward again through this mist, he went down the street of houses that backed against the river. Trees lined that road, huge trees in whose leaves the mist was congealing to water, and dropping in a slow rain to the dust beneath. A bad night for the comfort of a half naked man, but a good night for an elusive spy to wander about. Suddenly the houses stopped. He turned back. That one to the rear must be, according to the story of the girl, the same place in which she had seen her father standing at the door with the cat-faced man — El Tigre, he would lay his money.

And if El Tigre was there, he must enter and find the man. Yes, if El Tigre was there, Champion might be there, also, alive or dead. But how was he to enter?

He looked up, saw only three small windows, high up, and all of these barred. At the same time, he heard footfalls as if many men were sweeping down the street. He looked back and saw lanterns dimly gleaming and swinging. He did not hesitate. Before the house was one of those trees from which the mist was distilling, and now he laid his hand on the smooth bark and shook his head. No man could climb that huge trunk, now varnished over.

Off to the side, however, nine or ten feet from the ground, a branch dipped down with a sharp elbow. He ran forward, bounded high up, and in a moment he was secure, lying out along one of the great main boughs of the tree. There he stretched himself, his hands flung forward, and his legs straight out. If men looked very carefully up from the side, it might be barely possible for them to find him. Otherwise, he was posted just over what he took to be the door of El Tigre's house.

Under that tree went a mob of twenty searchers, talking loudly together, swinging their lanterns from side to side, almost as though they expected to find their quarry hidden under the dust of the street.

Jim Tyler smiled with scorn. It was not of a crowd that he had any real fear. Single men of brains and courage were the antagonists worth watching. From the rear of that running crowd, a man detached himself. As they moved on, he stepped to the door that was just beneath the watcher, raised the knocker, and let it fall with a brazen clanking sound. The door was pulled open instantly.

"Who's there?" growled a voice.

"A friend of the *señor*."

"How am I to know that?"

"By the bad weather," said the man in the street.

"Bad weather?" echoed the other.

"Aye, for the spring of the year."

"Well, come in," the man of the house said, and the other was admitted.

XI

"On the Bough"

There was no doubt in Jim Tyler's mind that he had overheard a password, and the instant the thought occurred to him he shuddered partly with fear and partly with pleasure. For he could not resist the feeling that he might be using that same phrase, sooner or later, to make his way into the house.

This thought had hardly come to him when the door beneath him opened again, and he heard the mounting hum of several voices. In the hall, a dull glow of light showed him that face which he most detested in all the world, the cat-like face of El Tigre. But he started and almost exclaimed aloud when he saw at the shoulder of the brigand the swollen jowls of Miguel Cambista. Cambista this far south, and with El Tigre!

Well, there were certain qualities and emotions in common between the pair of them. For one thing, they were both outlawed; still more important, they had in common a vast hatred for Tyler. No doubt it was this feeling that drew them together. With them was a fellow wearing a long cloak that covered him against the chill of the fog from head to foot.

"Walk up and down here before the house, Juan," said the voice of El Tigre. "But do more standing than walking. You have your guns?"

"A revolver, *señor,* and a sawed-off shotgun slung around my neck. I think that would do the business even of *Señor* Tyler."

"If you shoot, use both barrels," El Tigre ordered. "He has nine lives, I suppose, but I think that seven of them have been used up before this. Use both barrels, and make sure."

"Do you think, *señor,*" said the man, "that he would be fool enough to come to your house on a night like this?"

"What do you think yourself, Juan?" Cambista asked.

"Why, I think that he's been scared into some hole in the ground by this time. Perhaps he's slipped into the river and floated off down the stream."

"With the whole town roused against him, perhaps that would be the wisest thing to do, eh, Juan?" El Tigre said.

"Of course," said the other.

"However," Cambista interjected, "that's not what the *Señor* Tyler will do. He'll stay in town."

"And make himself invisible, then, *señor?*" asked Juan.

"He can do that, too, I suppose. Anything is possible for the devil, Juan. Mind you, stand more than you walk. Keep your eyes wide open. Walk when you feel yourself growing chilled, and look both up and down. He may drop out of the sky or that nearby tree, for instance." So saying, El Tigre stepped out from the house, bringing a lamp from the hall, and that lamp he raised above his head.

Tyler flattened himself more closely against the huge bough. Above him, a drip of water began to splash noisily between his bare shoulders. He trembled lest that sound should attract the sensitive ear of the great El Tigre. But, after all, it would be only the same sound as the drip of water upon the smooth bark of the bough.

"That tree ought to be searched?" said El Tigre.

"Come, come, man," scoffed Cambista's gruff voice. How the oil seemed to bubble and gurgle in his throat as he spoke. "Come, come, El Tigre, how could any man climb up a trunk like that?"

"Perhaps not," El Tigre agreed. "But still. . . ." He carried his light about the tree. Its brightness seemed to the hunted man greater than the glare of the sun. Then, he was tempted also by a frightful desire to draw his revolver and make sure of these principal scoundrels with two well-placed bullets. The imp of the perverse rose into his throat. In a half second, he could kill them both. To miss was impossible for him, at such a distance. He could afford to shoot for the head, knowing that he could not fail. It would be fatal for him, of course. Out of that dark hall, no doubt, other men would pour. But his own life was not the only consideration. There was the man for whom he had made this long journey; there was Harry Champion, now somewhere in that house, unless he missed his guess very badly. So he lay still, fighting against the raging of his nerves, for the desire to kill was taking him by the throat and shaking him.

"There's a branch that a man might catch and climb into the tree," El Tigre announced suddenly.

Jim Tyler slid his hand carefully down to his revolver, and waited. It would not be a question of choice, but of necessity on his part, if someone mounted into the tree, of course.

"Too high," said the voice of Cambista. "You couldn't catch that branch. Much too high for a man to jump to it."

"Hold this lantern and I'll see," El Tigre instructed.

Presently there was a light sound of a double blow on the ground. El Tigre had leaped, apparently, and missed his mark. "I jump as well as most people," El Tigre said. "No, I don't suppose that a man could catch hold of it. Then it would be hard to swing up into the tree after taking hold."

"Too hard," Cambista stated.

"Well," El Tigre said, "one of these days I'll have that tree chopped down."

"You talk, *amigo*," Cambista chuckled, "as though you intended to live in Patos del Oro the rest of your days."

"Well, we've made a mistake, you and I, Cambista," answered the bandit. "We've lived out in the hills farther than we needed to go. And I see that the safest hiding place, as a matter of fact, is right under the nose of the town-dwelling fools. No one has troubled me here. No one will for a long time, I think, unless our friend *Señor* Tyler smells us out."

They retreated, the precious pair, to the door of the house, and stood there together, brightly illuminated by the lantern that Cambista was now holding.

Juan moved off to a little distance and stood on guard, rigidly attentive to all around him except to his masters.

The voice of El Tigre went on softly: "Everything is perfect, and everything is just as I wished to have it, except that the idiots let him get to see the girl."

"There's no proof of that," said Cambista.

"There is proof," El Tigre contradicted. "A man has just come to me to report that, when they searched the garden of the Flores house, they found three or four prints of a naked foot, and the sign that someone had lain down behind a cactus bush just beside the fountain, where the girl was with her *duenna*. Not only that, but the *duenna* confesses that she was away from her charge only two minutes, she swears, but that's enough for the girl to tell everything that she knows."

"She knows very little, El Tigre."

"Bah! I told you that she rode down this street one day, and saw her father and me standing here in the doorway. What a fool I was to come to the door that day."

"Yes, that was very foolish," agreed Cambista. "What made you do it? What in the world made you do it?"

"You won't believe what a simpleton I was. But for a moment I'd forgotten who I was . . . El Tigre, with a blood price on my head, and the rest. I thought that I was simply a host saying good bye to a guest. I calmly walked to the door with Flores and opened the door, and at that instant the girl rode into view."

"But she could not know you, El Tigre."

"Perhaps no, and perhaps yes. I know that her eyes straightened at the pair of us as though she were aiming down the barrel of a rifle. If she describes to Tyler the man she saw here with her father, you see? He'll know at once that I'm here, and, if I'm here, he'll know that I'm probably behind the disappearance of the boy. That is why we must sleep with our eyes open tonight, Cambista."

"Sleep?" Cambista questioned. "I'd as soon cut my own throat as to fall asleep when that fiend is within a hundred miles of me."

"He is worth a little attention," agreed the small man. "He shall have it, too. Something tells me, Cambista, that before morning there may be an end to a long, long story."

"To what story, man?" asked the other.

"To the story of Miguel Cambista, El Tigre, and Harry Champion, as well as the stallion, Spring of the Year, and Tyler, too." He laughed a little, as he completed this list of names.

"Where do you keep the horse?" asked Cambista.

"Not far out of the town, at a little farm where I know the farmer. He is in good condition. If I need to move from Patos del Oro, I may have to move fast, and there is Spring of the Year waiting for me." He chuckled again.

Tyler, looking down into that detested face, marked the shifting of the round, bright, inhuman eyes.

"And now, El Tigre," said his companion, "what of the boy?"

"Champion?"

"Yes."

"What do you think?"

"That it's time."

"Tonight?"

"Well, why not? There is a fog on the river. No one would be able to see, when we paddle the boat out into the river and drop the body over the side."

"It has to be sooner or later," agreed El Tigre.

"Of course, it does. And why should you keep him any longer?"

"He has served his purpose," El Tigre stated, "and Tyler is in the trap, only the teeth haven't closed over him, yet."

"All in good time," Cambista assured. "But,

first, make sure of the boy."

"You can be the executioner, Miguel."

"I don't mind that. I know how to use a gun butt . . . one tap behind the ear . . . that is enough. Or at the base of the skull. You hardly see a mark, but the man is as dead as though he had been shot through the heart."

"Clever Cambista!" El Tigre stated gleefully.

He moved backward. The door closed, and only the dim mist under the moon filled the street, like a ghostly river.

XII

"The Tiger's Den"

Never had the heart of Jim Tyler so nearly failed in its beat as it did now. His scheme had worked perfectly. He was at the appointed place, he had seen his double quarry face to face, and he had heard them speak together, confessing all that he so far had merely suspected.

It was a trap for him, the whole complicated business. Having realized that in the old days Tyler was willing to risk his life to save Harry Champion, El Tigre and Cambista had put their fine wits together and evolved this scheme. It was a good scheme, not simple, but very far-reaching. And it had worked so smoothly, so indirectly, that he had been dragged this great distance south of the Río Grande, through the country of his enemies.

But now the end was close at hand. Yonder in the house they were preparing to murder Harry Champion. At any moment the thing might be done. A burning, electric convulsion mounted to Tyler's brain. Only to pass that door, and he might be able to affect something, anything. But the door was closed, and a man stood on guard near it. What could he, Tyler, accomplish? His mouth set in a grim line. The guard, in the meantime, had turned from his post and was walking slowly down the way, passing beneath the tree.

The thought was no sooner lodged in the mind of Tyler than he acted upon it. Out of the tree like a panther he dropped, his knees aimed at the shoulders of the Mexican, the revolver held by the barrel. As he dropped, he struck with the handle of the gun at the back of the man's head.

Juan slumped to the earth in a heap, and Tyler, his face pinched with remorse, instantly put his ear to the breast of his victim. He could find no heartbeat whatever. A wave of nausea passed over him. Murder was not his way. No doubt this Juan was one of the best cutthroats in the band of El Tigre. His brutal face seemed to proclaim all the evil of which a human being is capable. Still, to strike down a man when he is helpless was a frightful thing to the proud and high-strung soul of Tyler. It was not the first time that he had struck to stun rather than to kill. Perhaps he had not gauged correctly the momentum of his drop from the tree, together with the striking power of his hand. At any rate, he must turn his back upon this grim accident. His hands, he felt, would never be clean again, so long as he lived. But now there was other important work to carry forward.

He set his jaw hard, stripped the cloak from the fallen man, lifted him easily in spite of his bulk, and carried him to the brush that grew up in a small, low thicket beyond the house. There he laid down his burden and paused to arrange the body decently, the hands folded over the breast. Before this he had killed men, but never before in such a manner. There had been fights, man to man, but this was slaughter without a fair chance.

That feeling of horror was still on him as he went back and picked up the cloak that had fallen to the ground. He had to have that, whether it belonged to a dead man or not. He swung it over his shoulders thinking grimly that the very thing he had done to poor Juan was, in fact, what Cambista had proposed to do to Harry Champion. That relieved his heart a trifle. Still he was so sick of soul that he had to pause a moment, breathing deeply of the cold, dank air, before he stepped to the door, raised the knocker, and let it fall.

Instantly, as he had seen happen before, the door was jerked open. That porter had been taught to work like an automatic spring, it appeared.

"Who's there?" asked the man who was half lost in the darkness.

"A friend in bad weather," Tyler stated, forgetting exactly how the bit of dialogue had gone before.

"A friend in bad weather? That's nothing to me," said the man of the house.

"Not even when it's the spring of the year?" asked Tyler.

And he stepped forward, assuming the confident air of one who is very sure of himself.

"The spring of the year?" said the porter. He paused. "Well," he said, "I suppose so. What's your name, though?"

"José," Tyler said.

"José who?" asked the porter.

"Why, you fool," Tyler exclaimed, although he muffled his voice, "do you think that I use my second name in Patos del Oro?"

"*Humph!*" grunted the porter. He stood at full pause, staring at the figure before his door outlined in the dimness of the moon mist. Then he added: "Are you one of the brothers?"

"Who are you," Tyler questioned, "to ask me about the brothers?"

"Well, I can give you the sign," said the porter.

"Damn the signs," Tyler cursed. "I know the brothers," he went on, venturing boldly on to certain ground, "and I've never seen your ugly face among them."

The insult and the confident bearing of this man seemed to have a good deal of effect upon the porter, for he gave back half a step, but still he kept leveled the small gun that he carried in his hand. Only now did Tyler see the gleam of the steel.

"Some of the brothers are not in the hills, however," said the porter.

"Am I to be kept here all night?" Tyler answered angrily. "Call for your master, then, and let him speak to me."

"Hah?" said the porter. "Call for him? Well! I take no chances, and you gave the word in a queer way. Wait here, if you dare to face him." With that, he stepped back, and slammed the door shut.

The movement was so quick that Tyler could not entirely forestall it. He did, however, throw out a double fold of the cloak, between the swinging edge of the door and the jamb and, although the door slammed shut heavily, he heard only a partial click of the lock. Perhaps the bolt was not really or fully caught in the slot?

He heard the footfalls inside the hallway retreating. He counted to three, then pushed against the handle. The door remained fast. Was he to wait there and face El Tigre and El Tigre's guns? He might kill the great bandit, to be sure, but that would only insure the swift murder of Harry Champion. Again he grasped the handle of the door and pressed more strongly. Suddenly it opened before him. A breath of wind entered with him, whistling about his ears, and he found himself in the hall, with no light before him except the exceedingly dull glow from a lamp whose wick had been turned very low. He shut the door with caution and made sure that this time the lock was engaged.

Voices came from the other end of the hall. There was a door at his right, and through it he glided into the pitchy blackness. Close behind the half open door he posted himself.

The voice of El Tigre was saying, in the

hallway: "Either he knew the right words, or he didn't know them. And I told you that I'd have your fool's hide off and tanned for a saddle unless you kept off everybody except the right men."

"He was one of the brothers. By his talk I could have sworn that," the porter assured in a humble voice.

"The devil take you and your brothers," El Tigre hissed. "What have the brothers to do here tonight? I sent for none of 'em."

He reached the door and jerked it open. Tyler could hear the rush of the draft. There was a breathless moment. "There's no one here," El Tigre announced.

"*¡Dios!*" exclaimed the porter.

"Are you drunk, you sheep's head?" El Tigre asked with a snarl.

"*Señor,* I swear there was a man there, a tall man, in a cloak. A tall man with big shoulders, wrapped in a very long cloak. And he spoke almost the right words. I remember him perfectly. There was no hat on his head."

"Would one of the brothers come to Patos del Oro without a hat on his head?" exclaimed the master of the house. "What sort of foolery is this, Gomez?"

Panting desperately in his fear of the master, Gomez replied: "*Señor,* it was some scoundrel, then, who did not dare to wait for your coming."

"I'll teach you not to wait for my coming, either," El Tigre spit.

"*Señor,* I swear that I have been faithful and careful in everything. He spoke and gave most of the words right, but not exactly right. I remembered what you had said. The words must be perfect, or no man must come in. I was on the verge of letting him come, and then I hesitated. He demanded to see you. I thought it would be safer. I went for you."

"Did you close the door?"

"Yes, *señor.* What do you think I would do? Go to fetch you and leave the door standing wide open, for the whole street to walk in on us?"

"I could expect anything from you," declared the master of the house. "Anything at all! Dolt of a Gomez! You closed and locked the door behind you, eh?"

"I slammed the door shut."

"True," El Tigre said. "I heard you slam it, for that matter. Well, Gomez, never let such a thing happen again. You've fumbled something, I don't know what. Tell me, just how long has that door been open?"

"Which door, *señor?*"

"That door, fool!"

"I don't know, *señor.* All the evening, I dare say."

"You dare say, do you?"

Suddenly the wick of the lamp was turned up, and a shaft of light entered the room where Tyler was standing.

XIII

"A Lowered Gun"

It seemed as though fate, like a perverse imp, were striving to make Jim Tyler choose between killing El Tigre out of hand and then saving himself from the danger of the town as well as he could, or holding back through crisis after crisis until he should have his chance to help Champion. Now, he made up his mind to do a very simple thing that, nevertheless, took more nerve power than anything he had done in all his adventurous life.

El Tigre, he foresaw, would give one glance around the room, a hasty, baffled glance, not really expecting to see anything. But the pale gleam of a face, even in that shadowy corner behind the door, would be very likely to catch his attention. Therefore, Tyler turned his face to the wall.

Behind him, there was a pause. He could not see, but he felt the movement of the lamp in the hand of the Mexican. And now, perhaps, El Tigre had seen the dark cloaked form, now he was drawing his revolver, now he was ready to press the trigger, now the report would crash against the ear of Tyler. Cold sweat drenched Tyler's face. But with all his might he held himself, moment after moment. It was only the space of three breaths, but it was like three deaths to that man who waited with his face turned to the wall.

The steps came straight toward him. Then the door closed, and the light was gone. He knew that he was saved, for this brief moment, at least, and he pressed both hands against the wall and steadied himself until the cloud lifted from his brain, and his breathing became easier. Then he set to work at once. He must not remain in that room until the porter came back from attendance on his master to wait again by the door for every summons that he answered so swiftly.

Still with an electric tremor fighting in every nerve, Tyler opened the door, softly, steadily, as a door moved when it is off the latch and the wind presses ever so gently against it.

Down the hall, there passed waves of light, as when a lamp sways slightly up and down, carried in the hand. Tyler was instantly outside the door, closing it without a sound behind him. Down the hall the light receded, the porter carrying the lamp to guide his master. Tyler followed with long, noiseless strides. He could be glad of his naked feet now; they were better and surer than softly padded slippers.

Straight out of the house went the light bearer, and Tyler glided behind the shadow of a pillar of the arcade that overlooked the long, narrow garden, leading down to the river. There he paused, flattening himself against the stone column and staring with his eyes, for before him he saw Harry Champion, in irons, hands and feet, and beside him, at the garden table, sat Miguel Cambista.

The porter turned back from his master.

"Watch that door as though it were your own heart!" El Tigre ordered the man, and the latter went back with a growled word of resolution.

The three at the table made an odd contrast. Beyond them, the garden sloped toward the palisade along the river, with the sound of the current murmuring there. The palisade itself was only just visible through the mist, and the same thin fog covered up the water lily pools that adorned the slope. Their flowers were closed now, tightly, the great blossoms being jacketed in smooth green, but the lantern light, striking down from the table, stronger than the moonlight that filtered through the mist, showed the lily pads as still as painted images on the black of the water.

Looking on this scene, a chill crept through the spirit of the watcher.

He heard El Tigre say: "This is good news, Miguel?"

"Eh?" queried the other.

"Good news! Tyler is dead!"

Tyler smiled a little, and, looking at Harry Champion, he was gratified to see that the boy had started as though a knife blade had passed through his heart.

Agape he sat, with horror in his face, and

watched his two companions exulting or pretending to exult.

"If Tyler's dead," Cambista said, "I can't tell whether to be glad or sorry. I wanted to have a hand in that."

"So did I," El Tigre confessed. "But, after all, we failed to get to the killing. The good people down here in Patos del Oro were too keen for us. Only our young friend, here, had anything to do with the finish of Tyler."

"What did I have to do?" asked Harry Champion, turning his drawn white face toward the bandit.

"What did you have to do? Why, you drew him down here, didn't you? If it hadn't been for you, the man would never have come into old Mexico, where every hawk is on the wing to catch sight of him."

Champion's head dropped suddenly, as though all heart had gone out of him.

Tyler saw the two Mexicans exchange pleased glances.

"Where did they catch him?" asked Cambista.

"Down by the river," El Tigre responded.

"Ah? By the river?"

"Yes, he was trying to sneak upstream, paddling a canoe on the far side of the river. But two boats were coming down the stream, and they met him . . . they hailed him, because tonight the people are hailing everyone, to make sure. There's enough money on the head of Tyler to make it worthwhile for the whole of Patos del

Oro to join in the search."

"Yes, of course," Cambista said. "And what did our friend *Señor* Tyler do when they hailed him?"

"He tried to paddle to the shore."

"But they headed him off?"

"Yes," El Tigre said. "They headed him off, and like a flash he dived overboard into the black of the river."

"How did they get him then?" asked Cambista.

"Why, one of the fellows in the first boat was a good fisherman . . . it was his boat. He had a two-pronged fish spear in the bottom of the boat, and he picked this up. Pretty soon he saw the pale shadow of the swimmer well under the surface. The fisherman reached down and drove the prongs right through the body of Tyler."

"Ah, good," Cambista whispered.

Harry Champion, with a groan, raised his hands and buried his face in them. The Mexicans exchanged open glances of triumph.

"That was the end of him, eh?" Cambista asked.

"No, there was still life in him to scream for a while," El Tigre continued with satisfaction. "They towed him ashore on the fish spear. As they began to pull the prongs out of him, his yelling split the ear, it's said. They called for a priest, but the *gringo* was dead before he could come, screeching and kicking up the bank, begging for mercy and a doctor."

Suddenly Champion lifted his head and exhaled a great, gasping breath. "It's all a lie!" he said.

"Ah, is it all a lie?" El Tigre asked coldly.

"All a lie! I tell you, I know Jim Tyler, and Satan himself would sooner kick and scream for mercy and a doctor than Tyler would."

"Oh, you know Tyler that well, do you?" El Tigre asked, that faint, cruel smile on his lips, but a shadow of disappointment dimming his rounded, cat-like eyes.

"I know him that well," Champion stated with an air of conviction.

"I wasn't there," El Tigre said, shrugging his shoulders carelessly. "But the fact is that men will change, when they find death coming at them suddenly. When the hope goes out of some people, the strength goes out of them, too."

"Not out of Jim Tyler," insisted the boy.

"A very brave man, but only a man," El Tigre assured him.

"I've seen too many heroes change when the rope is around the neck," agreed Cambista. "Even Tyler might turn into a woman at the end."

"Of course," agreed El Tigre.

Champion shook his head. Conviction showed more and more firmly seated in him. "If he really were dead," he said, "you'd both be singing, drinking, shouting, laughing like madmen. But he's not dead. You've brought me out to murder me tonight. And you want to torture me first by making me think that my friend is dead before me, horribly murdered. I see through you, El Tigre, and through you, Cambista!"

"He's a little giddy in the brain," Cambista confided to El Tigre.

"Besides," Harry Champion said, "if a man like Jim Tyler had been killed by this time, the whole crowd in the streets would be yelling with joy. Bells would be ringing. It would be a *fiesta!* No, you've lied, and I know it."

"Let him think as he pleases, the fool," Cambista said to El Tigre. "It's time to give him to the river."

"I'll take the irons off him first," El Tigre said. "They might fish the body out of the river, one of these days, and trace the irons on it back to this house, and from this house to . . . well, ropes leave less of a trace. Ropes and a stone to weight 'em down." He unlocked the irons as he spoke.

Cambista, muttering something under his breath about too much frugality and suspicion, obediently lashed the wrists and feet of the boy with cords.

"Now for your work, Miguel," El Tigre said.

He stood back, smiling, and Miguel Cambista took out a revolver, balanced it in his hand, and then grasped it by the barrel.

"Are you ready, *Señor* Champion?" he asked.

The young man, white as stone, rigid in his chair, looked straight at the murderer and nodded.

"Say it," Cambista said, "or is the breath frightened out of you?"

A heavy, wooden voice came from the lips of the boy. "I am ready."

"Any messages, *señor?*" asked Cambista.

"No messages that dogs could carry for me," said Champion.

The heavy gun was raised suddenly in the hand of Cambista, and he made a half step nearer, as though about to strike. A vital half step was that for Cambista, to the verge of his own death, for Tyler from the shadow of the pillar covered the man with an unwavering muzzle.

"Steady, Miguel?" El Tigre stated.

"Bend your head, *gringo,*" Cambista ordered, his oily voice thickened and bubbling with passion. "This is for the base of your skull."

"Do as you please, I'm helpless," Harry Champion stated, "but I won't bend my head of my own will."

"He has courage, the youngster," El Tigre observed, nodding with a grudging admiration. "And that makes it too bad. If the color of his skin were a little darker, and a few other things about him changed, then. . . ." He paused and shrugged his shoulders.

"Is it time, El Tigre?" asked Cambista.

"Well, I suppose that it's time."

"We give you a second or two for prayer," Cambista said, still gloating over his prospective kill, like a cat over a mouse, and grinning horribly.

"If I pray, it isn't aloud for you two to hear," Champion informed them. "If I pray, it's only that Jim Tyler can hear of what's happened here in this garden. Because I think that he'll find a way to come at both of you, for my sake."

"You fool," Cambista hissed, "don't you know that if Tyler is not dead now, he'll be dead before the morning?" He raised the gun butt to strike.

"Wait one moment," El Tigre said.

The gun in the hand of Cambista was lowered; the finger of Tyler relaxed on the trigger of his Colt. Then, inside the hall of the house, he heard the gruff voice of the porter muttering: "Steady, Juan. Lean on me. This way."

XIV

"To the River"

Into the garden patio came the porter, once more, and this time he supported at his side the staggering form of Juan, the sentinel. Tyler hardly knew whether to rejoice or be sorry when he saw that the man lived, in spite of the blow that he had received. Reeling, he came on, while El Tigre leaped up angrily from the table and exclaimed: "Who told you to come here again uncalled for? And what do you mean by getting drunk, Juan?"

"Not drunk," Juan said slowly, "but dead. I died, and I've come back into a dream."

He staggered and would have fallen, but the porter supported him. El Tigre was alongside the two men in one bound. He took the sentinel by both arms and shook him roughly.

"What happened to you?" he demanded.

"Look at the back of his head, *señor* . . . it is all blood and swollen. If his skull is not smashed, it's a lucky thing."

"Listen, Juan, fool, what happened?" commanded the master.

"I stood," Juan explained in a dull, slow voice, "for a long time, after you went in. Then I walked down past the front of the house. I went under the tree. A shadow dropped out of it above me." He paused.

"The tree!" El Tigre grimaced through his teeth. "I knew . . . I knew . . . a chill went through me when I came near it, and still I failed to search it. I am the fool, the prince of fools."

In the same mechanical voice Juan spoke again: "I only know that it was a man. I heard a faint sound, like the snarl of a man, deep in the throat. As I tried to look up, the blow fell on me. Then there was blackness."

"I'll go out to look," El Tigre said. He added to the porter: "Take the thick wit and put him to bed. Wash his head and tie it up. He'll be all right again. There are no brains inside that skull to be damaged, anyway. I'll look about the tree for the traces of the man . . . if it were Tyler, if it were." He drew himself up on his toes in a cold fury.

"I'll go with you. You must not go out alone, if there's a ghost of a chance that Tyler is there," Miguel Cambista said.

"Stay here with the boy," El Tigre snapped.

"He can wait till we come back," Cambista insisted. "There's no danger that he'll move, not after the way I wound those cords into his flesh." And he was off, at once, at the heels of his friend.

So, by a single gesture, the garden had been cleared, and Jim Tyler stepped to the side of his friend.

At the first appearance of that tall, cloak-hidden form, no recognition came into the eyes

334

of the boy. Not until Tyler leaned above him, not until the fold of the cloak fell away from the face of Tyler, did Harry Champion see and exclaim in a whisper: "Tyler! How did you do it?"

Two slashes with the edge of the knife set him free. He leaped to his feet and looked wildly around him, as though his first thought were not a flight of freedom, but overwhelming desire to lay his hands on his captors.

The iron grasp of Tyler on his arm awoke him to a sense of the dangers of the moment. "The river," Tyler said, pointing.

They fled toward the palisades, reaching them before any outcry came from the house. Attention was centered on the street, no doubt, at the very moment of the escape.

"You first," young Harry Champion said, as they reached the high palisade.

"Oh, nonsense," answered Tyler. "Now I have you at the door, are we going to start bowing and scraping?" Stooping, he caught Harry by the legs and hoisted him upward. The tops of the posts were very sharp, but Champion managed with heels and hands to work his way to a safe balance and then drop down on the farther side to the shelving bank outside.

He looked back, dismayed. How would Jim Tyler manage to get over? The answer came the next instant. There was a rush of softly padding feet, and then the half naked body of Tyler appeared, poised an instant at the top, and then dropped lightly down beside his younger friend.

They found themselves standing on a very narrow bit of the bank, with the river encroaching on either hand. From the bank, as was usual in the houses of Patos del Oro that backed on the water, a flight of steps went down to a little landing stage. There, tethered to an iron ring by a padlocked iron chain, was a beautifully modeled canoe, resting on the shelf of the bank, bottom side up, with the handles of the paddles thrusting out beneath it.

Tyler turned it instantly in his hands.

"If we had the key," Champion was saying.

"We'll manage without the key," said the other, and sank the edge of his keen knife into the gunwale that ran around the little craft, and into which, at this point, was sunk the strong staple whose ring held the chain.

A wild shout came from the garden at this moment, the voice of Cambista raised to a bubbling roar of astonishment, hate, and agony of surprise. "He's gone! He's gone! El Tigre! See! He's gone!"

The voice of El Tigre, likewise raised, made answer: "He's gone and that means that the hand that cut these ropes was the hand of Tyler. That devil has taken wings and flown over the top of the house. Or else, he turned himself into a mole and tunneled up through the earth and be damned to him."

"Where can they have gone?" Cambista cried.

"Back into the house, of course. They've only had two seconds."

"But the river?" exclaimed Cambista.

"Not the river! Well, take men and look there. Francisco, Pedro! You louts and half-wits! Arturo!"

Men came pouring into the garden.

"This way!" called the voice of Cambista.

"We can swim down the current!" Champion groaned. "Those devils will be here in ten seconds."

"The canoe is a lot faster and dryer," Tyler said calmly, "and here it is."

He stopped slashing with the knife, broke out the pit of wood that remained, anchoring the bolt at its roots, and slid the canoe into the water. They stepped into it and seized paddles as the rush of men reached the river gate of the garden, and the key turned in the lock. Two long thrusts of the paddles sent the canoe shooting out into the current, and it was beginning to dissolve in the moon mist when Cambista and his men suddenly broke out onto the bank.

The screech of Cambista, as he spotted the fugitives, curdled the blood of young Harry Champion. Then half a dozen guns roared. He heard bullets about his head, like wasps. He saw a long furrow strike across the face of the water near the prow of the canoe. Still desperately paddling, he was aware that he was working alone. Had his rescuer, then, been struck?

He turned his head, without remitting his labor, and saw that Tyler had squared about, with the long-barreled revolver raised. It spoke.

The muzzle of the gun tipped up from the force of the explosion, and on the riverbank the dimly seen, heavy body of Cambista threw up its arms and toppled face foremost into the river.

The firing ceased. The sweep of the paddle made the forms on the shore mere suggestions of shapes, rather than actual silhouettes of human beings.

"Straight across the river, now taper her up the current. That's better," said Tyler.

"Is he dead, Jim?" Champion asked, his voice husky.

"I think he had it between the eyes," Tyler said calmly. "It should have been El Tigre, but Cambista was overdue to die tonight as well."

Champion nodded. He could not forget the bubbling laugh of brutal triumph with which Cambista had handled the revolver like a butcher's cleaver.

"You're steering to the right, Jim!" he exclaimed.

"Of course," said the other. "We're going back into Patos del Oro. Do you think that we can leave Ines Flores behind us in this hole?"

XV

"Señor Flores"

In the house of *Señor* Flores there was silence. Few lights showed except in the big library, walled in with books. The master of the house was a man of letters, and now he sat in his favorite room, looking very much the part of a student of another century, with his thin, tapering white beard, the fierce blackness of brows and eyes, and the almost translucently thin fingers resting on the table before him.

Books, however, were not his interest at this moment, but the girl who sat just opposite him at the table, slender, proud, with her head up and dark shadows of defiance in her eyes. It was not exactly with hatred that she looked at her father, but a revolt that was close kin to that emotion. Then he said: "So the thing is ending, Ines."

"It will never end," she said.

"It is ending," Flores insisted. "Your young friend, the *Señor* Champion, is now well on his way out of the country. I have the word of a trustworthy man for that. It cost me a good deal of money, but he will be taken safe and sound out of the country and back to his own land.

After this experience, you may be sure that he won't return again."

"He'll come back," said the girl, "and, even if he doesn't, I'll wait for him."

"So you think now, so you think now," said her father. "But I tell you, my dear, although resolves are of the strongest iron, time is a stuff that will dissolve them like sand, and they'll melt away. In six months, only your pride will uphold you, and your interest in *Señor* Champion will have diminished to a ghost. In a year, you will be smiling at some other young man. I, also, have been young."

She shrugged her shoulders. "We'll see," she said. "In the meantime, watch me like a criminal, because, if I have a chance, I'll get away, Father, and go to his own country and his own people to find him."

He smiled back at her, calm, secure of himself. "You have great thoughts tonight, Ines," he said, "but as the days run by, the thoughts will not be so great. Tonight you are inspired, because you have spoken with that terrible savage from the north, that *Señor* Tyler whom they call The Wolf."

"You think that Don Enrique Champion is a person of no consequence," she said, "but it was only for the sake of *Señor* Champion that *Señor* Tyler put his head in the jaws of the lion and came clear down here to Patos del Oro."

"It was a long journey, and a dangerous one. He will be a dead man before the morning, my dear," said the father. "And for that I am sorry. I respect courage, even in the savage, cruel, untrustworthy men of the American republic."

"They are as brave, as gentle, as true as those of Mexico," said the girl. "They are ready to die for one another. What can men do that is better than that?"

"It is a great thing," answered her father. "But Tyler is a demon, not a man. Of that I am sure, or he could never have come into the garden as he did. How could he have climbed out again, except with wings? However, he will not come again."

"Are you sure?" she asked.

"Of course. I still have men on watch. Not outside, of course. That's not necessary. But inside the house there are several, and this time they know for whom to watch. Even at the door to this room, Ines, there is a man with a shotgun. He has instructions to open even this door and dash in ready to shoot, the first moment that he hears a strange sound."

She closed her eyes and shuddered. Then, as she opened them and was about to speak again, there was a commotion outside, hurrying feet, then a hand knocked at the door and pushed it open a few inches.

"A messenger for you, *señor*."

"Let him come in," Flores said, rising and standing with dignity.

At that, a cloaked, villainous-looking fellow skulked into the room, glanced at the girl with

341

singularly bold, keen eyes, gave a note to Flores, and slunk out again with a quick, long stride.

The door closed. Flores opened the letter and read:

The cage has been opened and the bird has flown. Only Satan himself or The Wolf, perhaps, could have done the thing. Look after your own bird, *Señor* Flores. All the work is to be done over again!

There was no more signature than there was formal heading to the letter, but Flores knew perfectly well from whom it came. It slid out of his nerveless fingers, and fluttered to the floor, while he stared gloomily, straight before him.

"It can't be. It can't be," he was muttering, while the girl, leaning from her chair, read the message in a few glances. Her heart leaped as she sat up straight again. It was not hard to guess the meaning, from the words and from the behavior of her stunned father.

"Father," she said, "it means that *Señor* Tyler has reached *Señor* Champion and set him free. And I am the bird that you are to keep with care, am I not?" She stood up with a ringing laugh. Even as she laughed, it seemed to her that she heard a dull scraping or scratching at the shuttered window behind her that opened upon the second alley that ran past the house. Hearing this, or dreaming that she heard it, she went on, more loudly than before: "If they are both free and together, how will you be able to keep me, Father? They have walked through walls before this. How can you keep me from *Señor* Tyler? That's what I'd like to know."

"What the future can bring," he said, turning his back to her, and extending his hands toward the fire that burned on the hearth, because of the damp chill that the river mist had spread through the house — "what the future can bring, I don't know, I'm sure. But at least no two human beings would dare to stay in Patos del Oro in such danger as are *Señor* Tyler and *Señor* Champion, but if. . . ." He paused, and lifted his head suddenly, for there was a sighing sound and then, from the window, a chilly breath of the outer night reached him.

Very slowly he turned, with a sudden realization of what he was going to see. There, by the open window, he saw standing a tall man, naked above the waist and below the knees, his body brown as the skin of an Indian, his shoulders wide and overlaid with a cunning network of muscles that seemed like small wires moving underneath the skin. Aside from his nakedness and the mist trickling down his body as over-weathered stone, he seemed terrible on his own account. There was the hawk-like face with the dark hair streaking down over his forehead and across his cheeks. In one sinewy hand he carried a revolver. Otherwise, there was nothing in his bearing or his posture that would indicate any violence whatsoever.

Almost more than the figure of this wild man, to the mind of *Señor* Flores, was the figure of the second person who was mounting through the casement and whom he recognized as Harry Champion. For it meant that the first man was that mythically terrible man, or spirit, known to their world as The Wolf. And the second man could have come for nothing except his daughter, Ines.

Now, as he saw these things a very odd change came over Flores. A certain smugness, that had been his before, dropped away suddenly from him. He made an outward gesture with both hands. He even smiled, as a man might smile when he confronts fate.

"*Señor* Tyler," he said very quietly, "I suppose that you have come here for a little taste of revenge?"

"We have come for Ines," said the tall man.

Champion stood beside him, never wasting a single glance on Flores, but looking with consuming intentness at the girl. It seemed to Flores a foolish thing that he ever had doubted the sincerity of this Northerner. It now seemed to him madness that he ever had offered a large sum of money to a bandit for the quiet removal of this man from the town and from the life of his girl. For he looked older, and the single dark line that immense trouble and danger had drawn between his eyes gave him an air of penetrating dignity that he had certainly lacked before.

"Flores, I want to ask you only one thing,"

Tyler said abruptly. "When you called in El Tigre, did you want him to keep Champion bottled up, or did you know that the beast would murder Champion?"

"Murder him!" exclaimed the old man. "Murder him?"

The very form of the answer was enough for Tyler, and he said to Champion: "It's all right, Harry. If there'd been murder in his mind, I wouldn't have wanted to see you take a wife from such blood. But I was wrong. It was only the devil working in El Tigre, not the idea of Flores."

"Wait," Flores said. "Do you mean to say that the man actually wished to . . . to. . . ."

"My friend came just in time," Champion said gravely. "Another few minutes would have been too late. Ines, I think you know why I'm here. Will you come?"

She did not answer him directly. She turned to the shocked face of Flores and first asked: "Will you blame me?"

"If you would stay here with me," he said, "and trust me to arrange everything for the two of you, but I can't ask you to do that. I've forfeited your trust, Ines, and yours, Harry. Go your way, if you please, and God be with you. You can have your blessing, now, as well as later."

Tyler, looking with his keen eyes at the Mexican, touched the shoulder of his friend. "Harry," he said, "do one thing for me."

"I'll gladly do anything under heaven," the young man answered with emotion.

"Leave it all to the honor and the promise of *Señor* Flores. It will be better that way, and he'll be true to his word, if I ever read a man's face correctly. To take her with us is going to make our escape ten times harder. She knows that we've come for her, and that's the main thing."

"*Señor* Tyler, God bless you," Flores stated.

Ines Flores took the situation suddenly in her hands. She hurried to Champion and said: "You've heard my father promise. I trust him more than I'd trust my own honor. Go quickly, Harry. Write to me as soon as you are in safety, and I swear that my father and I will come to you, even if it's to the ends of the earth."

XVI
"The Return"

That was why the guard at the door of the Flores library heard no unusual sound. A few moments later, down the face of the river, past the uproar of the re-awakening town went a canoe, driven by two paddles.

"We can be ten miles down the river in two hours," Harry said over his shoulder, for he was still the bow oar in the boat.

"There's one thing left to do," Tyler said.

Below the last house of the town they landed, therefore, and, with Tyler leading, they hurried up the bank and across the windings of a lane to a little farmhouse and barn that stood in the midst of sweeping fields. They avoided the house, but into the barn they went. At the door, Tyler found a lantern, lighted it, and held it up over his head.

There was an open space of stalls where cattle, perhaps, were usually fed in the winter of the year. Now, there were half a dozen horses, and the looks of the animals were not such as one would have expected in such a place, but rather in a racing stable, so long were the legs, so beautiful and slender were the quarters modeled. But one loomed above the rest, a stallion, a dark, dappled chestnut that, lifting his head, seemed like a king of horses.

An exclamation came from the throat of Champion. "It's Spring of the Year!" he cried softly.

The stallion, as though knowing that voice, whinnied gently in answer.

"Man, man," Champion asked, "how could you know?"

"Why," Tyler answered, "the fact is that a bird whispered the secret in my ear. You didn't know that I understood the language of the birds, did you, Harry?"

"By thunder," Champion said, with belief in his voice, "it's the only thing that you need to know to make you perfect."

The return journey from Mexico was not easily made. There were troubles, more than one, and dangers. Particularly, there was that celebrated passage of the Eagle Cañon about which certain Mexicans will tell you, if you find them at the right stage with their *pulque* or tequila. But that is not the point of this narrative, which has to do almost entirely with how Harry Champion was taken out of the hands of death and replaced, once more, in a certain small border town among the hills.

From there, the telegraph lines were suddenly burdened with long, eager messages to the town of Patos del Oro in old Mexico, and in due time equally long and very explicit messages that turned the world of Harry Champion into a rosy heaven of delight.

Into that town, not very long afterward, came three visitors, in two details. The first included a middle-aged man, or one sloping actually toward age, driving one mustang in a rattling buckboard, a man with a troubled face and haunted eyes. The second consisted of two riders on two fine horses, a man with erect bearing and pale, bushy, sun-faded eyebrows, over buried eyes, and a girl with a face rosy from travel through wind and sun, but prettier on account of it.

The two riders reached the hotel first and dismounted. Striding to the hotel clerk, the man said: "I'm Alexander Champion. Is my son Harry here?"

Harry Champion appeared down the stairs, running, then checked his haste, and approached his father with a grave, stalking stride such as men in Texas put on with their dignity. When he saw his sister, he lost his dignity completely. He lifted her feet from the floor in the strength of his embrace. As he put her down, gasping, it was with difficulty that he put back the iron mask upon his features and approached the older man stiffly.

Mr. Alexander Champion, whom five men and one woman in the world called Sandy, stood with his arms folded, one hand raised to twirl his mustache softly. His face was also like iron. But

Sally Champion whirled in between them and caught them each by a hand.

"What stuff and nonsense!" she cried. "What other father have you in the world, Harry? Ask his pardon for everything this instant!"

The dignity of Harry Champion dissolved slightly, but did not quite disappear.

"I have a telegram," he said, "saying that Ines and her father are coming to this place as fast as a train will bring 'em. That's the only answer I can make."

"Why, it's a damn' good answer," Alexander Champion announced. "If the pair of you brats are willing to die for one another, I'm not such an old fool that I'll put trouble in your way, my boy. But where's the great man? Where is he? I've heard enough rumors and whispers and head shakings about what happened to you in old Mexico. Now I want to know the truth. What happened down there?"

"About Jim Tyler, you mean?"

"Yes, yes. What else would I mean?"

They had found hands and gripped hard, in the brief interval, while Sally Champion stood by with a brightness brimming her eyes.

"I only knew that I was about to die," Harry Champion said. "And that Jim saved my life. It's an old habit of his, saving my life. He's so fixed in it that he can't change. You don't mind, Father?"

"He might find a better way of spending his time," said the other, as gruffly as ever. "But what happened? What's this I hear about the killing of Cambista and El Tigre both in an evening?"

"Not El Tigre. There wasn't that much luck. Jim Tyler doesn't kill men out of hand when he has the chance, not even an El Tigre. But Cambista, yes. I saw him fall. Cambista is dead, I know."

"A good riddance," said the older man. "But where's Tyler? God knows that I have a few things to say to him."

"And I," said the girl. "I want to see him and tell him. . . ."

Harry Champion said to the clerk: "Where's Tyler?"

"He just came down while you were talking together, Mister Champion. He went out the front door, carrying a bag."

"Carrying a what?"

"A bag," the clerk repeated, with a troubled air and staring eyes.

"After him!" Alexander Champion shouted.

They hurried out to the front verandah of the hotel, and down the street they saw a buckboard rollicking over the bumps and throwing up dust, while in the seat sat the shapeless back of an elderly man, and beside him a fellow sitting very straight, with extremely wide shoulders and a sombrero whose brim drooped all around.

"That's the fellow!" Harry Champion cried.

"After him, then, and bring him back," Alexander Champion said.

351

The young man caught his arm. "No, no," he said. "I know Jim. I know his ways. He chooses to fade out of the picture, now that he's ridden another death trail and brought me safely back. If you go to stop him, now, you'll only find The Wolf, and no trace of Jim Tyler at all."

About the Author

Max Brand is the best-known pen name of Frederick Faust, creator of Dr. Kildare, Destry, and many other fictional characters popular with readers and viewers worldwide. Faust wrote for a variety of audiences in many genres. His enormous output, totaling approximately thirty million words or the equivalent of 530 ordinary books, covered nearly every field: crime, fantasy, historical romance, espionage, Westerns, science fiction, adventure, animal stories, love, war, and fashionable society, big business and big medicine. Eighty motion pictures have been based on his work along with many radio and television programs. For good measure he also published four volumes of poetry. Perhaps no other author has reached more people in more different ways.

Born in Seattle in 1892, orphaned early, Faust grew up in the rural San Joaquin Valley of California. At Berkeley he became a student rebel and one-man literary movement, contributing prodigiously to all campus publications. Denied a degree because of unconventional conduct, he embarked on a series of adventures culminating in New York City where, after a period of near starvation, he received simultaneous recognition as a serious poet and successful author of fiction. Later, he traveled widely, making his home in New York, then in Florence, and finally in Los Angeles.

Once the United States entered the Second World War, Faust abandoned his lucrative writing career and his work as a screenwriter to serve as a war correspondent with the infantry in Italy, despite his fifty-one years and a bad heart. He was killed during a night attack on a hilltop village held by the German army. New books based on magazine serials or unpublished manuscripts or restored versions continue to appear so that, alive or dead, he has averaged a new book every four months for seventy-five years. Beyond this, some work by him is newly reprinted every week of every year in one or another format somewhere in the world. A great deal more about this author and his work can be found in *The Max Brand Companion* (Greenwood Press, 1997) edited by Jon Tuska and Vicki Piekarski.

The employees of G.K. Hall hope you have enjoyed this Large Print book. All our Large Print titles are designed for easy reading, and all our books are made to last. Other G.K. Hall books are available at your library, through selected bookstores, or directly from us.

For information about titles, please call:

(800) 223-1244
(800) 223-6121

To share your comments, please write:

Publisher
G.K. Hall & Co.
295 Kennedy Memorial Drive
Waterville, ME 04901